A FLAME PUT OUT

Sons of Odin Series

ERIN S. RILEY

SOUL MATE PUBLISHING

New York

A FLAME PUT OUT

Copyright©2015

ERIN S. RILEY

Cover Design by Fiona Jayde

This book is a work of fiction. The names, characters, places, and incidents are the products of the author's imagination or are used fictitiously. Any resemblance to actual events, business establishments, locales, or persons, living or dead, is entirely coincidental.

Published in the United States of America by
Soul Mate Publishing
P.O. Box 24
Macedon, New York, 14502

ISBN: 978-1-68291-130-3

ebook ISBN: 978-1-61935-903-1

www.SoulMatePublishing.com

The publisher does not have any control over and does not assume any responsibility for author or third-party websites or their content.

For my son Riley—

You are my hero, #11.

I love you more than all the sand at the beach.

Acknowledgements

Thank you to my husband and children for supporting my need to write, including a willingness to eat peanut butter crackers for supper without complaint whenever I'm on a roll. A special thanks to Carmen Vanscyoc, Nicole Armstrong, and Kelley Franks, three wonderful friends who were my first readers and are still my biggest supporters, and to Kim Freeman, a dear friend who never tires of discussing story ideas with me. Thank you to fellow writers Susan Ward and Terry Wilson for their positive feedback and encouragement through this sometimes overwhelming journey. Thank you to Regan Walker and Carol Cork for their support. And a heartfelt thank you to Diana Deyo, a friend who refused to let me give up. Above all, thank you to my mother, Karen S. Ward, who was taken from this world too soon but taught me what unconditional love truly is. Everything I am and everything I will be, I owe to her.

I am so grateful to Debby Gilbert from Soul Mate Publishing for providing the opportunity for me to pursue my dreams. A special thanks goes to Victoria Vane, cover designer extraordinaire. And finally, thank you to my brilliant editor, Char Chaffin, who understood my vision from the beginning and who polished my story with unwavering patience.

Prologue

Ireland
860 AD

Grainne heard the children whispering just after dawn, too early for them to be awake. She shushed them over her shoulder as she stirred the kettle of porridge, but had trouble keeping her face stern as Cassan grinned at her.

Deirdre climbed down from the bench she shared with her brother. She toddled over, with Cassan following as he always did. "'San is hungry, Mamai," she lisped.

She regarded her little daughter. "Is that so? And what is it he wants, then?"

"Cakes," Deirdre replied with a serious expression, referring to the oatcakes and honey Grainne would sometimes make as a special treat.

"Well. If Cassan wants oatcakes, we will have to send Dadai into the forest to chase down a bee and steal his honey."

Deirdre pouted, as though doubting her father would be willing to undertake such a task. But she stomped off to the barn to ask him, with Cassan following several steps behind.

Grainne shook her head as she watched them go. The twins had been born too early, and although Cassan was somewhat small at birth, Deirdre had been tiny, barely longer than her father's hand. Her cries were so weak she sounded more like a kitten than a human child, and her mouth was too small to properly suckle. No one had expected the fragile infant to live.

But live she did. Faolan had made sure of that, despite Grainne's misgivings. Shivering, she crossed herself at the memory.

Little Deirdre not only survived, but quickly exceeded her brother's development. She uttered her first intelligible word before she could walk. Soon, she could speak in sentences, and at two summers she remembered every word spoken.

The child's uncanny precociousness made Grainne uneasy. What if someone put the chain of events together and realized what Faolan had done? But he scoffed at her worries.

Even the village priest believed Deirdre's abilities were a gift from God. He came to their house nearly every evening after supper, reciting scriptures to the child in Latin. And she soaked it all in, her face solemn with concentration. The priest thought little Deirdre might become a nun.

Grainne and Faolan didn't speak of the irony of that plan.

Cassan barely said a word other than the unintelligible jargon he spoke with his sister. Grainne would sometimes lie awake at night, listening to them chatter to each other in the dark. And hated it.

Her son was good natured with an even temper, a direct contrast to his sister's more stubborn nature. He allowed Deirdre to take the lead in all things, content to follow and do her bidding. Although Grainne worried about Cassan's meekness, Faolan found great amusement in this and said it would prepare the boy for his eventual marriage.

The door opened and Deirdre entered, pulling her father by the hand. Cassan was several steps behind with his thumb in his mouth. "Dadai will find the bee," Deirdre informed her.

Faolan shrugged helplessly with a smile, and Grainne's heart nearly burst with the beauty of it. She had loved him since they were children, thinking him the most handsome boy in all of Ireland. A man such as Faolan could have had any woman who struck his fancy, but he had chosen her.

He handed her the pail of milk he had been carrying, cocking an amused eyebrow. "Am I truly to go hunting for honey, then? Or is Deirdre-"

Suddenly a woman's scream sounded outside, calling for Faolan. Both Grainne and Faolan jumped as Ionait, the widow who lived at the neighboring farm with her son, rushed in from the mist beyond, darting through the open doorway.

"Finngalls," she gasped, clutching her chest. "They are here! Aodhan is fighting them!"

Grainne heard faint shouting and the clanging of metal. Ionait sobbed and backed toward the door, but Faolan blocked her way.

"Stay here," he ordered, in a voice Grainne had never heard him use before.

He flipped open the leather chest that sat near their bench, pulling out an ancient-looking sword. He was a farmer, not a warrior, and much handier with the pitchfork or scythe. But Grainne knew her husband would not leave his family unprotected while he ran to the barn. His grandfather's sword would have to do.

Time seemed to stand still as Faolan gazed down at the faces of his children, before exchanging a long look with Grainne. "Bolt the door," he said. Then he was gone, out into the early morning mist.

She heard his raised voice, followed by incomprehensible noises that reminded her of the snarling of wolves. Was that the language of the Finngalls? They were close then, so close, and she ran to bolt the door.

There was a scream from outside-a male scream-and then silence. "Faolan?" she whispered hoarsely.

If the Finngalls were still out there, the door would be no match for their weapons. Grainne waited, each second an eternity. What if Faolan had killed the Finngalls, but was now outside, wounded?

She took a deep breath, slid the latch over, and opened the door. The thick mist hid all from her sight, and she hesitated. Should she search for Faolan or stay with the children, who were crying behind her?

A noise, footsteps just a few yards in front of her, made her heart leap.

"Faolan?" she whispered again.

It wasn't Faolan. The devil himself emerged from the mist, a Finngall as large as two men, wearing a mail shirt and iron helmet. He carried a battle-axe on his shoulder, stained red with blood. When he spotted her, the smile forming on his lips seemed the most chilling expression Grainne had ever seen.

Too late she tried to shut the door, but the Finngall pushed into it with such force that she fell. The children and Ionait sobbed hysterically, and the devil growled something to them in his wolf language. Grainne turned, crawling on her hands and knees, desperate to protect her children.

The Finngall picked her up by the neck to toss her upon the table. Bowls of porridge flew from its surface and hit the wall with a clatter.

The giant laughed at her screams as he laid his axe next to her on the table. Her gaze fixed on the black hairs glued to the blood that smeared it, and she stared, numb and still. Faolan.

She felt nothing as he lifted her gown. Her body was as cold as that of her dead husband.

But the children's screams intensified, and she turned hollow eyes in their direction. "Run," she choked out to Ionait. "Take the children!"

Ionait seemed frozen in fear, clutching the twins to her breast. Deirdre struggled to break free of Ionait's grip, but Cassan only stared, pale and open mouthed, wailing.

Grainne's attacker pulled off his helmet to wipe his sweaty brow with one massive forearm. She stared at his face, memorizing every line and plane. Without the helmet, she realized he was very young. For all his size, this Finngall devil was barely more than a boy. Yet his eyes were empty and cold, devoid of any human emotion.

Deirdre suddenly broke free from Ionait and rushed toward the giant devil, biting his leg hard enough to draw blood. He bellowed as he turned his unholy gaze on the toddler. As he reached for the axe, Grainne flung her hand to the side, pushing it to the floor.

He stretched to grab Deirdre, and Grainne wrapped her arms around one of his to slow him down. "Ionait, run— now!" she screamed at the woman.

Ionait sobbed as her eyes darted to the door. She couldn't reach it without getting within an arm's length of the Finngall. As she inched across the room, clutching the children, another gigantic Finngall demon entered the house. Foreign words tumbled from them as they both cursed each other.

The devil suddenly broke from her desperate grip, catching her by the hair, to sling her across the room.

Grainne's temple hit the hearth and the edges of her vision went dark. A burning log from the hearth rolled to the corner, then blazed bright as the willow branch wall caught fire. The flames crackled upward, hot and quick; smoke filled the room.

She stared, dazed.

A voice in her head that sounded like Faolan's urged her to get the children away from more danger, and she forced herself to her feet. The two Finngalls were still shouting at each other, and the bigger one shoved the other aside to make him stumble.

Then, in a motion so fluid and quick Grainne barely had time to react, the devil pulled his sword from its scabbard, bringing the hilt forcefully down upon the small curly head of her daughter, as though squashing a bug.

Grainne screamed as Deirdre's tiny body collapsed in the smoke. Her head bounced against the dirt floor, and her wide, sightless eyes stared into nothingness. The devil flicked the sword up and over in his hand, catching it so the blade now faced downward, then raised his arm to run the child through with it.

The second Finngall yelled and ran toward the devil with his shield before him as if to block the blow. But he used the shield as a weapon, bringing the metal edge of it down upon the hand of the devil. The room echoed with the sound of metal cracking bone.

The devil dropped the sword and stared at his mangled hand for a moment. With a roar, he overturned the table to pick up the axe that had fallen under it. The second Finngall lunged for him. They rolled on the floor, snarling at each other like wolves.

Grainne crawled to the body of her child. Deirdre was pale and still, limp, and Grainne sobbed as she clutched the tiny form to her breast.

Suddenly the second Finngall spoke to her in strangely-accented Irish. "Run," he panted, "before he kills the other one."

Grainne and Ionait turned to flee, each holding a child. The devil grabbed Grainne's ankle, pulling her to the floor, and she had to twist her torso as she fell to avoid crushing the body of her little daughter.

"Take her, Ionait!" she begged. If the devil meant to carry Grainne off into slavery, she would not leave the tiny body to be burned inside the house, or thrown to the ravens.

Ionait seemed to understand, for she grabbed Deirdre's floppy body and pulled it clear of the Finngalls. As the woman hurried into the mist, Grainne saw Cassan's terrified face peering over Ionait's shoulder.

"Mamai," he cried, holding out a tiny hand.

Chapter 1

Norway, 876 AD

Selia awoke to the faint, melancholy strain of a bird chirping. The silk bedding was soft against her cheek, Alrik's familiar body warm and solid behind her. She nestled closer, loath to open her eyes. All would be right with the world if she could just stay here, with her husband's arm covering her like a shield, the past events nothing more than an unpleasant dream.

Alrik's fingers grazed her arm, pausing near her shoulder. "Did I do this to you last night?"

She lifted her arm to look. There was a faint bruise, an outline of fingers and thumb from where Ulfrik had grabbed her in the heat of their argument. It stood out against the white of her skin like a brand for the entire world to see.

Her husband's brother knew how to play upon her fragile emotions, attempting to maneuver her as carefully as he would the pieces on a tafl board. Though she had spurned him, still she had come uncomfortably close to allowing him liberties.

Selia would carry that secret to her grave.

Now she simply answered, "Yes."

Alrik swallowed, visibly distressed. "You haven't been back for long and I've already hurt you."

"It is all right." She snuggled up to his chest. "You know how easily I bruise. And it was worth it."

He laughed, such a wonderful sound. How she had missed it. "Well, be that as it may, I'll have to be more careful now. For the sake of the child." His hand cupped the swell of her abdomen as he smiled down at the life that grew inside her. His face was achingly beautiful despite the red-rimmed eyes and unkempt hair.

Selia caressed his cheek. "I love you, Alrik." Her voice came out in a whisper.

His gaze met hers. "Even after all I have done to you."

"Yes. I knew I should stop loving you. But I could not."

He appeared to ponder this for a moment. "I have caused you so much pain. There is no way to make it right." He gestured despairingly. "You should have stayed away, Selia. I destroy everything I touch. You and the child would have been better off—"

"No," she replied firmly. "I cannot be without you, Alrik." She turned his chin to force him to look at her. "You cannot make me leave again."

His smile made her heart flutter. As he bent to kiss her, there was a knock at the bedchamber door.

"I hope you're decent, because I'm coming in," Hrefna called.

Alrik sat up. "Stay out, woman, or you're going to see more than you bargained for," he commanded in the booming voice he used when giving orders to his men.

But Hrefna entered anyway, grinning from ear to ear, and Selia pulled the blanket up just in time to cover her nudity. The woman ignored Alrik, rushing over instead to envelop Selia in a hug. She made a choked noise that was between a laugh and a sob. "I knew you would come back, child," she vowed, "even though Alrik didn't believe me." She shot her nephew a gloating look, and he snorted at her.

Selia blinked back tears as she embraced Hrefna. This woman was more a mother to her than Grainne could ever hope to be. She had missed her terribly, nearly as much as she had missed Alrik.

Hrefna held her at arms' length, her brow pinching together as she took in Selia's appearance. "Have you been ill, dear? You look much too thin. I know I sent plenty of provisions with Olaf, and when Ketill stopped by, he said he had supplies for your family as well."

So Ketill had known the appalling state his Hersir was in, but had not thought to mention it to Selia. Obviously he had told Ulfrik, though. And Ulfrik had taken full advantage of the situation.

The thought of such perfidy made Selia's stomach tighten into a knot of fury. She willed her face to stay expressionless. "There was enough food," she said. "I . . . I was ill, yes." She drew the covers tight against her belly to show the rounded outline. "I am still with child."

Hrefna reached out in wonder to touch her. "How can this be?"

"Because he is strong," Alrik asserted. "My son is a warrior."

"Humph," Hrefna scoffed. "Warrior or not, your wife lost so much blood she nearly died herself. I can't understand how the child still lives."

Alrik scowled at her. "She has the protection of Odin. Is it so hard to imagine the child does, too?"

Selia looked away in discomfort. This sounded a bit too much like Ragnarr's delusions.

Hrefna seemed unnerved as she studied them both. "Well," she said after a moment. "Let's get some food into you then, Selia. It doesn't appear Odin has been feeding you properly."

Alrik's frown deepened at his aunt's sarcasm. She turned to him. "And you need a bath, my boy." Hrefna wrinkled her nose in distaste. "It smells like a barn in here. You simply can't go around pissing on the floor."

Selia walked out the kitchen door, humming softly under her breath. She had eaten and bathed. Hrefna had combed out the knots in her hair, then styled it for her. Selia felt pretty again. She looked the way the mistress of a household such as Alrik's should look, and not like some undernourished thrall dressed in rags, with burrs in her hair.

She turned into the woods to look for her ring, plagued by the vague memory of throwing it at Alrik when everything had gone so horribly wrong. The likelihood of finding the exact spot in the woods where the incident had occurred was slim, and of actually finding the ring even slimmer, but she still wanted to try. Was it soft sentiment that drove her to look for the band of silver, or the harder reality of knowing the runes would keep her safe?

After searching unsuccessfully for some time, she gave up—the ring was gone. Maybe Alrik could have another one made for her. She turned to go back to the house, but as she approached a large boulder she heard the sound of someone crying. She peeked around the other side. And recognized the pale, unkempt hair of Ingrid.

The girl had her head buried in her arms but was not doing a very good job of muffling her sobs. Selia hesitated. Ingrid would be furious if she knew anyone had seen her like this. And it wasn't as though Selia could do anything to help her, even if she wanted to. The girl hated her with a passion.

She took a step backward to slip away, but the hem of her gown caught on a bush, rustling as she pulled it free. Ingrid's head shot up. The look on her face changed from despair to rage as she met Selia's eyes.

"You!" she shouted. "Get away from me, you Irish bitch!"

Selia's eyes widened at her stepdaughter's ire but didn't return the insult. The girl had obviously loved Ainnileas and was hurting. Maybe just as much as Selia herself had hurt after losing Alrik. That kind of misery was punishment enough. She turned to leave.

"Wait," Ingrid sniffled. Selia glanced back at her. "Did he . . . did Ainnileas say anything about me?"

She studied Ingrid's tearstained face. Ainnileas had not spoken of the girl, not even once, but that mean nothing. For as long as Selia could remember, whenever her brother was upset about something, he would withdraw. His typical lighthearted banter would vanish for a time, then he would return to himself once he had worked through whatever was bothering him.

Ainnileas had been unnaturally reserved the entire time they had stayed at Ulfrik's house. And Selia had been too caught up in her own sorrow to notice or care.

But Ingrid deserved an answer. "He was very sad," Selia said slowly, "but he did not speak of why."

Ingrid's sudden laugh rose into hysteria. Selia gasped as the girl pounded her fist into her own stomach. She continued to hit herself until Selia knelt to grab her arm.

"Ingrid, stop."

The girl pushed her backward. "Leave me alone!"

Selia stared as realization dawned on her. "Are you with child?" she whispered. She was sure the pair had lain together.

What would happen if Ingrid carried a babe?

And what would Alrik do to Ainnileas?

"No. I am *not*."

"But you wanted to be."

"Ainnileas would have married me if I was!" Ingrid shouted. "Even after everything . . . I know he would have married me if I carried his child."

Selia hesitated. How was she supposed to respond to this? The girl had all but admitted she had tried to force Ainnileas' hand. "I'm sorry," she said finally.

"You're *sorry*," Ingrid snarled. "You hate me. Why would you care if your brother doesn't want me?"

"I do not hate you, Ingrid. I understand how you feel. I felt this way when I was apart from Alrik."

The girl blew her nose in the hem of her shift. "Why did you come back?" she demanded. "You are a fool for returning to my father. I know what he did to you. Ainnileas wouldn't marry me because of it. If you're willing to come back to a bastard like Alrik Ragnarson then you two deserve each other."

Selia turned away. Several moments passed before she spoke. "I forgave him."

Ingrid snorted as she rose to her feet. She brushed the dirt from her gown, glaring at Selia with disdain. Her resemblance to her father was uncanny. "Then you really are the stupidest girl I've ever met. Stay away from me. It makes me ill to look at you."

Ingrid stomped off in into the trees, and Selia sat against the boulder for a few moments longer. At least her brother had escaped a marriage to this unstable and desperate girl. That was one bit of luck to be grateful for.

"Selia!" Alrik shouted through the forest. She heard a hint of fear behind the impatience in his voice.

"I am here, Alrik," she called back to him.

There was a rustling of leaves as he came into view. He too had bathed and dressed in fresh clothes. As the late afternoon sun dappled through the canopy of branches overhead, his hair gleamed like silk. She was reminded of how he had looked the first time she had met him on the hill in Dubhlinn. He had lost weight during their time apart, and his skin possessed an unhealthy sallow tint. But he was still an undeniably beautiful man.

"What are you doing up here?" he asked. "I've been looking for you everywhere."

She made a face at him. "Alrik, I came back to you. Do you still fear I will run away?"

He crossed his arms with a glower. "No. But the woods aren't safe for you to wander alone. There are wolves, and bears—"

"And boars," she reminded him.

Alrik nodded. "And boars." He was biting back a smile now.

Selia laughed as she went to him. She wrapped her arms around his waist and breathed in his scent. "I missed you, Alrik."

His hand caressed the back of her head. "I missed you too, little one," he said quietly.

She craned her neck to meet his eyes. "Come with me and help me find my ring. I think it is over there, somewhere." She pointed in the direction she had come from.

"Your ring?"

"Yes." She blushed. "I . . . took it off, remember?"

"Oh, I remember," he assured her as he reached into the pouch on his belt and pulled out the ring. He took her hand to slip it onto her finger, and it felt warm and comforting against her skin. She rubbed the familiar runes and smiled at him.

He closed her hand into a fist. "Don't take it off again, Selia."

"I won't."

He leaned over to kiss her, and she melted into his embrace. Selia wrapped her arms around his neck and twined her fingers in his hair. How she had missed the feel of his mouth on hers, the lips soft yet hard, the scratch of his whiskers against her cheek. He groaned and started to pull away. She held on, and when he stood he took her with him. She kissed him again.

Alrik laughed as he untangled her arms from around his neck. "Later, I promise. Now, we have to get back or Hrefna will have my head. She sent me to find you before supper gets cold." He paused and added, evilly, "She made blood pudding and sheep's liver, especially for you."

Chapter 2

The Irish ship returned a sennight later.

Selia and Hrefna worked the looms in a companionable silence as Ingrid lay like a slug on her bench, pouting as usual. Selia's mind had wandered, as it did so often now, to thoughts of the babe, and she jumped when she heard a shout from one of the thralls outside. She and Hrefna hurried to the door to see what the commotion was about.

She caught her breath at the sight of the Irish ship, maneuvering into the bay. Niall's men would assume Selia's return to Ireland with them—willingly or unwillingly—where they expected to be paid handsomely for her safe return to Buadhach.

She didn't want to contemplate what they would do to Ainnileas when he told them she would be staying in Norway after all. She wiped her clammy hands on her gown. She had a plan, but she would have to act quickly before Alrik saw the ship.

"Get back in the house, Selia." Alrik came up behind her, a bit out of breath. He had been overseeing the barley harvest in one of the fields a good distance from the house. One of the thralls must have run for the master the moment the ship was spotted on the water.

She looked up at him and swallowed. What was she going to do now? "You will need me to translate for you, to tell them where Geirr's house is," she said. It was Ulfrik's house now, of course, but she was loath to even say his name.

"One of the Irish thralls can do it," he replied. "I don't want you out here." He kept his hand on the hilt of his sword.

It was obvious he still anticipated some treachery on the part of Ainnileas or his men.

She hesitated. Should she tell him the truth and ask for his help, or would it be safer to leave Ainnileas to his own devices? Although Alrik had been remarkably stable since her return to him, experience had taught her how his moods could shift like quicksilver.

He narrowed his eyes as though sensing her uncertainty, then grabbed her hand and headed toward the house. Selia had to run to keep up with his long strides. "Are you having second thoughts already?" he hissed.

"No, Alrik. It is not that. Please . . ."

But he continued to the house, dragging Selia into their bedchamber. He sat her in the chair in the corner, then turned to flip open the large chest containing his battle gear, muttering to himself all the while. He must have thought she'd change her mind about staying with him. Now, his odd behavior confirmed it.

"I won't let you go again." His voice escalated as he pulled out his mail shirt, helmet, and axe.

"Alrik—" she began, rising to move toward him.

"You sit down and don't move from that spot!" he shouted, pointing to the chair with his battle axe.

Selia blew her breath out in exasperation. "Stop, you stupid man. You are angry over nothing! I do not want to leave. I am afraid for Ainnileas."

He lowered the axe and looked at Selia for a long moment. "Stupid?" he asked finally. "Who taught you that word?"

"Ingrid."

Alrik snorted as he pulled the mail shirt on over his head. "Why are you afraid for Ainnileas?"

She hesitated. "You must promise me you will not hurt him."

He turned to her with suspicion. "I do not often make such promises."

"Please, Alrik." Selia laid her hand on his arm. She tried to think of a reason that might appeal to him. "If I do not do something, then Ainnileas might have to stay in Norway. With Grainne."

He stilled. She knew he wanted the woman gone, far from them both. Now that Grainne was a freedwoman, she could come and go as she pleased, and if she stayed in Norway the odds were high they would see her again. Alrik wanted to avoid that at all costs.

"I promise no harm will come to your brother," he said. "Now tell me what you're hiding from me."

She looked into his fierce blue eyes. He was still angry, at the tipping point where he could easily slip over the edge into a mindless rage. But she was running out of alternatives.

"There is a man in Ireland who wanted to marry me. He will pay well if I am returned. The ship came back to claim me, and I am afraid Ainnileas will be in mortal danger from his crew if I do not go back."

Alrik's jaw clenched so hard she could hear his teeth grinding, and his hand twitched against the hilt of the battle axe. "So you were going to go back with them to save your brother?" His voice sounded like gravel. "You *were* going to leave me again."

"No," she insisted earnestly. "I was going to give them my jewelry. Ainnileas also has silver in Ireland. My bride price. I thought it would be enough, together."

His eyes narrowed to slits. "By all rights I should kill your brother for his deceit."

"You promised, Alrik!"

"I did. But hear me now, woman. If I make this right for Ainnileas, he will never be welcomed on Norse soil again. I will not tolerate such treachery as he has shown me. Do you understand?"

Relief made her knees go weak. Her brother was safe; Alrik wouldn't hurt him. She nodded, eyes downcast.

Alrik remained quiet for a moment. "Did you love him? The man in Ireland?" He tilted her chin up so she was forced to look at him. There was hurt in his eyes behind the anger.

"No," she whispered. "I told you, I have never loved another before you."

But he wouldn't let it rest. "Did he touch you?" he asked. Selia shook her head but he persisted. "Tell me his name."

She jerked her head away. "So you can kill a helpless old man? No, Alrik. I will not."

He made a guttural noise deep in his throat as he glared down at her. She stood her ground and remained silent. "Stay in the house," he said finally, then turned to storm out, battle axe in hand.

She watched from the main doorway as Alrik, Olaf, and one of the male thralls approached the ship as it docked. Ingrid had decided it was worth her while to rise from her bench after all, and she stood next to Hrefna near the docks, close enough to hear whatever conversation the men would have. Selia felt a twinge of resentment as she watched them. Alrik still didn't trust her enough to stand with the other women.

Three of the Irish sailors met Alrik at the dock, and even from a distance she recognized Niall's men. Ainnileas' men now, but would they would remain so?

Alrik, the mighty Hersir, towered over the Irishmen. He was a menacing sight indeed as the sun glinted off his mail shirt and the axe he carried at his broad shoulder. And instead of tilting his head as he did when he regarded her, he kept his chin angled in a hostile manner and simply looked down his nose at them. He was trying to intimidate them. Judging from the frightened reaction of the Irish sailors, his tactic appeared to be working.

Alrik spoke to the Irishmen as the thrall translated. Then he leaned back, crossed his arms, and gave them the disdainful glare Selia knew very well. The conversation was over as far as he was concerned.

Suddenly there was a scream from Ingrid. Selia's breath caught. Had Alrik done something after all—had he killed one of them and she hadn't seen it? She scanned the scene, cursing the fact that she wasn't down at the docks. Alrik hadn't moved and no one seemed to be hurt. But Ingrid ran into the woods, wailing, with Hrefna calling out after her.

The discussion concluded quickly. The three Irishmen hastened to board the ship. They wasted no time sailing out of the bay, as Alrik stalked back toward the house.

"What happened?" she called to him, but he pushed past her without a word. She followed him into the bedchamber, where he threw his axe to the floor with a clatter and ripped the mail shirt off over his head.

"*Buadhach*," he snarled, running his hands through his hair. The Irish name sounded strange spoken with Alrik's strong Norse accent. "Did you think I wouldn't learn his name? I will kill him, Selia. I will rip his lungs from his chest—"

She gasped. "No, you promised!"

He turned to her. "I promised not to hurt your brother. I made no such promise about the man who would take you from me. And for someone you claim to care nothing about, you seem quite concerned for his safety."

"He is an old man, not any threat to you. Buadhach is, um . . ." she paused, blushing, "unable to bed a woman."

"And how would you know that?"

"Eithne told me. She said my father was afraid I would die in childbed, so he would give me to Buadhach."

He continued to pace, undeterred. "Yet he would rob me of you, Selia—he would pay those Irishmen to steal you away! I should have killed every one of them, to the last man." Snarling in frustration, Alrik bent at the waist to be face to face with her. "Never in my life have I swallowed my pride this way, woman. Do not ask me to do such a thing again."

Selia stilled, looking into his blazing eyes. She hadn't been able to see past the threat to Ainnileas' safety to realize that the Hersir would consider it an achievement of unbearable restraint not to slay the crew of the Irish ship for their part in the deceit. She hadn't understood the situation would be an affront to his Finngall sense of honor.

His body shook with the effort it cost to maintain his self-control, and she touched his face to soothe him. "I'm sorry," she murmured consolingly.

"Do you have anyone else to tell me about?" His voice was curt. "Any other thwarted suitors I should be aware of?"

None beyond your own brother. "No," she whispered. She slid her hand behind his head and placed a soft kiss on his lips. Alrik's mouth remained hard. "Will Ainnileas be safe?" she asked, looking into his eyes for the truth.

He drew back. "He will be safe as long as he stays out of Norway. I told those Irishmen I would grant them the gift of their lives, which is more than they should hope for after such treachery. If your brother does not make it to Ireland safely, I will find and kill every one of those men, and I will take their women as my thralls. This was my vow."

She shuddered, knowing the threat was not exaggerated. "Why did Ingrid scream?" she asked.

Alrik glared at her for several moments. "Because she knows I will never allow Ainnileas to have her. I swore on Odin's blood if your brother or any one of those Irishmen sets foot upon Norse soil, it will be the last step they will ever take. I will not show mercy a second time to those who would steal from me."

Selia drew her breath in sharply as realization dawned on her. So this was it, then. She would never see her brother again. She felt a sense of lightheadedness that had nothing to do with the child growing in her belly, and she moved away from Alrik to steady herself on the edge of the table.

Although he had said earlier he would not allow Ainnileas to return to Norway if he helped him, she had assumed Alrik's statement was simply a product of his anger, and that when it burned off she would be able to reason with him. But no, this was final. Her husband was furious that his honor had been compromised, and he would never forget nor forgive.

Ainnileas, her twin, her once-constant companion, would very soon be on the Irish ship sailing away from Norway. Forever. She had not even said a proper goodbye, and now would never be able to. The bitter words they had exchanged when she departed from Ulfrik's house clawed at her mind, refusing to be pushed away.

A suffocating panic rose inside her and she had difficulty forming the Norse words. "I did not get to tell Ainnileas goodbye—"

"No, Selia," he growled, as if he already understood what she was about to ask.

"Alrik! If you are to keep him from returning to Norway, I must go to him. I must see him one last time. He is my brother. He is my twin." Selia sank onto the chair, forcing air into her lungs. *Breathe.*

He studied her for a moment, his expression fierce. "Why should I do this? Tell me why I should let you see that traitorous boy. A boy who deserves nothing from me other than a blade through his belly."

"Because there is good in you," she pleaded. "And because you love me."

Alrik took a very long time to respond. He looked away, and when he turned back to her his face was shuttered. "If I take you, then this will be the end of it," he vowed. "You will never ask me to reconsider. Ever. Understood?"

"Yes," she whispered.

The trip that had taken Selia so long by foot was made much faster by horse. Alrik had asked Olaf to accompany them in case the Irishmen decided to try to take her after all, despite his grim threats.

She rode in front of Alrik as they galloped at full speed, the horses churning up clumps of dirt with their hooves. She gripped the saddle with white knuckles as the wind forced tears from her eyes. The power of the animal beneath her was terrifying, and she was grateful for Alrik's strong arm holding her tightly to his body. But even traveling at such a breakneck speed, there was a good chance they wouldn't make it in time and would arrive to find an empty house. The ship could travel much faster than the horses.

As they drew near the dwelling, she saw another horse tied to a tree. It danced with a nervous whinny as they approached. Selia's stomach tightened. Was it Ulfrik's horse? She had assumed he had gone back to Ketill's farmstead after she had refused him. Why would he have stayed here? And more importantly, what was she going to do when she saw him?

Alrik reined the horse, then dismounted, turning to lift Selia down as well. She rushed to the edge of the cliff, leaving the men to tie the horses to the tree, and let her breath out as she saw the Irish ship. The fact that the Irishmen were sailing through unfamiliar territory must have slowed them down just enough to allow the horses to reach the house in time. The water was too shallow for the deep ship to pull up to the dock, so it was positioned in the middle of the bay, waiting, while two Irish sailors in a small boat rowed toward the dock.

She heard the sound of raised voices as she peered down to the beach. She saw not only Ainnileas and Grainne, but Ingrid as well. So the horse belonged to Ingrid, not Ulfrik. The girl must have come in a desperate attempt to run away with Ainnileas.

As Alrik came up behind her, he obviously reached the same conclusion. He bellowed with rage as he drew his sword to rush down the hill toward the beach. Selia took the shorter way, climbing down the cliff, and reached the group on the beach before he did.

Ingrid, frantic, eyes wild, cried incoherently. She appeared to have pulled out fistfuls of her own hair. Ainnileas' body language was more subdued. Although he held himself in a slightly defensive posture against a sudden attack from Ingrid, the expression on his face seemed to be one of pity. Grainne stood closest to the water, veering back and forth between her son, the mad Norse girl, and the small Irish boat on its way to grant her freedom.

Ainnileas' gaze landed on Selia. "What are you doing here?"

"Alrik knows what you tried to do," she said, gasping for breath. "He won't let you come back to Norway, and I needed to see you one last time—"

Ainnileas looked up sharply as Alrik crashed through the brush. "Why did you bring him here, Selia? Now he'll think I planned this!" His gaze flickered toward Ingrid where she crouched in the sand, sobbing.

Selia turned as her husband rushed toward her brother with his sword drawn. "No, Alrik!" she cried. "He had nothing to do with this!" She stood in front of Ainnileas to block the attack.

Ainnileas pulled the dagger from his belt and shoved Selia aside. Grainne screamed.

There was a blur of motion as Ingrid launched herself at her father. She grabbed his sword arm so tightly that she came off her feet as he tried to shake her loose. "This is your fault!" she screamed. "Ainnileas won't have me because of you!"

Alrik's eyes were lit up like the devil himself as he glared at Ainnileas. "Is it not enough that you mean to steal my wife from me, but now you would steal my daughter as well?" he snarled.

"No!" Ainnileas shouted, gripping his dagger. "I do not want Ingrid."

The girl wailed again. "He loved me until you ruined it! You ruin everything!" she screeched at Alrik.

He grabbed Ingrid by the hair to pull her free of his arm, letting her dangle for a moment before dropping her unceremoniously on the ground. "You are an embarrassment to me, daughter," he sneered down at her. "This boy is a coward and a deceiver, and yet you throw yourself at him like a whore. As long as there is breath in me, I will never give you to him."

Ingrid cried out as though she were in physical pain as she collapsed onto the sand. Alrik motioned to Olaf, who came forward. "Take her back to the horses until the ship is gone," he ordered. "Restrain her if you must."

Olaf hoisted Ingrid to her feet. She put her head into his chest, sobbing. He held her for a moment and spoke softly to her, then half-led, half-carried the girl up the hill toward the house.

Grainne and Ainnileas stood close together, watching Alrik. He gave them both a scornful look before turning his gaze to the small boat. The sailors had tied it loosely to the dock but appeared fearful to get out, and so they sat in the boat as it bobbed like a cork in the water.

"Get in the boat, woman," he ordered Grainne, pointing with his sword. "My wife would say goodbye to her brother, but not to you."

Selia had told him, without going into detail, how there was no love lost between her and Grainne. If she never saw her mother again it would not be a hardship.

The woman shared a sneer between Alrik and Selia. "You are dead to me, child," she said in a harsh whisper, spitting on the ground. "The flames of hell will rise up and devour you—"

Ainnileas made a cutting motion with his hand. "Enough. Just get in the boat, Mother."

She did so, muttering under her breath all the while, and Alrik turned back to address Ainnileas. "Listen well, boy. You will never see Selia again. If you attempt to return to Norway, I will kill you. Do you understand?"

Ainnileas remained motionless, and Alrik turned impatiently to his wife. "Tell him in Irish—"

"I understand," Ainnileas retorted, visibly bristling.

Selia stepped between them and frowned at Alrik until he moved aside. He cursed as he sheathed his sword. "Then say your goodbyes," he commanded.

She touched her twin's cheek with a rueful smile. "I love you, my brother." She used the language that was theirs alone.

His face crumpled as he pulled her to him in a fierce embrace. "I can't leave you with him."

"Yes you can," she whispered, blinking back tears. "You only see the bad in him, everyone does. But I can see the good. He loves me, and I love him."

"He'll end up killing you, you foolish girl. Even Ulfrik said so—"

She shook her head. "Do not speak that name to me. He is a liar. Everything he said was a lie."

He stared at her for a moment. "Did he do something to you, Selia?"

"No," she retorted. "But if you ever see him again, don't believe a word he says. Promise me."

Her brother nodded slowly. "I'm sorry for trying to take you back to Buadhach. I'm sorry for everything. Now I've lost you, and I've lost Ingrid too."

"You do love her, then."

He averted his gaze toward the beach path Ingrid had taken. "It doesn't matter now, does it?"

Not if Alrik had anything to do with it. "No," Selia sighed. "It doesn't." She stroked his chin where a few more dark hairs had sprouted recently. Her brother was turning into a man overnight. "I'm sorry too, Ainnileas. I know you can't understand why I'm staying in Norway, but I hope you'll be able to forgive me."

"I already have," he murmured, then pulled her close again to kiss her on the forehead. "I love you, Selia."

She slid her arms around him and held on, choking back a sob. Ainnileas finally stepped away from her with a sad smile. He wiped his eyes on his sleeve as he turned to climb into the boat next to Grainne.

Hot tears streamed down Selia's face as she watched the boat slowly make its way toward the ship. Although Grainne refused to look in her direction, Ainnileas didn't take his gaze from hers. As she watched them climb up into the ship, Alrik took Selia by the arm, ready to leave.

"Wait," she whispered. "Not until the ship is gone."

He grimaced but released her arm. The ship's sails unfurled with a flutter, catching the wind. Ainnileas stood white-faced as he gripped the rail, his gaze locked with Selia's.

The craft sailed out of the bay and disappeared into the cleft in the cliffs. A cry escaped Selia's lips as she stared at the empty space where the ship had been. Her brother was gone.

"It's time to go, little one," Alrik said quietly, reaching for her hand. His eyes had lost their blaze of fury, and now studied her with something approaching compassion.

Selia met his gaze briefly. This was it, then; her decision was permanent now. She would never leave Norway. She nodded, sniffling, and placed her hand in his to return home.

Chapter 3

Selia awoke at dawn. She lay quietly for some time, listening to Alrik breathe beside her. The seasons had shifted from late summer to autumn, and the light had begun to change as well. The darkest part of the night now lasted longer than it had during the summer.

At her request, Alrik had postponed his fall trip to Ireland for as long as possible. But the time had come; the war band would leave tomorrow morning. The sea could be unpredictable this late in the season, and if they waited any longer the men might have to winter over in Dubhlinn.

Selia stared at the form of her sleeping husband in the semidarkness. She studied him, memorizing the curves and planes of bone and muscle, burning the image in her mind until he returned. Her eyes focused on the pulse in his neck, beating almost imperceptibly. He was a huge man, stronger than any she had ever known, yet she could not fool herself into thinking he was impervious to the ravages of battle. A well-aimed blade could still the Hersir's pulse just as easily as it could that of any other man.

Aside from the occasional, mild mood swing, he had been surprisingly stable since she had returned to him. She suspected it was because both Ulfrik and Ainnileas were gone, and therefore he had less to be jealous of. He was still the same Alrik after all—selfish enough to be resentful of any competition for her affections, even those of a platonic nature. In that way he was very much like a child, overwhelmed with the intensity of his need for her.

He had gone to Bjorn's for the blacksmith to sharpen his weapons, and while there had run into Ketill. Upon Alrik's return home he had shared with disdain that his brother had left Ketill's farmstead and had gone to Bjorgvin to join with Gunnar One-Eye's crew.

Selia had startled at the name. Gunnar One-Eye was the warlord who had raided Muirin's village in Ireland, selling her into slavery. Gunnar had the reputation of being the single most violent and bloodthirsty of all the Vikingers in Norway, which of course infuriated Alrik.

Gunnar concentrated his efforts on slave-trading. He chose only the most beautiful, exotic specimens to sell at a high price as concubines. Everyone else he killed, which rubbed against Alrik's practical nature. A homely, yet strong-backed slave could fetch a reasonable price at market. Alrik had grumbled that Gunnar's methods were wasteful and smacked of laziness.

She was shocked that Ulfrik would join with such a man, but then again she had been fooled by Ulfrik before. His gentle nature had been nothing but a ruse. Every kindness he had shown her had been a deception to lure her away from Alrik. Why should this new evidence, that he wasn't the man he pretended to be, surprise her?

The light from the smoke hole intensified as the sun rose, and Selia watched as the blaze touched Alrik, giving his skin and hair a golden glow. She reached for his face, unable to resist, and drew her fingers over the glittering hairs of his eyebrow.

He squinted in the sunlight, his irises a ghostly blue. "What are you doing?" he mumbled. The heavy muscles rippled under his skin as he stretched.

Her breath caught in her throat at the beauty of him. She felt tears prickling in her eyes and she blinked them away. "I am looking at you, Alrik. I love you so much it hurts."

He chuckled. "I'm sorry it's so painful for you."

"Do not laugh at me," she said hotly. "I could not bear it if you got hurt again. I do not think I could live without you." She rolled over to stare at the rafters.

He caught her gaze as he rose up on his elbow. "Do you think I want to leave you, Selia?" He drew his thumb across her bottom lip. "Do you think I can bear the thought of being apart from you again?" He ran his hand down her throat, over her breast, finally resting on her pubic bone. The rough skin of his hand left a trail of heat where he had touched her.

He flashed his devilish smile and bent to kiss her. A small noise escaped her lips as Selia opened herself to him, unable to resist him any more than a moth could a flame.

She felt his erection pressing into her leg, but he didn't enter her immediately. Alrik instead worked his way down her body, kissing, licking, and occasionally biting, until she felt she would explode. She grabbed his shoulders in an attempt to pull him on top of her, but Alrik took her wrists, pinning them by her sides as his mouth moved over her belly, and lower.

"Please, Alrik . . ." she begged.

He laughed, biting her inner thigh, and Selia squirmed to no avail. "Soon," he said. "I will give you something to remember while I'm gone."

His silky hair brushed against her sensitive skin as his mouth moved with maddening precision. She arched toward him with a moan. He lingered slowly, unusual for him, and she was vaguely amazed he had held himself back this long. He continued his torture until Selia's body shattered with pleasure, and she lay dazed.

Alrik smiled at her, proud of his achievement as always, and finally moved on top of her. But he entered slowly, with incredible self-control, and she looked up at him in confusion.

"Alrik," she panted, "What are you doing?"

"I thought you would like this." His jaw ground audibly with the effort of holding back.

So he was doing this for her, as a gift before he left. Selia's heart nearly burst with love for him even as her body rebelled. She had become so accustomed to his primal intensity that nothing else would do.

She wrapped her arms around his neck, pulling his face down so he was forced to look at her. "No," she whispered. "I want you . . . I want all of you. Do not hold back, Alrik."

There was a flicker of astonishment in his eyes before they shuttered over and he allowed himself to let go with a groan. Selia cried out, swept away by the intensity of his passion. She was his willing vessel, opening her very soul to his thrusts, and her body trembled as he buried himself inside her with one final grunt.

He didn't move for a moment and she could feel his heart pounding against her cheek. She clung to his broad back, missing him already. He shifted his body again so he could look down at her.

"You . . . prefer it that way?" There was doubt in his voice.

"Yes." How could he not know that already? Couldn't he tell from her body's response to him that she did? "I love you, Alrik. When you are careful, it feels like it is not you."

He shook his head as though unconvinced. "I thought women preferred the other way."

Selia smiled up at him as her face heated. Why did she feel so shy? She ran her fingers through his hair, twining a lock of it around her finger. "Not me. I like it."

She craved the strength and power of his body. She craved the unpredictability of the beast that raged within him. How had he not known this? Had he thought she had been doing him an act of kindness by allowing him to ravage her, instead of understanding she wanted him just as much as he wanted her? His expression changed as realization dawned on him.

He gazed down at her in silence for several moments, looking as stunned as she had ever seen him. "You were truly meant for me, Selia," he marveled. "Now I understand why Odin put you in my path."

"Yes," she agreed, with some reluctance. It was better not to argue with him when he spoke of his conviction that she was some sort of prize or reward from Odin. This belief made her uncomfortable, and not just because it went against her Christian upbringing. If she had been compelled by Odin to fall in love with Alrik, then did that mean she had no free will, no choice in the matter? Was her love less genuine if it had been forced by a heathen god?

Alrik lay back on the pillows, appearing lost in thought. Selia suddenly felt cold, as though he had already left her alone in an empty bed. She nuzzled her face into his warm neck and inhaled his scent.

"Promise you will come back to me, Alrik. Promise."

"I promise, little one. Not even the gods themselves could keep me from you."

Ingrid was still asleep—as usual—when Selia went out to the kitchen. Hrefna was nowhere to be found, which was more unusual. Maybe Hrefna and Olaf were doing the very thing she and Alrik had been doing only moments ago. Or maybe . . . maybe Hrefna had been called to the slave quarters? The thought sent a shiver of anticipation up her spine.

She hummed to herself as she began the makings of the morning meal when Olaf hurried past her on the way to the privy. "Oh," Selia said, feigning nonchalance. "Is Hrefna still asleep?"

Olaf ran his hand over his bald head in the manner of one who is still surprised his hair was gone. "No, one of the thralls came for her in the night," he replied. "Muirin's time is at hand and she is having trouble."

She gasped. "Is everything all right?"

"I don't know," he said over his shoulder. "Hrefna hasn't come back yet."

Selia hurried to the slave quarters. Muirin was having trouble. What did that mean, exactly? Would the child be all right? Her hand hesitated briefly on the door, and she closed her eyes and took a deep breath. Her own unborn babe kicked inside her, and she caressed the swell of her belly before she walked in.

Muirin was in the back corner of the house, crouching naked on her hands and knees in a pile of straw. Hrefna wiped the girl's brow with a rag as another thrall, Keir, knelt behind Muirin to rub her lower back. Muirin's enormous belly seemed to undulate. Selia gaped for a moment, then dismissed it as a trick of the flickering light.

Muirin cried out; a loud, strong bellow that was surprising given her timid nature. Her face purpled with effort as she bore down, changing the sound into a grunt. Keir placed her hand between the girl's legs. She held it there momentarily, then looked up at Hrefna as she shook her head.

As the pain passed, Muirin's body sagged and her head drooped toward the ground. She appeared to almost be asleep. The thrall continued to rub Muirin's back and speak soothing words to her, but Hrefna noticed Selia standing silently in the doorway. She handed the rag to Keir as she walked over.

"Is everything all right?" Selia whispered, unable to stop gawking at Muirin. The girl was clearly exhausted. Was this a normal part of childbirth or had something had gone awry?

The woman hesitated a moment too long. "Yes, my dear. Everything's fine."

Selia was unconvinced. "Is there anything I can do to help?"

There was another cry from Muirin, a higher pitched scream that made the hairs rise on Selia's arms. Hrefna seemed uncomfortable. "This could take quite some time," the woman whispered. "I was planning to pack supplies for the men. Maybe you could do that for me?"

It was obvious Hrefna wanted her away from the slave quarters. Selia studied her for a moment before looking back to Muirin.

"If the babe is coming now . . . then it is probably Alrik's after all," she said.

"Yes." Hrefna nodded. "I'm sorry."

Selia walked out without another word. She closed the door on the blood-chilling sound of Muirin's screams as she headed back to the house.

A strange sense of calm enveloped her as she searched out Alrik. She found him on the dragonship with Olaf, examining the ropes in preparation for tomorrow's journey. He was so busy with his task that he didn't notice her standing on the dock. She watched him for several moments.

"Alrik," she called. "I need to speak with you."

He looked up and met her gaze. "I'm busy. We can talk later."

"It is important. Please."

Grunting his annoyance, he tossed the rope he was scrutinizing in Olaf's direction. He jumped over the rail of the ship, landing on the dock just a few feet in front of Selia. She pulled him farther down the beach so they could speak privately.

"I don't have time for this, Selia. What do you need?" There was an edge to his voice. Olaf must have told him about Muirin, and now Alrik probably thought she was angry at him again.

She looked up at him and took a deep breath. "Muirin is having her babe."

Alrik gave a curt nod.

"The child is yours, then," she prodded.

He frowned. "Yes. But that means nothing. It doesn't matter."

"If you freed Muirin now, her child would be freeborn. If a boy-child, could he be Hersir?"

Hrefna had explained the difference between a freeborn man, and a freedman. A freedman, such as Ulfrik, would always be somewhat under the guardianship of the family who had freed him. In Ulfrik's case, his brother. He was expected to ask permission before making decisions that a freeborn man could make alone, such as marrying or moving his household. He would also be expected to show deference to freeborn men, and could, by law, never be Hersir.

Ulfrik was older than Alrik, and therefore could have claimed the title of Hersir after Ragnarr, if only he had been freeborn. Alrik would have had a sound dispute to his brother's claim, however, since he had been born to Ragnarr's wife, and Ulfrik to his concubine.

Alrik stared down at her for a time before he spoke. "Why are you asking me this?"

"Because . . ." she paused, cupping the curve of her belly protectively. "If I could keep this child from killing my people, I would."

Alrik blew out a breath as if speechless, with a look on his face she had never seen before. It was clear she had deeply offended him.

"He can still learn to fight," she said quickly. "He will still be a Finngall. But if he is your second son, perhaps he can learn a trade?"

Blacksmith, merchant, farmer . . . she didn't care which. Just as long as his occupation didn't require him to lead a bloodthirsty war band across the sea to slaughter her people.

He just blinked at her and remained silent.

"Besides," she continued, now desperate, "Muirin is much bigger than I am. Her child will be large and strong. He will make a good Hersir."

Alrik scowled. "It could be a girl. Then I would have freed Muirin for nothing."

"Yes," she agreed. "It could. But so could my child."

His scowl deepened. She knew Hrefna had initiated a serious discussion with him about the unsuitability of Selia's slender hips for childbearing. Unless Alrik wanted his wife to eventually die in childbed, they needed to ensure their first child would be their last. And so he had agreed to allow Selia to take Hrefna's tea after the child was born, a drink that prevented a man's seed from taking root in a woman's body.

"Are you sure you want this?" He narrowed his eyes. "After you were so angry about Muirin, are you sure you now want me to claim the child?"

She lowered her gaze to the ground. "Yes. I am sure." It would be awkward for a time, having Muirin around as a freedwoman. But after the child was weaned, his mother would leave the farmstead and the child would stay. Perhaps Muirin could go with Ulfrik. Wasn't her child a fair trade for her freedom and her ability to be with the man she loved?

"If I do this, I cannot change it, Selia. You cannot change your mind."

"I know," she whispered.

Alrik shook his head in exasperation. "All right. I'll claim the whelp."

"Then you must hurry before Muirin has the child." She took his hand, pulling him in the direction of the slave quarters.

"I'll have to send for Bjorn first, to remove the collar."

Selia held back a sigh of frustration. If they waited too long, Muirin would deliver the child and the entire proposition would be for naught.

She watched anxiously as Alrik went in search of one of the thralls to find Bjorn, and hoped they wouldn't be too late.

Chapter 4

Later, Selia followed Alrik and Bjorn into the slave quarters. Muirin squatted over the straw with Hrefna and Keir on either side, supporting her under her arms. Hrefna looked up with a frown at Alrik and Bjorn. It was not fitting for men to be present at childbirth.

"Why are you here?" she asked her nephew.

He ignored her and strode over to Muirin, regarding her with what appeared to be indifference. The girl was too exhausted to even attempt to register surprise at the appearance of her master. Her head lolled to the side and her weary gaze fixed on his boots as he spoke to her.

"Muirin. You are no longer bound to me as thrall. I grant you your freedom so that my child will be freeborn. You may leave this household if you choose, but the child stays with me." Alrik clenched his jaw as he spoke.

Was he simply annoyed at the necessity of setting free a valuable slave, or did he still have some residual feelings for the girl? Selia suppressed a flash of jealousy as she eyed them both.

Muirin's face drained of color. She licked her parched lips as two tears trickled down her cheeks, landing in the straw below. Selia looked away and swallowed back the bile that threatened to rise in her throat. Even though the girl had agreed to this, it was still difficult to watch.

Muirin tried to kill your babe, she reminded herself. This was better than she deserved.

Hrefna blinked at her nephew as though he had lost his mind. "What?" she sputtered, looking back and forth from Alrik to Selia. "What madness is this?"

"It's none of your concern, woman," Alrik replied. "The child is mine and I'm claiming it."

Muirin's belly seemed to ripple again, and she screamed as another pain hit her. She bore down, grunting and red-faced, and Keir leaned over to look between Muirin's legs. "I see the head," she whispered encouragingly to Muirin.

Alrik turned to the blacksmith. "Remove the collar before the child is born."

Bjorn's gaze had been averted since they had walked in the door, and he coughed uncomfortably into his hand now. "The woman will need to lie on a hard surface." He scanned the room with uncertainty. "The table will probably do."

The pain passed, and Muirin's body again sagged to the floor. Alrik hoisted her to her feet. He dragged the naked girl to the table and bent her over it, face down. With Alrik's large hand pinning her head to the table, Bjorn drew out a chisel and small sledgehammer from the bag he carried over his shoulder. He turned the collar around on the slave's neck until he found the iron rivet that fastened it. He placed the chisel over it, eying the spot where he would need to strike.

The pains seemed to be coming faster, and Muirin's body bucked as she was overcome with the next one. Alrik pressed her to the table. "Stop squirming," he ordered, "or the blade will cut you."

Choking back a sob, she stilled and closed her eyes. Bjorn held the sledgehammer up as he aimed, then brought it down with a swift, precise motion.

Selia flinched as the sledgehammer made contact with the chisel, just inches from Muirin's head. The rivet snapped in two and Bjorn pulled the collar free from her neck. The girl's hand snaked up to her throat, running her fingers over the area where the collar had been for a decade of her life. She sank to the floor with an audible sigh.

Alrik turned to address Hrefna. "Notify me when the

child is born." He walked over to where Selia stood in the corner, and took her arm as if to leave.

"Alrik," she whispered, laying her hand over his. "I will stay here and help if I can."

He frowned down at her. "Do as you wish, then. I have the ship to ready." Ignoring Muirin and her pains, Alrik left, followed by a relieved-looking Bjorn.

Hrefna stared at Selia in silence for a moment. "Was this his choice or yours?" she asked finally.

Selia felt her cheeks flame. "Mine," she admitted. "And Muirin agreed. I . . . I do not know if I can give him a son." Her eyes flickered over the exhausted mother-to-be. "Maybe she will."

Despite the brief appearance of the child's head, the labor continued well into the afternoon. Hrefna tried everything she knew to make the babe come, ranging from different labor positions to runes written on Muirin's hands and body with a charred stick, to no avail. The child refused to be born.

Although Hrefna assured Muirin first labors typically lasted quite a while, and its length didn't indicate something was wrong, Selia could tell from the look on Hrefna's face that all was not well. And as Muirin became more and more drained and actually lost consciousness in between contractions, the woman would mutter to herself and shake her head.

This was no longer just an unborn slave, but the freeborn child of the master of the estate, Hrefna's great-nephew or niece. The potential loss of the babe weighed heavily on her.

Muirin was asleep again, with her chin on her chest and her body supported by Selia and Keir as Hrefna knelt down to examine her once more. She came back up, looking worried. "The child is too large."

"Pull it out . . ." Muirin mumbled, and the three women jumped. The girl's eyes were still closed but obviously she was alert enough to have heard Hrefna. "Please, Mistress. I cannot do this any longer."

Hrefna placed her hand on Muirin's sweaty brow until she looked up at her. "I can try. But it will be painful, and it may not work."

Her face pale and drawn, Muirin's beautiful green eyes were dulled with pain. "Will the child live?"

Hrefna hesitated. "I don't know. You have been pushing for a long time."

Selia swallowed. There was a good possibility that the babe was dead already, then. But if it wasn't dead it would be soon, and Muirin along with it. Something had to be done.

Muirin nodded again with a strangled sob, and Hrefna indicated to the women that they should lay her back on the straw. "You will have to hold her," she instructed, "and do not let go."

Selia put one hand on Muirin's shoulder and gripped her hand with the other.

The girl glanced up at her. "I'm sorry, Mistress," she faltered. "God is punishing me for what I did to you."

"No, Muirin," Selia protested, squeezing her hand.

Muirin stared with her green cat eyes. Then she gasped, overcome with another pain. "If I die," she panted, "will you tell Ulfrik I loved him?"

"Of course," Selia assured her, "but you will not die."

Keir looked away uncomfortably. She truly thought this was the end for Muirin, then. Suddenly the poor girl let out a piercing shriek and fought against the women with unexpected strength, and it was all Selia could do to keep her from coming up off the floor. Hrefna, working between Muirin's legs, had managed to slip one hand inside her and was pressing down on the top of her belly with the other.

The girl's body bucked as she screamed. Her belly undulated with another contraction, Hrefna struggling to deliver the babe. The sound that Muirin made was inhuman, and Selia's arms shook with the effort it took to restrain her.

There was a triumphant grunt from Hrefna, and Selia looked down to see what appeared to be a dark, bloody ball emerging from between Muirin's legs.

"The head is out," the woman informed Muirin. "One more push, and the child will be free."

Muirin's eyes rolled like a panicked animal. She bore down hard with the next pain, and Hrefna cursed in frustration as the babe didn't move.

"The shoulders are stuck," she declared grimly. "Hold her again. I will have to pull once more."

Muirin's scream was desperate as she pushed with the next pain that came over her. Hrefna tugged on the child's head while using her other hand to adjust the shoulders which were still inside. There was a sickening sound that reminded Selia of fabric being ripped as the woman finally pulled the child free.

A final, awful cry burst from Muirin before the girl slumped in the straw, completely spent. Hrefna took a cloth and rubbed the child briskly with it for what seemed to be a very long time, until finally the babe emitted a weak mewl.

Selia let her breath out. The child's cries escalated and Hrefna laughed in satisfaction. There was a faint smile on Muirin's lips as she reached for her babe. "Is it a boy or a girl?" she whispered.

"A boy," Hrefna replied. "He looks healthy."

"Can I hold—" Muirin began, then her voice faded away. Selia stared as Muirin's face drained of color and her eyes lost focus.

Hrefna thrust the babe at Keir. "Get him to suckle," she ordered, as she put both hands on Muirin's belly and pressed in with all her weight. Selia had a vague memory of the woman doing that to her the night she had nearly bled her child out, and she gasped as she watched the straw between Muirin's legs stain with bright red blood. *No.* It was coming out of her at an alarming pace, and by the reaction of Hrefna and Keir this was not a normal part of childbirth.

She bit back a scream.

The thrall held the child up to Muirin's breast and was attempting to force it to suckle, which confused Selia even more. It seemed inappropriate to worry about feeding the child when its mother was obviously at the point of death. "What are you doing?" she hissed at Keir as the woman tried to pry open the protesting babe's mouth with her finger. "You are going to hurt him!"

"It can stop the bleeding, Selia!" Hrefna snapped. She grabbed Selia's hand and placed it on Muirin's belly. "Push down as hard as you can, child. I need to try to pull out the afterbirth."

She pushed down into Muirin's soft, boggy flesh, gaping in horror as Hrefna put her hand inside the girl. After several long seconds, she drew back her arm—now slick with blood—and pulled out a large, purplish mass that resembled raw liver. It was attached to the babe's navel by a ropy cord. Hrefna placed the bloody thing on the ground. A few wisps of hair had escaped from the woman's fillet, and she swiped the hair from her eyes with the back of her arm, leaving a smear of Muirin's blood on her forehead.

Hrefna swallowed as she looked at Muirin. The girl was fish-belly white, and although her eyes were still open, they stared back at her mistress sightlessly. The expression on her beautiful face was one of mild surprise. "It's too late," the woman said quietly. "She is gone."

It took a moment for Hrefna's words to sink in as Selia gazed down at the motionless girl.

Dead.

Muirin was dead. Selia had held her hand as the girl's soul slipped from her body, and had been powerless to stop it. Covered in blood from the waist down, Muirin's body looked as though it had been butchered.

She'd had only nineteen summers.

Selia felt the bile rise in her throat. She stood quickly, stumbling in her haste to get outside and into the fresh air. She slung open the door and breathed deeply, willing herself not to vomit. The early evening air felt soothing on her overheated skin.

This couldn't be happening. Muirin had been strong and healthy, with hips made for childbearing. Selia had prayed the child would be born before Alrik left for his fall trip; prayed Muirin's labor would start. If it did, the child growing inside the thrall's belly was more than likely Alrik's. And— if Muirin were to be granted her freedom—the future Hersir.

Had Selia's prayers been answered, but at the cost of Muirin's life?

Now, a new worry. Selia had gotten only a brief glimpse of the babe, but nevertheless had been struck by his size, especially the width of the shoulders. Both Alrik and Ulfrik had incredibly broad shoulders. If Muirin had been unable to survive childbirth, how could Selia expect to? Would she be dead as well, nothing more than a butchered body lying on a bed of straw?

Hrefna came out, wiping her hands on a rag, and approached Selia with caution. "Are you all right, child?" She drew her eyebrows together. "I'm sorry you had to see that."

Selia sniffled and wiped at her eyes. She rubbed her belly, shielding the babe from the carnage inside the slave quarters, and it kicked back at her hand as though sensing her distress. Her gaze locked on the open doorway as she heard the muffled squalls of the child from inside. Alrik's child. Her step-child. Keir made hushing sounds and the babe quieted.

Hrefna reached out to squeeze her arm. "It will be all right, my dear," she assured her, but Selia sensed the uncertainty in her voice.

"It will *not* be all right, Hrefna!" she cried. "That child ripped Muirin apart. How can I hope to birth a babe that large?"

Hrefna avoided her gaze and didn't answer. A loud wail arose from inside the slave quarters, and the woman snapped to attention. "Well. We must find Alrik in order for him to examine the child, so the poor thing can be fed. I will send Keir to find Hallveig. Her own child appears old enough to be weaned. And she seems rather intelligent as far as thralls go. We don't want a stupid girl feeding the Hersir's son."

Selia nodded. The woman went inside to fetch the babe, emerging a moment later with the wriggling bundle in her arms. Hrefna had cleaned the blood off the child, and Selia looked down at him curiously. He had the broad cheekbones and wide mouth common to both the sons of Ragnarr.

But the child's eyes appeared to be long and slightly slanted, like a cat.

Alrik and Olaf had finished readying the ship. The women found them back at the house, enjoying a freshly opened cask of ale. They were chuckling about something, but quieted as the women entered with the fussing babe.

Alrik noted their blood-covered gowns and Selia's dazed expression. He pulled her close, and she buried her face in his neck for a moment. "Muirin is dead," she whispered.

"And the child?" he asked over the top of Selia's head.

"A boy. He appears healthy." His aunt laid the babe on the floor carefully, then unwrapped the blanket so he was naked for inspection.

Selia stepped to one side as Alrik rose to his feet and studied the child. "He's scrawny," he said with a slight smirk. "No child of mine has ever been so small. Maybe he is Ulfrik's."

She blinked. Small? He thought this child was small?

"Thralls' children are usually smaller," Hrefna reminded him. "You can't compare him to your girls."

Alrik cocked his head at the babe. "Do you think he looks like me, or Ulfrik?"

His aunt peered down at the child, lips pursed. "I honestly don't know how you would tell."

He glanced over at Selia. "Are you sure you want this? Once it is done it cannot be undone."

She felt Hrefna's eyes on her but kept her gaze averted. "I am sure," she affirmed.

Alrik shrugged and mumbled something to himself. He knelt to gather the child from the floor. "Bring me some water," he called to one of the thralls. The woman hurried to do so, keeping her gaze lowered as she held a bowl out to him. He dipped his fingers in it and sprinkled droplets of water over the babe.

The child let out a howl of rage. "Maybe he is mine after all," Alrik said with a laugh. In more formal voice, he continued. "I own this child for my son. He shall be called Geirr." He made the sign of Thorr's hammer over the child. "My gift to him shall be the sword of his namesake, Geirr Jorulfson. A better man has never lived."

Selia was surprised at the emotion she heard in her husband's voice as he spoke of his grandfather. As if in reply, the babe grunted, then let loose a stream of urine that shot straight up in the air and arced down onto Alrik's shirt. Scowling, he held the child up, facing outward, as Geirr continued to relieve himself all over the floor. "Take him, Hrefna," he commanded, and the woman swaddled the babe in the blanket.

The slave Hallveig entered, a blond, sturdy-looking woman with a generous bosom. She stood a respectful distance from the family group with her head lowered.

Hrefna walked to her and looked her over. "You are still nursing your child?" she asked.

"Yes, Mistress," the woman replied.

Hrefna nodded as she handed over the wrapped bundle. "You will wean your child immediately and be nurse to this one," she stated. "He is Geirr Alrikson, a freeborn child. His life is in your hands, Hallveig. If he dies Alrik will hold you responsible."

The slave woman swallowed, and her gaze met Hrefna's momentarily before lowering back down to the babe in her arms. She looked terrified. "I understand, Mistress," she whispered.

As though deeming the thrall sufficiently frightened, Hrefna's face relaxed. "Bathe him then, Hallveig. And you will sleep here in the main house. It would not be fitting for the child to sleep in the slave quarters."

Hallveig hesitated. "Mistress," she said tentatively. "My own child . . . where will he sleep?"

"In the slave quarters. I will not have him competing with Geirr for your attention. The other thralls can look after him."

The slave's lip trembled. "Yes, Mistress." Her voice tightened with emotion.

Hrefna regarded Hallveig for a long, thoughtful moment. She glanced over at Selia calculatingly.

Oh, no. Selia didn't like Hrefna's expression one bit.

"On second thought, Selia will look after Geirr when you're at your chores. You will be able to see your own child then. But do not feed him," Hrefna warned sternly. "Your milk is only for the babe."

Hallveig nodded as her tears spilled over. "Thank you, Mistress," she whispered, hurrying into the kitchen to prepare the child's bath.

Alrik raised an eyebrow at his aunt. "You're getting soft in your old age, woman."

Hrefna turned to him. "Your wife needs to practice caring for a babe since you've gotten her with child." Ice coated her voice.

Alrik slapped his hands on his hips and loomed over his aunt. "You're still angry at me for sowing my seed in my own wife," he demanded.

"Yes." Hrefna scowled. "I think you are the biggest fool to ever walk the earth, Alrik Ragnarson." She headed for he door. "Now excuse me while I have the thralls bury the girl who just died birthing your child," she hissed over her shoulder, slamming the door behind her.

In the bedchamber at last, Selia stripped off her bloody clothing, then took a quick bath with a basin of cold water and a rag. The water was tinged pink by the time she finished, and she turned away from it with a shudder. She pulled on a fresh shift.

Selia climbed into bed. She lay on Alrik's pillow, breathing in the scent of his hair. It seemed as if she could still smell Muirin's blood.

Alrik strode in, rummaging in one of the chests for a clean shirt, but stopped short as he saw her in the bed. "What's wrong?" he asked. It was still early in the evening and they hadn't eaten supper yet. "Are you not feeling well?"

She met his regard. "Were Ingrid and your other girls much bigger than Geirr when they were born?"

His face changed as though he realized what she was worried about. "No," he hedged, "not much bigger."

"You are lying," she accused, and rolled away from him.

He sat on the edge of the bed, pulling her back to face him. "Selia. You are the strongest woman I have ever known. You have survived things that would have killed grown men. If anyone can birth my child, you can."

She blinked back tears. "You did not see it, Alrik. It was horrible. The child tore Muirin apart. He was stuck, and Hrefna had to pull him out." And that sound, that dreadful *ripping* sound . . . could she ever get that sound out of her head?

He grasped her shoulder. "You will be fine, little one. Odin chose you for me because you will not die. I destroy everything I touch, but not you."

Selia considered this. His fixation on such an idea sounded much too similar to the story she had heard from both Ulfrik and Hrefna about Ragnarr's delusional beliefs regarding his concubine, Treasa. But what if there was a grain of truth to Alrik's assertion, after all? What if fate had truly brought them together for a reason?

Though she was small, she did seem to possess a surprising resiliency. She had survived a blow to the head and a fall from a cliff, not to mention the volatile temperament of her Finngall husband.

She chewed on her lip. "You think I can do it?"

"Yes," he asserted. "I do. I told Hrefna so."

"She was very angry."

"That woman is always harping about something," he scoffed.

"Is she angry a thrall's child will be Hersir?"

"No. But I'm sure she would have rather been consulted first. You know how she is."

Alrik moved his hand down from her shoulder to her belly. His hand was so large it covered her from pubic bone to sternum. It gave her an inexplicable feeling of security, as though he actually could protect her and the child from the ravages of childbirth.

"If this one is a boy, I hope you won't come to regret he won't be Hersir," he mused. "You might think differently when he's grown."

"No," she said, "I will not. Geirr will be Hersir, and this one will just be a Finngall."

"'*Finngall*,'" Alrik repeated, looking amused. "You've never told me what that means. Surely it can't be too bad if you're willing to call your own child that."

"It means 'white foreigner.'" She reached up to finger a lock of her husband's blond hair.

"Well. I suppose that's better than *bastard*." He used the Irish word, chuckling, then leaned over to kiss her, his mouth warm and persistent. Selia relaxed into his embrace, allowing desire to push aside her fear of the future.

At least for the moment.

Chapter 5

Time seemed to pass in a miserable blur. Selia missed Alrik with a deep ache that made it difficult to think about anything else. Her haze of depression was intensified by dealing with Geirr, who already seemed to be a child very particular about who met his needs. He liked Hallveig. He liked Hrefna. He even seemed to like Ingrid when she could be coaxed into holding him. But whenever Selia held him, he screamed.

Geirr grew plump and sturdy on the thrall's milk. He was a beautiful babe, with creamy skin and a head as bald as Olaf's. Except for the cat eyes, he bore a striking resemblance to both Alrik and Ulfrik. She would probably never know who had actually fathered him, and the uncertainty was maddening.

Often she resented Geirr's very existence—what had she been thinking, choosing to raise the child of a slave? But sometimes she held the sleeping babe to her breast and imagined what it would be like once her own child was born.

Ingrid lay on her bench most of the time, nearly mute with grief since her plan of running off with Ainnileas had been thwarted. She refused to bathe or change her clothes, and the smell that emanated from her would set off Selia's gag reflex whenever she got wind of the girl. Not only was her nose still acutely sensitive due to the child she carried, she had grown accustomed to the meticulous grooming habits of the Finngalls. She found her stepdaughter's filthy state revolting.

Other than a few idle threats to drag Ingrid out to the bathhouse by the hair, Hrefna didn't do much about her. Surprised at the older woman's indifference, Selia finally asked, "Why doesn't anyone take the girl to task?"

Hrefna had shrugged. "It's not the first time Ingrid has fallen into a state of melancholy. And it won't be the last. She'll come out of it on her own as she always does, and until then I am enjoying the peace and quiet."

Quiet was relative, however, with Geirr around. At least Hallveig slept with him, so Selia didn't have to rise all throughout the night to take care of him. But when Hallveig was at her work, the brunt of the child care duties fell on her shoulders. If Geirr wasn't wet, he was dirty, and if he wasn't screaming in hunger he was spitting up all over himself. She would take him to Hallveig to nurse, then carry him back to the house where she would inevitably end up either changing his nappy or his gown, or both. Geirr would proceed to scream at the top of his lungs until Hrefna finally took him with exasperation. The woman would have him back to sleep quickly. All of this, combined with Selia's lingering sickness, made her thankful she would not be having more children after this one.

One particular morning, when she had changed Geirr's gown three times already, and had done her best to placate the sweating, red-faced, screaming child, he grew suddenly quiet. She looked down at him, wincing for what would inevitably come next. With his face a mask of deep concentration, the child loosed his bowels, an explosive mess that ran out the sides of his nappy and down the front of Selia's favorite gown.

She held him at arms' length, trying not to breathe in too deeply. What to do now? Hrefna had gone to the dairy as soon as Geirr had begun to cry, and had not returned yet. Probably on purpose.

"Ingrid," Selia shouted at the lump on the bench, "Help me!"

Ingrid had a pillow over her head to muffle Geirr's cries. She didn't move. The babe's face turned redder, and with a powerful grunt he released another mushy stream of excrement which oozed down his leg and landed at Selia's feet.

"Oh!" she cried. "Ingrid, I know you can hear me, you horrible girl!"

Ingrid took the pillow off her head and rolled over with a slow, infuriating stare. The corners of her mouth twitched as she took in the sight of Selia holding the babe out in front of her. "He can shit all over you for all I care," she drawled.

"*Please*, Ingrid. He is your brother," she implored.

"If you think that child is my brother, you're stupider than you look." With a snort, Ingrid rolled back to face the wall.

The movement unfortunately caused her ripe aroma to waft aloft. Selia gagged, desperate to cover her nose but unable to do so while holding on to Geirr. She sprinted outside and fell to her knees, trying not to drop the babe.

And broke into sobs. This, all this, was too much to ask of her. She knew nothing about caring for babies. And Hrefna refused to let her hand Geirr over to one of the thralls. The woman said it was to give her practice, but Selia felt completely inept.

Hrefna approached and took the child from her arms. Geirr's fussing stopped almost immediately, and Selia glared at him as he chewed on his chubby fist. Traitorous babe. If it wasn't for Hrefna, Geirr would be living in the slave quarters.

"I cannot do this," she moaned. "Geirr hates me!"

Alrik's aunt raised her eyebrows but didn't disagree. "He senses your ambivalence, I think."

Selia made a face. "I do not know that word."

"It means you are unsure. You don't know your own mind."

She stood, sniffling. Yes, she was ambivalent, but not about becoming a mother as Hrefna thought. Instead, she refused to allow a bond with Geirr. Because letting herself care for the babe, and in return to have his love for her, seemed unfair to her own unborn child. She had traded her child's birthright for Muirin's freedom. Now poor Muirin was dead, and Selia was left to raise a thrall's child as Hersir. Had she made a terrible choice?

"I must change my clothes," she mumbled, trudging toward the house.

The weather shifted with a vengeance, turning the pleasant autumn conditions cold and damp almost overnight. The storms that occasionally swept in from the water were shockingly violent. The wind blew so hard, the roof rafters groaned above them like a restless ghost. Although the family stayed warm and dry in the solidly-built longhouse, Selia couldn't help but fear for Alrik on his dragonship. Visions of the ship being tossed to splinters arose in her mind, intensifying her guilt about encouraging her husband to delay his fall trip. Her reasons, wanting him with her for as long as possible in her confinement, now seemed so selfish.

On just such an evening, as the wind whipped outside and the rain pelted sideways, there came a sharp rap at the door. Selia and Hrefna exchanged a startled glance. Ingrid had left for Bjorn's, stating she could take Geirr's incessant crying no longer. Obviously she would not knock at the door of her own house, but Selia knew Hrefna was concerned about the girl's emotional state.

Whoever was outside might bear troubling news.

Hrefna rushed to the door and pulled it open, with Selia two steps behind, carrying Geirr. The babe had just gone to sleep, but she knew from experience that if she laid him down too soon he would wake up immediately, screaming in fury. It was easier to simply hold him, even if it did spoil him as Hrefna insisted it would.

The woman cried out as she threw her arms around the large figure outside. For a brief second Selia thought the war band had returned, and her heart leapt. But the timbre of the man's voice told her it was Ulfrik.

Ulfrik, here?

Selia stood frozen as he bent his head to clear the doorway and stepped inside. He stared down at her, his face expressionless.

"Hello, Selia," he said softly. His gaze traveled over the babe in her arms.

She could neither force her feet to move nor her mouth to form words. Why was he here? What could he possibly want? Ulfrik was no fool, but the idea of him showing up at Alrik's house now was completely mad. Unless, of course, he knew his brother had left for Ireland on a raid. What better time would there be to come and carry Selia off?

Ulfrik was soaking wet, and he pushed his dripping hair out of his eyes as he turned back to Hrefna. "There are forty men out there in the rain. Could they come in until the storm blows over?"

"Gunnar One-Eye's crew?"

He hesitated but a moment. "Yes."

"Alrik wouldn't like that." Hrefna frowned.

With a nod, Ulfrik stepped back. "I understand. We will sail to my house to wait out the storm. I would ask to see Muirin though, before I leave." He turned back to Selia, his gaze again resting on Geirr. "Is that the child?"

Hrefna looked up at him with a sigh. "Ulfrik. Muirin is dead, my boy."

His face blanched, and for a brief second Selia felt sorry for him. Hrefna laid her hand on his arm and gave it a squeeze. Then squared her shoulders as if making up her mind about something.

"Have the men come inside. They are welcome to stay the night and fill their bellies. What Alrik doesn't know won't hurt him."

The nightmare began in earnest as forty wet Finngalls took over the longhouse. Gunnar One-Eye was introduced to Selia as Gunnar Klaufason. The man was surprisingly young, about the same age as Alrik and Ulfrik. He was built like a bull, square and solid with muscle, and his hair was nearly black, uncommon among the Finngalls. His face, which might have at one time been handsome, was marred by a thick scar that began on his forehead and ended just above his beard. His left eye socket was sunken and the eyelid appeared to have been sewn shut. His other eye, however, was strangely beautiful; a pale violet-blue, surrounded by a bristle of thick black eyelashes.

The contrast of the perfect eye with the mangled one unnerved Selia, who found herself reluctant to look at him directly.

Gunnar's right hand man, tall and blond Einarr Drengsson, possessed the distinctive sharp bone structure shared by Alrik and Ulfrik. Selia was not surprised to learn that his father and Ragnarr had been cousins. Gunnar was married to Einarr's sister. It seemed to Selia nearly every Finngall in Norway was related by either blood or marriage. Sometimes even both, although uncommon. It was not unheard of for cousins to marry if necessity dictated, but her head spun trying to keep the various connections straight.

All of the men, but Gunnar and Einarr in particular, stared at Selia in open curiosity. This too was unnerving. Since marrying Alrik, she had become accustomed to men not looking at her directly. If any did meet her gaze, their faces filled with fear, not desire. Their apprehension about Alrik's jealousy squelched whatever interest they may have felt under other circumstances.

These men, however, were not operating under that same concern, and she was taken aback at the blatant desire she saw in many of their faces.

Hrefna, on her way to the kitchen to oversee the assembly of a supper for forty unexpected guests, whispered to Selia "Stoke up the fire quickly and then join me in the kitchen. And don't go to the privy alone tonight. Ulfrik or I can walk with you if necessary."

Selia stifled a cynical laugh at the thought of asking Ulfrik to accompany her to the privy to protect her from the advances of Gunnar's men. But she nodded to Hrefna, understanding the danger all too well.

Holding the babe in one arm, she stirred the coals of the fire to warm the men. They stripped down to their breeches, laying their wet shirts and cloaks on the floor to dry, and the air was soon filled with steam from the damp wool.

Not at all comfortable at being surrounded by nearly naked men with lust in their eyes, she hurried toward the kitchen to help Hrefna. She stumbled slightly as she stepped over the wet clothing, and a big hand went around her arm to steady her. She'd been in no danger of falling, yet the hand remained on her arm.

Selia looked up into the eerily familiar face of Einarr Drengsson. Although he had the strong build that seemed to be a given in Ragnarr's bloodline, Einarr was not quite as tall as Alrik and somewhat thinner. And younger than he appeared from a distance—only a few summers older than Selia. He had the same intense blue eyes as his cousins, as well as the same wide, sensual mouth.

Einarr leaned closer, looking directly into her eyes, and smiled Alrik's smile. It made her skin crawl.

"Selia. What a rare beauty you are. But then, Alrik Ragnarson has always had good taste in women. If I had known about you I would have visited long before now. To partake of my cousin's hospitality." His fingers pressed into her flesh in a slow, deliberate massage.

She narrowed her eyes at him. Cousin or no, Alrik would never have stood for this man's insolence. She gave a pointed look toward his hand on her arm, then glared up at him. "You do not know Alrik very well, I am afraid. You would lose that hand if he were here."

Einarr's eyebrows went up as his smile deepened. He released her arm. "I see you are not faint of heart," he said. "Even better. I should have known Alrik would have chosen a feisty one."

As he stood upright again, Selia noticed the tattoo on his chest. It was in the same location as Alrik's and appeared to be the same design. Was it some sort of family symbol?

Einarr saw what she was looking at and puffed his chest out a bit. "Ahh, you like berserkers, little Irish cousin? They do say once a woman lies with a berserker, a normal man will never do again." He gave her a knowing wink and lowered his voice to a whisper. "I would be happy to oblige you if you find your bed is cold tonight."

Selia would have slapped his face if she wasn't holding the babe. "No. But I will be sure to tell my husband of your offer when he returns," she hissed.

Ulfrik's voice came from behind her. "Einarr," he warned, "I would advise you to mind how you speak to Selia. A man could find himself in a shallow grave for disrespecting the wife of Alrik Ragnarson." His voice was deceptively calm, but the threat was clear.

Einarr grunted, eying his cousin over Selia's head for a long moment. He finally stepped back. Ulfrik took her by the elbow to steer her toward a quieter corner of the room.

"Let go of me," she demanded when they were out of earshot of Einarr. Just being in the same room with Ulfrik made her uneasy. She shook her arm free.

"I mean you no harm, Selia. I just want to talk to you," he said in Irish.

"I have nothing to say to you," she snapped.

He sighed. "Give me my child, then. I haven't even had a chance to see it. Is it a boy or a girl?"

She hesitated, torn between a desire to inflict pain on him the way he had hurt her, and acting with kindness. She looked down at the beautiful babe sleeping in her arms, biting her lip in indecision. Why should she care about Ulfrik's feelings? He was a liar. He deserved to feel pain. "He is a boy," she told him. "His name is Geirr . . . Geirr Alrikson."

He went still and quiet, until she finally brought her gaze to meet his.

Ulfrik's face had shuttered. "My brother is a spiteful bastard, but I wouldn't have expected *you* to go along with something like this—"

She cut him off. "Alrik did nothing out of spite. This is his child and he claimed it."

At his narrowed gaze, she squirmed, willing him not to read her mind.

"Why are you doing this, Selia? Not that long ago you were eager for me to take Muirin and the child away. Now you're willing to raise a child that isn't yours, and probably isn't even Alrik's. Do you hate me so much that you would steal my child from me?"

She clutched Geirr to her breast. "I didn't steal your child. When Muirin was dying she told me the babe was Alrik's. She only let you believe it was yours because she was in love with you."

Ulfrik didn't take his eyes from hers. "I can tell you're lying, Selia."

"Why?" she retorted. "Because you're such an accomplished liar yourself?"

Ulfrik leaned in, thrusting his face so close to hers that she took a step backward. "It would be unwise to anger me. Do you realize how easily I could take both you and the babe right now, and sail off with Gunnar?"

She swallowed. "Alrik would find us," she whispered, "and he would kill you."

"He could try," Ulfrik retorted.

"I would kill myself before I would go anywhere with you."

He blew his breath out forcefully as he rose to his full height. "Why can't I just be through with you, Selia?

Why do I keep doing this to myself?" he muttered. "All I wanted was to make you happy. And I could have, if you had only given me the chance."

Ulfrik slumped on the bench behind them, looking forlorn. A tiny flicker of sympathy arose in her, unbidden. Once, he had been her only friend and confidant. He'd understood her in a way no one else ever had, maybe not even Ainnileas. She thought of how patient he had been as he taught her Norse, and their games of tafl, and the laughter they had shared.

Her heart gave a bit as she met his gaze. How could she hate him? He was still Ulfrik. He was still her friend. Tentatively, she opened her mouth to speak. Then she saw a glimmer of anticipation in his eyes as though he sensed her uncertainty.

Selia's mind suddenly flooded with the memory of those blue eyes glinting in the same way just before he had kissed her. She fought back a flush, remembering the unwilling response of her body.

No.

What was she doing? Ulfrik tried to manipulate her, exactly what he had done to her before . . . what had ultimately led to the incident at the cove.

She hardened her resolve and her voice. "I won't fall for your tricks again, so you can stop." She shifted the heavy Geirr to relieve her numbed arm from carrying him for so long, reluctant to put him down with so many men milling around.

"Tricks. You think it's a trick, when I tell you I love you?" he asked. "Is it a trick when I tell you I think of you endlessly? The scent of your hair, the sweetness of your mouth, and the softness of your skin—"

"*Stop*," she growled. "You have no right to say those things to me."

"If I've done anything to hurt you, I will be sorry for it until my last breath. But mark my words, Selia. Alrik won't live forever. The instant he dies, I'll be there waiting."

She blinked at him as her mind sorted his vow. Surely he wasn't threatening to harm Alrik? Her grip must have loosened on Geirr, because suddenly the babe was lifted from her arms.

Startled, she looked up to find Gunnar One-Eye holding the infant against his burly chest.

"Irish is such a beautiful language," Gunnar said to her in perfect, unaccented Irish.

Selia gasped. How much of the conversation had he heard between her and Ulfrik?

"So very soft," he added. "Not unlike its women."

He *had* heard. Selia's cheeks grew hot in mortification. She wanted nothing more than to run into the bedchamber and hide, but she couldn't leave Geirr in the hands of this man. "Give him back to me. You'll wake him up," she said, hating that her voice shook.

The despicable man cocked his head at the babe. "He's already awake. He looks just like you, Ulfrik, except for the eyes," he said with a crude wink in Selia's direction. Obviously he assumed the child was hers, and from the conversation he had overheard thought the babe was the product of an affair between her and her husband's brother.

She straightened her shoulders and looked directly into Gunnar's disfigured face. "That child is not my son. His mother is dead." She spoke coldly.

Ulfrik stood, peering over Gunnar's shoulder at the babe. "He has Muirin's eyes. She did have beautiful eyes." He reached over to stroke the child's hand, and Geirr wrapped his chubby fist around Ulfrik's finger.

"Hmm," Gunnar mused. "What a shame I didn't get to meet her."

Something snapped inside Selia, and her body nearly vibrated with fury as she hissed, "Oh, you met her—you murdered her family and you sold her into slavery. You have *no right* to touch her child. Give him back to me now."

The man stared down at her wide-eyed like a fool, as though completely unaccustomed to being spoken to in such a way. She took advantage of his shock by yanking Geirr from his arms.

Gunnar's face grew stony as he looked over at Ulfrik. "Are you going to let a little Irish girl decide who can and cannot hold your son?"

Ulfrik's gaze locked with Selia's. "He's not my son after all. He is Alrik's."

Chapter 6

Selia managed to successfully avoid Ulfrik while she helped Hrefna prepare the meal, although she could still feel his watchful regard. Hallveig came in to feed Geirr, and Selia handed him over with firm instructions not to put the babe down or let any of the men hold him.

When it was time to eat, she hesitated to sit at the head table with Hrefna, Ulfrik, Gunnar, and Einarr. She had never met a more vile man than Gunnar, and Einarr was a very close second. She'd had her fill of leering stares for the night and no desire to attempt polite conversation for Hrefna's sake. Not to mention having to face a room of bare-chested men, since their clothing was still damp. Forced to dine, eye level with their tattooed, scarred, and hairy midsections would be more than unbearable.

Ulfrik and Einarr sat on one bench and Gunnar and Hrefna the other, so she would have to sit next to someone she detested, either way. She shifted from one foot to the other, seriously considering feigning illness to avoid the entire situation. Her hand went to her temple, rubbing slowly.

Before she could announce she had a headache, Einarr stood with a smile and fetched her, placing one hand on her shoulder and the other on the small of her back.

"Come, little cousin, sit next to me." He steered her to the bench, then sat her in the middle, next to Ulfrik. Einarr crowded the other side of her, much closer than necessary. With the semi-naked bodies of two large men bracketing her, Selia felt near to suffocating, trapped in a prison of male bone and sinew.

Hrefna leaned in toward her. The room was filled with the good-natured shouting and laughter of the men, and she had to raise her voice to be heard. "Are you all right, my dear?"

"My head pains me. I think I will go lie down," she replied, and began to rise from the table.

"You really should try to eat something first, Selia. To keep your strength up," Hrefna said with concern.

She stared at Alrik's aunt, willing her to understand that her condition was not a topic she cared to discuss in the presence of these men. Although she recently had to let her gowns out in the waist and bust, her condition wasn't obvious when she was fully clothed. She'd prefer to keep it that way while Gunnar and his crew were here. The humiliating situation of carrying Alrik's babe while caring for his child by a thrall would surely be pounced upon by Gunnar One-Eye.

"Have you been ill?" Einarr asked, tearing off a hunk of warm bread and eying her as he chewed.

"No," Selia answered curtly. She looked directly at Hrefna as she spoke, and although the woman appeared a bit perplexed by her shortness, she didn't press the issue.

Gunnar leaned in with an unpleasant smile. "What part of Ireland are you from, Selia?"

She paused. It was a simple question and not posed threateningly, but she was loath to answer him. She had insulted this man when he had been holding Geirr, and she had a sense that Gunnar Klaufason was not a man who let insults slide off his back. Selia did not want him to know where she was from, and where Ainnileas and Eithne still resided.

"She is from Árd Srátha," Ulfrik answered casually, then took a long draught of ale. As angry as Selia was with Ulfrik, she felt a glimmer of gratitude as he lied for her.

"Humph," Gunnar grunted. "I would have guessed Baile Átha Cliath by her accent." He looked down his nose at Selia, one black eyebrow cocked.

She kept her rebuttal at a single, "No," picking at her stew for a moment before adding, "How is it that you speak Irish so well?" Perhaps a change in subject was in order.

Gunnar smiled. "My mother was Irish. The granddaughter of the great Irish chieftain Cian Ó Riain. Ulfrik's mother and my mother were sisters."

Here was an unexpected bit of information. That would make Ulfrik and Gunnar cousins. It did explain Ulfrik's surprising willingness to sail with a man known for being the most brutal Vikinger in all of Norway. He was family.

But Selia's blood ran cold upon realizing Gunnar was half-Irish. This was exactly why she would do anything to avoid a similar situation with her own child. What could be worse than teaching her child the language and customs of her homeland, only to have him grow to manhood and return to that homeland to raid and kill?

Unconsciously, her hand snaked up to her belly to cover it in protection; then as she realized what she was doing, she dropped her hand back into her lap.

"How does your mother feel about what you do?" she inquired, trying to keep her voice from shaking with emotion.

Gunnar regarded her with his icy-violet gaze. "She died when I was a boy. But she did marry a Vikinger, so I doubt she would be surprised to know she had raised one as well." He uttered a sardonic laugh.

Despicable bastard. Selia could feel herself heat with anger, and wanted very much to fling her bowl of stew into his good eye.

Ulfrik set his cup down on the table with a clatter and turned to her, giving her the shrewd expression she knew all too well from playing tafl with him. He had obviously figured out what her interest in Geirr was.

Selia cringed.

"So, Selia," he began, "how will you feel when the sons you bear Alrik grow up to raid your people? How will you feel knowing they are half-Irish Vikingers like Gunnar . . . and like me?" Ulfrik's voice was calm but she could see the anger in his eyes.

She fidgeted under his gaze. Hrefna was staring at her too, with a shocked expression on her face. Selia turned to avoid the woman's reproachful eyes. "I do not know. I have not thought about it," she hedged.

"Surely you have," Ulfrik pressed her. "Alrik will need a male child to succeed him as Hersir. A child who isn't born of a thrall." When she didn't answer, Ulfrik turned to Hrefna. "Did my brother free Muirin before she gave birth?"

Hrefna hesitated. Her gaze flickered to Selia, then back to Ulfrik. "Yes," she said finally.

"And whose idea was that, I wonder?" he asked, with a hard look at Selia.

A sudden flash of Muirin's glassy stare, frozen in death, swept over Selia and forced tears to form that she hastily blinked back. Muirin had been more than willing to exchange her child for her freedom, Selia reminded herself. So why did she feel so guilty?

Einarr drew his pale eyebrows together and glared at his cousin. "You're upsetting her," he said, reaching around her to shove Ulfrik's shoulder. "Leave the poor girl alone."

"Poor girl," Ulfrik mocked. He took another deep pull of his ale, draining it, then held his cup out. One of the thralls came around to refill it. Selia glanced at Einarr and flashed him a small but grateful smile.

Which was a mistake.

Einarr grinned down at her and patted her hand where it lay in her lap. He kept his large hand on hers under the table as he spoke. "Selia. I'm curious to know how you ended up married to Alrik. A pretty little Irish girl like you, married to someone like him, seems unlikely. Was it a love match, or arranged?" His thumb stroked her hand in a slow circle. "I imagine the wedding night was interesting, to say the least," he added.

Hrefna gasped and Ulfrik paused with his cup halfway to his mouth. Gunnar burst into laughter. Selia jerked her hand from Einarr's, her cheeks hot with mortification.

Hrefna recovered first. "I don't think that is any of your business, Einarr Drengsson." Ice coated her voice.

"Forgive me." Abruptly he changed tactics. "My question was misunderstood. I am having a somewhat difficult time finding a wife, as I know Alrik did. I just wondered if she knew her intended was a berserker, beforehand."

Selia swallowed, her unwilling regard on the tattoo decorating his chest. Faded, it appeared to be stretched out of shape the same as Alrik's. "No," she said quietly. "I did not."

The expression on Einarr's face reminded her of Alrik's, just before he pounced. Her instincts urged her to move away from him, but unfortunately that would press her up against Ulfrik. She was trapped.

"And you do not fear him? You are not afraid he'll hurt you?" Einarr asked with a predatory smile.

She shrank into the bench. Ulfrik snorted into his ale but said nothing. He was either so angry at her over the situation with Geirr that he was unwilling to stop the insistent questioning by Einarr, or too drunk to care.

Taking charge, Hrefna slapped her hand down on the table. "Your questions are inappropriate. Storm or no, you will be sleeping with the goats tonight if you do not stop this immediately. Am I understood?"

"I was only—" Einarr began, but she cut him off.

"If you have questions about the details of Alrik's marriage, I suggest you take them directly to him, rather than to his wife," Hrefna snapped.

Selia could imagine the battle that would ensue if Einarr was stupid enough to confront Alrik. She shuddered to think of these two men attacking like wild beasts, tearing each other to shreds.

Einarr scowled into his ale, but Gunnar cocked his head at him, smiling. "I, for one, would greatly enjoy seeing Alrik Ragnarson again. I would like to thank him personally for his hospitality. What say you, Einarr—shall we return when our host is home, so you can get an answer to your question?"

Again, Gunnar spoke in a mild tone of voice, but Selia sensed the veiled threat. She suspected Hrefna did as well, as the woman's face drained of color. Hrefna's gaze caught Ulfrik's and they exchanged a look that Selia didn't understand.

Ulfrik placed his cup on the table. "No, Einarr," he said. "As I told you earlier, any man foolish enough to show the slightest interest in the wife of Alrik Ragnarson has a death wish. I strongly suggest when we sail away tomorrow, you never return. Unless, that is, you are stupid enough to think you can challenge Alrik and win."

Although Ulfrik had addressed Einarr, his words seemed to be meant just as much for Gunnar. The threat behind them was unmistakable. Gunnar raked his good eye over Ulfrik and leaned close. "One would think Alrik was still your Hersir, cousin," he sneered.

"Then one would be wrong." Ulfrik met the man's stare. "But I know my brother well. He will fight to the death if his wife's honor is disparaged."

Gunnar glowered. "The business I have to settle with Alrik Ragnarson has nothing to do with his wife," he rumbled. "But if it's a fight he wants, I'll be happy to oblige him."

The words Ulfrik had spoken to Selia earlier came flooding back. *Alrik won't live forever, and the instant he dies, I'll be there waiting.* Was this part of his plan—to have another man kill Alrik, so he could then step in and take her for his own? Although it would seem to an outsider that he was discouraging Gunnar and Einarr from returning, nothing Ulfrik said could be taken at face value. It wasn't much of a leap to imagine the master tafl player planting seeds of dissent, then standing back to wait for them to germinate.

A sickening fear gripped Selia's belly as she stood. "You should have left them out in the storm, Hrefna," she spat, then switched to Irish as she addressed Gunnar. "I find it highly offensive that you would come into Alrik's house and make threats against him. You are a dishonorable man, Gunnar Klaufason. When you take your leave tomorrow, know that none of you will be welcomed back." Selia gave Ulfrik a pointed look. "Ever."

Gunnar's face flushed blood red, and his fists clenched the edges of the table. Neither Hrefna nor Einarr knew enough Irish to understand what Selia had said, but it was clear she had reprimanded him, and they both reacted with stunned expressions.

Selia turned to Einarr, addressing him in Norse. "And you. I tell you now I have no interest in any other man but my husband. I think you cannot find a wife because you are ill-mannered, not because you are a berserker."

Einarr's jaw dropped. "Allow me to apologize. I meant no offense," he sputtered, looking very contrite. "Please forgive me."

Selia glared at him for a moment, then gave him a terse nod. Anything to be through with this conversation. But as she stepped over the bench she saw his eyes widen at the brief flash of her ankle, and he smiled at her. Did this dim-witted man think she was playing games with him?

Disgusted, she strode into the bedchamber, shutting the door firmly behind her. Despicable Finngalls. What had Hrefna been thinking, letting them in the house? She lay on the bed and hugged Alrik's pillow tightly to her body, breathing in through her nose, needing his scent. But he had been gone for so long, his pillow no longer smelled like him.

It smelled like nothing at all.

At Hrefna's insistence, Selia slept with her that night, in order for Hallveig and Geirr to have Selia's bed. Gunnar's men took up every available bench in the main room, with overflow on the floor by the hearth, and Hrefna was concerned lest an overeager, drunken man take Hallveig by force. Selia wasn't sure if the woman's anxiety was for Hallveig's sake or Geirr's, since the potential rape of his nursemaid would leave the babe unsupervised. But she agreed to the change in sleeping arrangements without an argument.

Although more than ready for sleep, she lay awake, and tossed, longing for her own familiar bed and Alrik next to her in it. She missed him with a terrible, gnawing ache. The fact that Ulfrik, and now Einarr, resembled him to such a degree was like salt in her wound. It seemed wrong for them to be here and Alrik not. Selia cried hot tears of self-pity as Hrefna snored beside her.

Since seeing Ulfrik again, she'd had an unpleasant feeling deep in her gut which had nothing to do with her unrelenting nausea. It was an ugly sense of guilt that worried at her, and she couldn't shake it no matter how hard she tried to rationalize her actions.

As angry as she was with Ulfrik, there was no denying she *had* claimed Geirr for her own selfish reasons, as a way to keep her unborn child from suffering the fate of Hersir. Although there was as much chance Alrik was indeed Geirr's father, the fact remained that Ulfrik had been willing to claim him, and had returned to the farmstead accordingly. Alrik would not have thought to declare the boy as his own unless encouraged to do so, and Ulfrik probably knew it.

Hrefna had suggested Selia was ambivalent about her feelings for Geirr, and she supposed the same could be said about how she dealt with Ulfrik. He could not be trusted, yet she couldn't bring herself to truly despise him. Even if his every kindness *had* been a calculated act meant to steal her away from Alrik, he had also saved her life as a child. Saved her from Alrik's sword.

Ulfrik professed to love her; that everything he had done was to keep her safe. Selia rubbed her belly. All her actions had also been meant to keep her own child safe. Could distasteful deeds be justifiable if performed in the name of love?

Selia startled as she heard a stifled female scream coming from another part of the house. She sat up in bed and shook Hrefna awake.

"What?" Hrefna mumbled. Then they both heard the shouting of men and a sudden ruckus, followed by a piercing cry from Geirr. Wearing only her shift, Hrefna leapt from the bed to race from the room. Selia followed close behind as she wrapped a blanket around her shoulders.

Lit by the dim light of the hearth, two men were in a heated argument. Ulfrik and Einarr. Several other men restrained them as they lunged toward each other, snarling insults. Hallveig stood in the doorway of Selia's bedchamber clutching the wailing babe, and Hrefna rushed up to the slave woman.

"What happened?" she demanded, taking Geirr from her and examining him closely.

The frightened thrall stammered, "I was half asleep after nursing, and someone crept into the room and climbed into bed with me. I thought it was Selia or you, come to check on Geirr. But then I felt a man's hands on my body, and I panicked. He was drunk and I was afraid he would smother the babe, so I screamed for help."

Hallveig cast her eyes to the floor, obviously upset to have caused such a scene. Hrefna patted her on the shoulder as she attempted to quiet the babe.

Einarr and Ulfrik were still shouting and struggling to get at each other. Einarr had a bloody nose but was so drunk he didn't appear to feel it, and when he saw Selia out of the corner of his eye he stopped his slurred ranting to leer at her. His eyes wandered from her loose curls to her bare feet and back up again, the hunger on his face unmistakable.

Selia clutched the blanket tighter around her, and Ulfrik's eyes flashed with fury as he lunged again for Einarr. "Do you expect anyone to believe you were only after the thrall, you shameless bastard? I ought to run you through right now—"

"Ulfrik!" Gunnar shouted, scowling into his cousin's face. "Enough. No harm was done to your brother's wife." The emphasis on the word 'brother' was not lost on anyone. He continued in a lower voice. "By your reaction, one would think your own wife had been dishonored."

Ulfrik clenched his jaw with such force that his teeth ground together audibly. Enraged as he was, his sudden resemblance to Alrik was uncanny, and both Selia and Hrefna gaped at him. Shaking with the effort it took to contain himself, he spoke in a rasp. "If you do not remove this white-livered man from my sight, Gunnar, I swear I will kill him."

The crowd of men reacted visibly. To call a man white-livered was to call him a weakling and a coward. When he was teaching her Norse on the ship, Ulfrik had told Selia this was the reason the Finngalls dubbed the Christian son of God the 'White Christ,' as they considered a religion based on forgiveness pathetic. As far as the Finngalls were concerned, a society who worshipped a God who refused to fight back deserved everything it got.

Ulfrik's insult to Einarr would not be forgotten.

But the man was so drunk it was doubtful he could lift his sword. "I'll run you through, Oath Breaker," he bellowed, and lunged toward Ulfrik. Einarr staggered and nearly fell, and the men holding him by the arms had to hoist him back to his feet.

"Not tonight you won't," one of them laughed.

Gunnar eyed Ulfrik for several long moments before turning to his wife's brother. "Einarr, although you were only after the thrall, the woman was not yours to take. You have disrespected Hrefna Erlandsdottir with your lack of

manners, and she is a fine woman who gave us shelter in the
storm. You will sleep outside for the remainder of the night."

Einarr gave a drunken snort. "Where?" he demanded.

"I believe Hrefna suggested the barn." He steered the
man toward the door. Einarr snarled over his shoulder at
Ulfrik, just as Gunnar shoved him outside. He slammed the
door on Einarr's protests.

"I apologize on behalf of Einarr Drengsson," Gunnar
said with a nod in Hrefna's direction. He gave Ulfrik a
culminating glare as he passed him on his way to his bench.
"*And* on behalf of Ulfrik Ragnarson."

Chapter 7

Selia remained sleepless for the remainder of the night. There was an odd energy in the air that refused to dissipate even after the howling wind and pelting rain finally stopped. The house seemed eerily quiet after the constant noise of the storm. Finally, a streak of thin, pale light from the smoke hole in the roof revealed dawn's arrival. Blurry-eyed, she arose from the bed and dressed.

She jumped in surprise as she opened the door to find a pair of male legs stretched out across the floor in front of Hrefna's chamber. Ulfrik, wrapped in his cloak, lay with his head pillowed by his arm. Even in sleep he frowned, as if dreaming of the previous night's events.

Ulfrik had chosen to protect her from any further mischief from Gunnar's men. She studied him for a moment before stepping over him, then headed out the kitchen door on her way to the privy. She glanced around in the watery morning light, watchful for Einarr, but he was nowhere to be seen. As drunk as he was last night, he would probably have to be carried onto the ship when they departed.

The foggy dampness of autumn had given way to an early winter. The morning was clear and very cold, and the rain had turned to snow sometime in the night. A glittering blanket of white dusted each dark, slender tree, giving the forest an unnatural stillness. She hurried from the kitchen to the privy, crunching through the snow with every step of the warm fur boots Hrefna had made for her.

Back in the house, she stirred up the coals in the kitchen hearth, and added a small pile of sticks to get the fire going again. As Selia blew into her fingers to warm them, she felt a presence behind her. She turned to find Ulfrik standing in the doorway.

"What do you want?" she whispered in Irish.

"You shouldn't be outside alone," he admonished her. "Einarr can't be trusted."

Selia busied herself with the fire so she wouldn't have to look at him. "And you can?"

He remained silent, but she could feel his gaze on her. "You'll end up being the death of me, Selia," he finally murmured. "I almost killed my own cousin over you last night. You love a man who doesn't deserve it, you tell me you care nothing for me, and you conspire to keep a child who very well could be my son. I want nothing more than to wash my hands of you." His voice grew tight. "But yet I cannot. You consume me in a way no woman ever has."

Selia's cheeks burned. She stirred the coals of the fire to gather her thoughts. "Whatever you feel for me, I did not wish it so. You were my only friend, like a brother to me. I missed Ainnileas so much . . ." She met his heated gaze squarely. "If I ever did anything to lead you to believe I cared for you in that way, then I'm sorry."

Before he could reply, Hallveig entered the kitchen, carrying Geirr. They had fallen into the routine of Hallveig giving the child his morning feeding before she handed him off to Selia. Then the thrall could do her work without having to take Geirr outside with her.

But she hesitated when she saw Ulfrik in the kitchen with Selia. "Mistress," she said, "would you like me to keep him a while longer?"

"No." Selia took the babe from Hallveig. Typically she was less than enthusiastic about handling Geirr, but this morning she was glad for the distraction of the child. If he screamed or spit up on her, it would be a perfect excuse to end this unsettling conversation.

The thrall hurried out the door, no doubt anxious to see her own child. Selia examined Geirr. Rosy-cheeked and content from his morning milk, he stared up at her with a solemn expression, studying her face. This wouldn't last long. As soon as he realized who was holding him he would begin to fuss as he always did. She tensed, waiting for it. The child had a singular hatred for her.

But for reasons unknown, this morning was different. Geirr focused on her intently, then without warning broke into a wide, toothless grin. Caught off guard, she smiled down at him. "So, you've decided you like me?" she asked the babe. "Or is this a trick so you can vomit in my hair again?"

Ulfrik was suddenly next to her, standing much too close as he gazed at the child. "Let me hold him, Selia," he said, the longing in his voice tangible.

But she hesitated to hand over the fragile bundle. Distressing visions danced in her mind; of Ulfrik dashing the babe against one of the stout wooden beams of the kitchen, or running off to the ship with him, to sail away with Gunnar. She hugged Geirr tighter and forced the images away. What on earth was wrong with her?

"Do you think I would hurt him?" he asked quietly. "I am Ulfrik Child Lover, remember?"

She knew only too well how he had received that nickname. It was anyone's guess how he managed to sail under Gunnar One-Eye, a brutal man who surely took pleasure in the slaughter of children. But she pushed the thought from her mind. What Ulfrik Ragnarson did or didn't do was no concern of hers.

She handed Geirr over, watching Ulfrik for any sign of deception. But his face was gentle as he held the child he believed to be his son. Geirr pondered the new face quizzically, with one eyebrow cocked. Selia had frequently seen just that expression on the faces of both the sons of Ragnarr.

Geirr offered a gummy grin—he was in rare form this morning—and Ulfrik responded with a low chuckle. Selia was struck with a wave of remorse so strong it took her breath away. Regardless of how she felt about Ulfrik, she found herself questioning the wisdom of the bargain she had struck with Muirin.

"Ulfrik," she began, "I'm sorry."

He held her gaze firmly. "Muirin never told you Alrik was the father, did she?" he asked.

"Not outright," she whispered, shifting from one foot to the other under his intense scrutiny. "She said she couldn't be certain. But when the babe came as he did, I thought he must be Alrik's. So I asked him to free Muirin and claim the child. Muirin agreed to it, to secure a future for her son."

Ulfrik thought for a moment. "This child is at least half Irish. If he's mine, then he's more Irish than he is Norse. Did you not think of that?"

She looked away without answering. In her desire to protect her own offspring from following in Alrik's footsteps as a warlord, she'd not considered Geirr's heritage. Ulfrik's words hit home. Muirin's child could have more Irish blood flowing through his veins than did the babe growing in Selia's belly. How could they ever know for sure? Would her actions send Geirr the man out on a massacre to her homeland, slaughtering his own people? In attempting to protect her unborn child from such a future, she could very well have made things worse.

Sudden shame cut through Selia like a hot knife.

"No," she whispered. "Or maybe yes. I don't know. Lately I've been making one bad decision after another, it seems." Starting with events at the cove.

Ulfrik shifted the child in his arms. The expression on his face made her think he'd guessed her thoughts. "Selia." He paused. "I need to tell you how sorry I am for what happened at the cove. I came to you with honorable intentions. Whatever else you think of me, please don't think *that*."

She studied him. It was impossible to tell if he was lying.

"And I should have told you the truth about your mother. About Alrik. I thought at the time I was doing the right thing." He stared down at Geirr. "I was protecting this child, Selia. Alrik would have killed Muirin if he knew I told you. He would have murdered the child out of spite."

How was she supposed to respond to this? Was he manipulating her again, knowing she also felt protective of Geirr? Selia turned away. "I don't know what to believe anymore, Ulfrik. I don't think I can ever trust you again. When I look at you all I see are lies."

Silence hung heavy in the room after her vow. He studied the babe, as though memorizing Geirr's features. Then he sighed, "I understand."

Ulfrik handed Geirr back to her, his face expressionless as he stood. "I do not want to hurt you any further. I am leaving and I will not return unless you wish it."

A wave of relief washed over her. "I will not wish it," she said quietly.

"But if you need me—if Alrik hurts you—"

"That won't happen."

"You haven't seen what he's like during the winter," Ulfrik cautioned. "You may yet change your mind."

She shivered as he urged, "Listen carefully, Selia. If you need to get away, go to my house and dig next to the rock you were sleeping against at the cove. I buried your bride price there after Ainnileas returned it. Take it to Bjorgvin and you can buy passage out of Norway. But don't go back to Ireland because that's the first place he'll come looking for you."

She trembled in earnest now. "Stop, Ulfrik."

He started to reach out for her, then dropped his hand to his side. "I know you don't trust me. But I swear to you on my life—if you ask for my help, I won't expect anything in return." He paused for a moment. "If you ever need me, go to Ketill and ask him if he's heard from me. He'll know what that means. He'll send word and I'll come for you."

There was a stirring from the main room as the men arose and began preparations to depart. Ulfrik stroked a gentle finger over Geirr's downy head. His hand brushed Selia's, his calloused skin lingering on hers just a moment too long.

Her heart hammered in her ears as he made eye contact with her, his face only inches from her own. "Goodbye, Selia," he whispered, then turned away to join Gunnar and his men.

The house was very quiet after the men departed. Even Geirr slept soundly following the excitement of the night before. He lay upon one of the benches next to where Selia and Hrefna worked the looms, making faces in his sleep. Selia kept one eye on him, worried he might try to roll over and fall out.

Hrefna also kept to herself. Yet Selia could feel the woman's questioning eyes on her as her fingers methodically wove the thin strands of wool. "Selia," she finally said, in a hushed voice, so as not to wake the babe, "even though Ulfrik is not my nephew by blood, I care for him very much. I raised him from the time he was eight."

Selia glanced up. Why did Hrefna feel the need to share this with her? "I know," she replied.

"The boys were always so different from each other. Alrik was hotheaded and impatient, and Ulfrik was quieter. More thoughtful. Though Ulfrik looks exactly like Ragnarr, I assumed he was going to be the easier child to raise."

"What? He looks like Ragnarr?" Whenever she had pictured Ragnarr in her mind's eye, she had always envisioned a more deranged version of Alrik.

"Yes. He is the very image of his father. I believe that's why Ulfrik keeps his beard so short, because Ragnarr always wore his own beard long. Alrik resembles his father too, of course, but if you look closely he favors his mother as well."

Oh, my. How difficult it must be for Hrefna to see the image of her sister's murderer every time she looked at Ulfrik.

Hrefna sighed. "After a time I realized there was more to Ulfrik than I at first thought. An intensity he kept hidden. He wears a mask most of the time, so people don't realize it's there, but he feels his emotions with more force than anyone knows. He just keeps himself under control better than Alrik does."

Selia nodded, trying to stay focused on her work. Couldn't they talk about something other than Ulfrik? Even the wailing of Geirr would be a welcome interruption.

"Ulfrik is in love with you." Hrefna's bald utterance caused Selia to jerk and drop the strand of wool. "I've known this for quite some time. I always hoped he would take Muirin and the babe far away from here before Alrik saw it for himself."

Selia drew in a sharp breath. Her first impulse was to deny the allegation, but then she thought better of it. What was the use? "I did not do anything to cause Ulfrik to care for me, Hrefna—"

"I know, my dear. I wasn't implying that you did. But the way he behaved around you last night . . . he wasn't trying to hide his feelings at all. It was clear to me, and to every one of Gunnar's men, that Ulfrik is in love with you. And men do gossip, just as much as women do, although they won't admit it." Hrefna finished a line of weaving before stating, "I think if something happened between you two while you were apart from Alrik, you should tell him. Before he hears it from someone else."

Selia felt suddenly lightheaded. Hrefna couldn't have discovered anything about what happened at the cove. The woman might have a sixth sense that told her something was different, but she didn't *know.*

Struggling to clear the bile that rose in her throat, Selia sank onto one of the benches. "Nothing happened, Hrefna. I have never loved anyone but Alrik."

Hrefna took a seat next to her. "You used to be comfortable around Ulfrik. But last night you were jumpy, like a scared little mouse. It was clear to me that something has changed between you two."

Obviously, complete denial wasn't going to work. Selia wiped her sweaty palms on her gown. "He . . . he wanted to marry me. To go to Ireland with me and my family. I told him no, and then I came home to Alrik," she said.

Hrefna cleared her throat. "That's it? Nothing else?"

She shook her head. "He stole a kiss. I spurned him. That was all. And this morning, he told me he was leaving and not coming back. So we will not have to worry about it anymore, Hrefna. There is no reason to tell Alrik anything."

The woman nodded slowly, still uneasy. "I never should have let them in last night, knowing what kind of man Gunnar is. He and his crew are nothing but lawless pirates. If it weren't for Ulfrik I would have left them outside and hoped they froze to death before they hacked their way into the house."

She met Selia's regard and sighed. "Truth be told, you are far too pretty for your own good, my dear, and Alrik is right to be jealous. If Gunnar gave the word, Einarr or any one of those men would think nothing of carrying you off, do you know that? As soon as I let them in I realized it was a mistake."

Selia fought back sudden anger. She had been told all her life—mostly by Eithne—that her beauty was a dangerous thing, capable of arousing the lustful appetites of men. This had always struck her as tremendously unfair. Why should she be held responsible for the behavior of men who couldn't control themselves?

"I cannot help what I look like, Hrefna," she protested. "I did not *do* anything—"

The woman wrapped her in a hug. "Oh, my dear, I know you didn't. I am angry at myself more than anything. The hatred Alrik and Gunnar carry for one another goes far back. Knowing what kind of man Gunnar is, I wouldn't put it past him to think of hurting you or Geirr to get back at Alrik. I should have known better than to let them in. I thought if I kept Gunnar in check, everything would be all right, but I wasn't counting on Einarr to be so impulsive. If you had slept in your own bed, Einarr would have forced himself on you, and it would be my fault."

Selia pulled back. "If a man does a bad thing, then it is *his* fault, no one else's."

"Yes." Hrefna studied her. "Yes, you're right, of course."

Selia returned to her loom and changed the topic of conversation to something less personal. "Why is it that Alrik and Gunnar hate each other, Hrefna?"

"Well, Gunnar told you his mother and Ulfrik's mother were sisters, yes?"

Selia nodded.

"Klaufi Leifson—Gunnar's father—he was one of Ragnarr's men. On the same raid to Ireland where Ragnarr took Treasa, Klaufi also took her sister. Her name was Ide, I believe. Klaufi married her, and Gunnar was born around the same time that Alrik and Ulfrik were born. So the three boys were the same age, and competed fiercely amongst themselves, as boys are known to do. Although at that time Ulfrik was still a thrall, and therefore couldn't raise a hand in his own defense to the other two."

There was a stirring from Geirr on the bench, and both women stopped what they were doing and watched him for a moment. Geirr, still asleep, screwed up his face and let out a startlingly loud fart for such a small babe, then relaxed. Selia stifled a giggle and looked back at Hrefna.

"Just like a man." Alrik's aunt waved a dismissive hand at the babe as she went back to her story. "Ragnarr's men were putting a tattoo on one of them, and the boys overheard Ragnarr boast that he had gotten his own berserker tattoo when he was only seven, after bashing in another boy's head with a rock." Hrefna paused for a moment, pursing her lips. "According to Alrik—if he can be believed—Gunnar then said he would have a berserker tattoo as well, and he picked up a rock and hit Ulfrik with it, knocking him senseless. Alrik took a rock of his own and beat Gunnar so severely that he lost his eye."

Selia gasped. Ragnarr had died when Alrik and Ulfrik were four, so the boys couldn't have been any older than that when this incident occurred. The thought of small children brutalizing each other in such a way was almost unimaginable. "So that is how Alrik got his tattoo?"

Hrefna nodded. "Yes. Although Ragnarr beat Alrik to within an inch of his life for what he had done, secretly he told him he was very proud. He put the tattoo on the boy himself." She shook her head in disgust. "Soon after, Ragnarr died and Klaufi was the first of his men to turn on him. He wanted vengeance for his son's eye. And Gunnar himself has been plotting his own revenge for a long time."

"But surely if Gunnar is as bad as you say he is, he would have tried to do something to Alrik before now."

"Oh he has, my dear. More than once, I'm afraid. He attacked when the boys were living with their grandfather, but Alrik pushed him down a cliff and broke Gunnar's leg. And then Gunnar tried again after Olaf and I moved here, but before Alrik married Eydis. Gunnar was pursuing Eydis as well, you see, but she was put off by his eye. I'm sure it was like salt in his wound when Ketill turned down his proposal for Eydis, but accepted Alrik's. Gunnar came here in a blaze of fury, looking for Alrik. And Alrik laughed at him. He beat Gunnar and left him lying in the dirt. I took pity on Gunnar, cleaned him up, and had Olaf take him home."

Hrefna shrugged. "I almost wish Alrik had killed him, as coldhearted as that sounds. That man is crafty and unpredictable, and I don't like him knowing about you and Geirr."

"Then why did you let him in the house?"

The woman gestured wearily. "Child, Gunnar's men are like a pack of wolves. They will sniff and circle and pace, but they will not attack unless their leader signals them to. I knew Gunnar felt indebted to me for my small kindness to him long ago, and I counted on him honoring that. Which he did. If I would have denied him our hospitality, the respect he felt for me would be finished, and he would have had no qualms about sacking the house and carrying you and Geirr off, or worse. Do you understand?"

"Y-yes." Selia's mouth dried up in a sudden panic. She herself had not once but *twice* insulted Gunnar. And that man had been holding Geirr—a man who clearly would take immense pleasure in inflicting pain or humiliation on Alrik. He could have dashed the infant's head in without a second thought, and thrown the tiny body out into the snow.

Hot rage arose in Selia. "Ulfrik should have known not to bring him here."

"Yes," Hrefna agreed. "Which makes me wonder why he did."

Chapter 8

Time passed with no sign of Alrik's ship. The Finngalls' fall trip was usually shorter than what they planned in the spring, due to the unpredictable nature of the sea so late in the season, so there could be no good excuse for why the men hadn't returned.

The apprehension Selia felt was mirrored in Hrefna's eyes, and even in Ingrid's. The girl of course couldn't care less about her father. Her fears were for Bolli and Olaf.

Hrefna refused to speak of the delayed return of the ship. After the severity of the autumn storms, the sea had calmed and remained as placid as a lake. The woman could easily have said the men were delayed because there was no wind for the sail and they were too tired to row. She could have said Alrik decided to winter over in Dubhlinn.

But Hrefna voiced no hollow reassurances. It seemed clear she believed the ship had been lost.

The unrelenting nausea that had plagued Selia for many moons began to ease, although she found her constant worry was just as much a suppressor of her appetite as the sickness had been. But their lives revolved around food nevertheless. In preparation for the long winter, the women spent a good deal of time making cheese and butter, as well as smoking, salting, and drying meat and fish. This could have been left to the thralls with minimal overseeing by Hrefna, but Selia sensed Alrik's aunt needed something to occupy her mind other than spinning and weaving.

Selia took it upon herself to walk through the forest

whenever the weather permitted, on a stated purpose of stockpiling firewood for the winter. She carried a small dagger with her for safety—although Ingrid scoffed that she was more likely to stab herself than to kill any animal hungry enough to attack such a scrawny meal—and promised Hrefna she would stay close to the house. But as soon as she was out of sight, she always climbed the steep hill that overlooked the fjord, to scan the sea for any sign of the ship.

This was one of the few places where she allowed her tears to fall freely. Ingrid had caught her crying, once, when Selia had thought she was alone in the kitchen, and the girl had proceeded to unleash a torrent of condemnation on her. In her opinion Selia was a stupid, foolish girl, not only feeble-minded but spineless, wasting her tears on a man who would rather bed the thralls than lie with her.

Selia, too exhausted and depressed to argue, had only cried harder, and Hrefna had come into the kitchen and slapped Ingrid to make her stop ranting.

But it was the last time Selia would cry in front of Ingrid, and so she saved her tears for the darkness of her bedchamber or for her trips to the hill behind the house. She imagined pushing Ingrid off the cliff and into the sea hundreds of feet below, but even that couldn't lighten her mood.

There was a ledge on the hill that stayed relatively dry, and she sat there as she cried. Alrik must be dead. What other reason could there be for his absence? Although her mind believed it, her heart refused to. She had gone through so much to be with Alrik and it seemed such a cruel twist of fate to lose him now. She loved her Finngall husband more than she would have ever thought possible, and he had been snatched from her in the blink of an eye.

Selia twisted the ring on her finger. He had loved her as well, to have given her such a thing to protect her from his rages. Yes, he could be amazingly selfish a good deal of the time, but with the gift of the ring he had proven himself willing to give up his life to keep her safe.

She had prayed over and over for Alrik's safe return. But her prayers had been in Irish, as of course her thoughts were naturally conducted in her native language. Her prayers had neither been directed at God or at Odin. She was hesitant to pray to her Christian God on behalf of a heathen, but was nevertheless fearful of the consequences of praying to Odin. So she prayed to a nameless, faceless deity. Now she realized this deity was probably insulted by her indecisive nature.

Selia sat up straighter, wiping her face with the hem of her shift. She examined her ring and rubbed the runes with her finger. How could she expect to get her husband back without some sort of sacrifice on her part? In marrying a Vikinger she had probably condemned her Christian soul anyway. She could sit around and wait until her death to burn for all eternity, or she could use what soul she possessed to bargain for the safe return of her husband.

Swallowing, she mentally apologized for what she was about to do. She doubted God would understand, but it made her feel slightly better if her reasons were made clear.

Selia spoke aloud in Norse. "Odin," she said in a whisper, then cleared her throat and spoke with more conviction. "Odin. I am praying for the return of my husband, Alrik Ragnarson. He is . . ." She hesitated. To call Alrik a good man was a lie, and Odin wouldn't care about goodness in any event. "A good fighter. He has killed many people in your name. If you let him live he will kill many more for you."

There, it was done. She took a deep breath, feeling as though the flames of hell were licking at her feet. She had a nearly uncontrollable urge to cross herself and had to sit on her hands to stop the motion. She had committed yet another mortal sin by praying to a heathen god. Would it be worth it?

Selia waited, looking out onto the water expectantly, until the cold seeped into her bones and she felt frozen to the rock.

When she finally descended the hill to return home, she heard the piercing screams of Geirr before she even opened the door. It was not his typical cry of hunger or of anger, but one of pain. Selia picked up her skirts and sprinted inside.

Ingrid was holding the squirming, red-faced babe, and appeared to be trying to soothe him, although it was obvious her jostling movements were only making things worse. "What is wrong with him?" Selia shouted over the noise.

"Nothing." The girl scowled. "He rolled off the bench, that's all."

Geirr had been remarkably strong from the moment of his birth, and as soon as he learned to roll over, had done so constantly. They had no cradle in the house—Alrik had smashed it to bits after his children died—and so the women had resigned themselves to watching the babe closely to keep him from landing on his head whenever he woke from a nap. Every time there was a close call, Hrefna would press her lips together in exasperation. She had repeatedly vowed that as soon as Alrik walked in the door, she would hand him a block of wood and a saw, and demand that he make a cradle for his son.

Selia snatched Geirr from Ingrid's arms, glaring at the infuriating girl. "You were supposed to be watching him!"

"No," Ingrid sneered. "*You* were supposed to be watching him, you stupid cow. This thrall child is not my responsibility."

Hrefna came through the kitchen door, on her way back from the smokehouse. She looked tired. "What's going on?" she asked.

"Ingrid let him roll off the bench," Selia said through gritted teeth.

"It's not my fault he won't lay still," the girl argued. "It's not my fault Selia goes who knows where and leaves me alone with her husband's bastard child."

"Well." Hrefna huffed with resignation. "I suppose we can see if Bjorn will make a cradle for him. Ingrid, ask him about it tomorrow."

Selia and Ingrid stopped their argument and both turned to the woman, open-mouthed. It was true, then.

Hrefna didn't believe the men were ever coming back.

Selia learned later that night how prayers answered by Odin always came with a heavy price. As she cried into her pillow and ruminated on raising not one, but two babies without a father, there was a noise from the main room. She choked back a sob to listen.

There it was again; the distinct timber of Alrik's voice.

She leapt from the bed, barefoot and clad only in her shift, and ran into the room. *Alrik.* He was home. Her mind rapidly took stock that he looked thin and tired, and his head was bandaged, but all his body parts were intact. He saw her at the same moment, and stopped talking as she launched herself into his arms.

Time stood still for a moment as they held each other. His arms were around her so tightly she could barely take a breath. She refused to pull back, however, but instead buried her face into his neck and held on tighter. She whispered his name, over and over, feeling his pulse beat under her lips. Alrik was home. He was alive.

She slowly became aware of her surroundings, and her dazed mind took in the fact that Hrefna was crying. Selia looked around the otherwise empty room as a cold fear gripped her insides. "Where is Olaf?"

Alrik didn't answer right away. He sat on one of the benches, pulling Selia into his lap as though loathe to let her go. "There was a storm." His voice sounded cracked and hoarse. "It snapped the mast. We lost nine men. Olaf is dead."

A wail escaped Selia's lips. "No!"

"There was nothing I could do," he rasped. "He was there and then gone. There was nothing I could do."

Hrefna burst into fresh sobs. Selia climbed down from Alrik's lap to put her arms around the woman. "Oh Hrefna, I am so sorry," she choked out. It felt odd to be comforting she who was typically so strong; the backbone of the family. It was as if the world had crumbled and fallen apart around them. What would they do now?

Suddenly she realized Ingrid wasn't in the room. The girl slept in the main room, and therefore would have been the first one to speak to her father when he returned. Where had she gone? Selia turned back to Alrik. "Bolli?" she asked hesitantly, unsure if she wanted to know the answer.

Alrik looked away. "He is alive. But the mast crushed his foot. He may lose it."

"Oh," she gasped. Poor Bolli. Only sixteen summers, not even a man yet. Crippled.

Hallveig must have awoken when she heard the commotion in the room. Now she returned from the kitchen carrying mugs of warmed ale, which she served to the family. Geirr stirred and cried out. Hallveig sat on the bench, lifting the babe with one hand and pulling her bodice down with the other. Geirr attached himself to her nipple and began to suckle vigorously. Alrik watched them for a moment with a look of vague surprise, as if he had almost forgotten about the child's existence.

He turned to contemplate the flickering coals of the fire with a look of defeat, then spoke the names of the nine dead men, his voice a low monotone. Selia closed her eyes and saw their faces as he went through them, one by one. "Olaf Egilson," he began. "Mani Nefbjornson and his two sons, Falki and Hallgrim. The brothers Vegeirr and Afrald

Skallagrimson. Asleif Ingjaldson. Rodrek Sialfson. And Riki Ketilson."

Her mind reeled. Nine men, fierce Vikingers all, strong enough to defeat three times their number in battle. Killed not by a blade, but by a wave that washed them overboard and down into the cold, shadowy depths of the sea.

From previous conversations with Hrefna, she had learned Finngalls considered death at sea one of the most ill-omened ways to die, especially if the bodies weren't recovered. A man's death was a reflection of how he had lived his life, and so the most honorable death was one that occurred in battle. 'Thor's red gift,' it was called.

For the Finngalls, to die in battle was proof that a man had been fierce and unwavering until the end, and was deserving of a place with the gods in the afterlife. To die of an accident was less honorable, but nevertheless depended on what the man had been doing at the time of the accident. If Alrik had died of his wounds inflicted by the boar, it would still have been considered a brave and respectable death. Illness, or worst of all, old age, was a passive and unmanly way to die. Many a sickly or elderly man talked his son or grandson into taking him on one final raid in search of Thor's red gift.

A funeral for a Finngall killed in battle was conducted on a grand scale. The man's widow and children would have the comfort of knowing he had died the death of a hero and had a place in the afterlife befitting his bravery. Songs would be sung in his name and vats of ale would be opened in his honor. His courageous death would be revered by all.

For Alrik's nine dead, there would be no funerals to prepare for. There were no bodies to bury or to burn. No caches of treasure, no food, and no sacrifices to send along with the dead men to ease their journey to the afterlife. A death at sea portended nothing but ill luck and misfortune. Many a tale was told of restless corpses who rose from watery graves to search for their loved ones. There were rituals that must be conducted before and during a funeral to stop the dead from rising, and without a body, no rituals could be performed.

Hrefna stared down at the mug of ale in her hand, blinking. She appeared to be in shock. The woman probably needed the tea she had made for Selia when she had learned of Niall's death, except Selia didn't know all the ingredients to make it. "Hrefna," she said, "I will make you some tea if you tell me what to put in it."

Hrefna regarded her with empty eyes, then blinked at Alrik. "No," she said, rising slowly. She shook her head as if to clear it. "No. I must examine Alrik's wound."

Setting her mug aside, she unwound the bandage from Alrik's head. The wound was jagged and swollen, running horizontally beneath his hairline, beginning in the middle of his forehead and ending at the temple. It had been sewn shut by someone who was by no means an expert. Selia could see several areas where the white of his skull showed through the stitches.

Hrefna pressed her lips together as she inspected the wound, her movements practiced and careful. She was all business now, completely closed off from anything other than the task at hand. Selia's heart ached for her.

"This will need to be re-stitched." Hrefna turned to thread a needle.

Selia didn't argue with her. She brought Hrefna a bowl of water and a cloth, and assisted as the woman cut out the old stitches and washed the wound. Alrik sat still, stony and quiet, as his aunt worked. He didn't flinch when the needle pierced his flesh to draw the edges of the wound together. When she was finished he had a neat row of perfect stitches across his forehead. It gave him a surprised look, like an extra eyebrow.

Hrefna finished her work and dabbed a few droplets of blood from Alrik's head. She folded the cloth neatly, laid it on the table, and wiped her hands on her gown. "I believe I'll go to bed now," she said quietly. *Too quietly.*

"Hrefna—"

But the woman held out her hand to stop her. "I'm fine, my dear. We will talk in the morning." Wraithlike, she left the room.

Selia swallowed and watched as Hrefna shut the bedchamber door behind her. It seemed wrong for her to be by herself. Shouldn't they try to do something to comfort her?

Alrik took her wrist, pulling her to him. "Selia. Leave her. She needs to be alone."

She turned back to him with a sigh. The flickering light from the hearth illuminated Alrik's gaunt face. His skin had a waxy pallor to it and his eyes looked sunken. How long had it been since he had eaten? Or slept? She reached up to trace her fingers lightly across the line of fresh stitches on his forehead. She drew them across his cheek, feeling the sharp outline of the bone and the hollow beneath it.

Alrik might look half-dead, but he was alive. He was home. She leaned in to feel the warmth that radiated from his skin, and placed a soft kiss on his mouth. The wave of desire that overtook her was strong and unexpected, and she had to close her eyes for a moment to steady herself.

But he didn't move, and Selia dropped her hand and stepped back. Maybe it was too soon. The deaths of Olaf and his men were too fresh for him to be interested in anything else. "Do you also need to be alone?" she whispered.

The intensity of his gaze shook her to the core. "No," he rasped. He pressed his hand to the back of her neck to pull her closer, his fingers digging in. "I need you, Selia. But I don't want to hurt you. It has been a long time."

She studied him. Alrik's desire was dark, restless for release. The beast was pacing. Had he indeed been true to her, then? Had he not taken advantage of their time apart to sample the charms of whatever woman caught his fancy? Selia shivered as she felt his craving, her body answering the primal call.

She cupped his face and kissed him, all her pent-up longing coming to a head. She moaned into his mouth, craving him, and the heat emanating from Alrik intensified and exploded into urgency. His hands were on her, crushing her body to his. The sound that came from his throat sounded like a growl.

He pulled her shift up and his roving fingers found what he needed. Selia's knees went weak and she thought for a moment he was going to haul her into his lap to take her then and there. But he rose to his feet, lifting her, and carried her into the bedchamber. The candle had burned out and the room was in darkness. Alrik bolted the door, then bore her to the bed.

His mouth on hers was demanding, possessive, and the pitch blackness of the room intensified Selia's rush of desire. She tugged at his shirt, finally pulling it over his head, and sighed with satisfaction as she felt the solid muscles of his torso under her hands. She fumbled to unfasten his trousers as he pushed her back on the bed.

He tore off her shift and his hands found her breasts, but he faltered as he bumped into the unyielding mound of her belly. He hesitated for a moment, then rolled her over. Alrik lifted her hips and sheathed himself inside her.

Selia cried out at the sensation of being filled completely. It had been too long; she had missed him so much, and she met him now, thrust for thrust. The frustration and worry she'd suffered heightened into frenzy, and she gripped the blankets with both fists as her body shuddered with release. With a final groan, he buried himself inside her and went still.

He let her go and collapsed on the bed next to her, breathing hard. Her eyes had adjusted to the darkness and she could see the outline of Alrik's massive body against the pillows. She had lain in this bed, alone, night after night, praying for him to return. And now he was here. The simple pleasure of lying in bed with her husband beside her caused her tears to well up again.

But her happiness came at the expense of others' sorrow. Hrefna would never lie next to Olaf, and Alrik's men would never be with their families again. Selia burrowed into the crook of Alrik's arm, needing the comfort of his embrace. She breathed in his scent and held on to him, listening as his racing heartbeat slowed.

Something was different. Bedding her almost always lightened Alrik's mood, but now he was quiet and withdrawn, closed off from Selia even as he held her. As though his body had returned from the voyage but his soul was trapped with nine dead men at the bottom of the sea.

"I missed you so much, Alrik," Selia whispered into the darkness.

It took him a moment to respond. "I missed you too," he echoed.

Chapter 9

An air of melancholy settled over the house with Alrik's return. His ruined dragonship sat on the water with the end of the splintered mast rising from the wreckage like a broken bone. The railing on one side was smashed to bits, part of the decking crushed as well. It looked to Selia as though the ship would never sail again.

And Alrik seemed as broken as his ship. He had the thralls bring him a steady supply of ale, and he stayed in the bedchamber, brooding, irritable; restless. Only the ale seemed to take the edge off. Even at night he only slept after he had drunk himself into a stupor.

Selia did everything she could to distract him, but not even she could bring him out of his gloom for long. She had been right about his emotional state. Bedding her was now nothing more than a physical release for him, after which he would stare silently up at the rafters.

Finally he rose from the bed with something approaching purpose. He opened all the chests and dumped the contents out onto the floor, muttering to himself. Selia watched him warily.

"What are you doing?" she asked. It was just after dawn, but she knew he had been awake most of the night. When he turned to look at her, she cringed. His eyes were sunken and red-rimmed, his hair a tangled mess around his face. He looked like a madman.

Alrik shook his head but didn't answer. He knelt on the floor and began to divide the horde of treasure into piles. Selia wrapped a blanket around herself against the chill and walked over to him. She watched him for a few moments as he picked up each piece and made a careful selection of which pile to put it in. Selia counted the piles; there were eight. Nine dead men, minus Olaf. Eight piles.

"Are these for the families of your men?" she asked quietly.

Alrik grunted, and she took this for a yes. She knew most of the bounty the men had collected from the raid had been lost in the storm, and what was left had been divided among the surviving members of the war band. It was Alrik's duty as Hersir to ensure the survival of the families of all of his men. Although winter hadn't hit with a vengeance yet, it soon would, and many of the families could not get by without the yield of the twice-annual raids.

Selia hesitated. "Can I help you?"

"No. Just stay out of the way."

She knelt next to him. "What about food?" she asked. "They will need food for the winter."

He stopped for a moment, grimacing as if annoyed at the distraction. "Yes," he snapped. "Go to the pantries and bring the surplus here. Only leave what we need to get by until spring." He turned back to his piles, dismissing her.

Selia rose to dress. As she was leaving she spotted a golden ball that had rolled away when Alrik had overturned the chests, and she picked it up to hand to him. Then stopped short and frowned as she got a closer look at it. Not a ball but rather a knob in the shape of a lion's head, sized to fit in the palm of a hand. The lion's eyes were glittering rubies.

She stared at the lion's head. *No.* No, it couldn't be. She turned it over in her hand and cried out as she saw the hole on the other side. It was the top of a cane, and the hole was meant for the wooden end of the cane to fit in. Selia had seen this particular cane many times before.

Alrik looked up at her with narrowed eyes. "Give that to me."

"Where did you get this?" she whispered.

Alrik snatched the lion's head from her hand. He didn't add it to the piles but instead set it aside on the floor. "You know where I got it, Selia."

Her heart hammered in her chest. "Did you kill him?"

"Of course I killed him," he retorted impatiently. "I told you I would."

"Alrik! He was an old man. What threat was he to you?"

Her husband stood and crossed his arms. His face had lost its despondency and now—for a moment, at least—his anger made him look more like himself. More like the Hersir.

He glared down his nose at Selia. "Any man who would take what is mine is a threat to me. He paid men to try to steal you away. Did you expect me to let that go unpunished?"

Selia didn't reply as her tears spilled over for Buadhach. Had the poor man suffered? Had Alrik at least made it quick? She was afraid to know the answer. She turned away, hoping God had shown mercy on the soul of the man her husband had murdered.

Later that morning, Alrik packed one of the little boats to overflowing, then set off from the bay to distribute the provisions to the families of the dead men. The house was shrouded in silence after he left. Ingrid was staying at Ketill's house with Bolli. She had made it very clear she blamed her father for Bolli's crushed foot. Hrefna remained silent, quieter than Selia had ever known her to be. Did the woman also blame Alrik for the death of Olaf?

Or did Hrefna blame Selia? It had been at her behest that Alrik had postponed the fall trip. She had of course been reluctant for Alrik to leave so soon after she had returned to him. But the darker reason was because she had hoped Muirin would go into labor before he left, ensuring he was there to free Muirin and claim the thrall's child as his. The thought of Hrefna being upset with Selia made it difficult to focus on anything else.

Geirr woke fussing from his nap, and Selia dropped her spinning to go to him. She held the babe more than was necessary now, but she needed the distraction. She looked down at his beautiful face, chewing at her lip.

As she held one child, the other—as yet unborn—kicked in her belly. He was getting stronger, for sometimes he would kick her so hard she nearly lost her balance when she was walking. Her condition was impossible to hide at this point; the rounded outline of her belly protruded just past her breasts. Hrefna said she had about three more full moons until the babe was born. Selia didn't like to think about how large the child could grow by then.

Geirr looked up at her with a somber expression and she gave him a small smile. He cooed and smiled back, wide and toothless, and kicked his legs in infant joy.

She bent to kiss his head. The thought of any harm coming to Geirr made her sick and anxious. Selia loved him, there was no denying it now. It had taken the threat of Gunnar and his men at the farmstead for her to finally realize it. The only thing she could do at this point, the only thing that would approach making this right, was to care for—and love—this motherless child.

As if reading her thoughts, Geirr turned his head and began to root at her bodice, searching for milk. She repositioned him. "None yet, little boy," she said, and left the house to find Hallveig.

On her way back from the slave quarters, Selia turned into the woods to set a snare. She had seen Ainnileas do it often enough to know how. She needed a sacrifice for Odin, but was reluctant to kill one of the farm animals. That would necessitate telling Hrefna what she done, and she was sure the woman wouldn't be pleased. Odin granted great power to the Finngalls who prayed to him, but the god's gifts were dark and always came with a price.

Selia returned that evening to find a rabbit struggling in the snare. It was young and rather small, and its thrashing intensified as she approached. She watched it, her hands growing clammy with sweat, and fought back a wave of nausea as she knelt down beside the animal. "I'm sorry," she whispered.

She took a deep breath to steady herself and wiped her hands on her gown. It was no different than killing a chicken for supper. No different. And to deny Odin the blood required to answer her prayer to bring Alrik home would surely bring dreadful consequences. The god might take a sacrifice of his own.

"Odin," she called out in Norse. "I thank you for the safe return of my husband." Her voice sounded hollow and thin, and a sudden wind blew her words away as it whipped through the trees. "I give you the blood of this animal as tribute." She unsheathed her dagger.

The rabbit seemed to sense her deadly intention. Its thrashing took on an air of panic, and she stared down at it, wavering. Its eyes rolled up to her, and it made small squealing noises as it struggled. Selia's mind rebelled.

What was she doing? How had she come to this—an Irish Christian, preparing to slaughter an animal in the name of a heathen god who had cursed Alrik's family with nothing but misery? Odin had brought her husband home to her, yes, but at the cost of the lives of men he loved. And possibly at the cost of his sanity.

Odin did not deserve a sacrifice. He didn't deserve anything more from this family than he had already taken. Grabbing the rabbit, she wrestled to hold it still, then slipped the tip of the dagger under the rope around its hind leg. The rabbit squirmed and twisted in her hand, squeaking. It sunk its teeth into her flesh just as she cut it free from the snare.

She screamed and dropped the rabbit. The animal's teeth had laid open a small gash on the pad of flesh beneath her thumb. The creature skittered away as Selia's blood dripped onto the white of the snow.

She brushed her tears away, then took a handful of snow in her injured hand and squeezed it to stop the bleeding. Now would be the time to pray, to ask God for forgiveness for what she had almost done. But the words wouldn't come. Her throat felt as dry as ashes.

She stood up, sniffling, and steadied herself on a tree for a moment. The babe squirmed inside her as he always seemed to do whenever she was upset. Selia rubbed her belly to comfort the child, and turned to go back to the house.

There was a fluttering of wings as a raven settled on a branch above her and studied her with its beady black eyes. Selia's skin crawled at the sight. She hated ravens. A sudden stench of smoke and rotten flesh permeated the air, so strong she felt as though she were choking on it. An unreasonable panic arose inside her. She wanted to run.

Run from what, exactly—a silly bird?

She threw the bloody ball of snow at the raven, but although it fluttered its wings again, it didn't fly away. It cawed at her as it paced along the branch. Ravens were sacred to Odin. Had he sent this one to ensure Selia completed her task as promised?

"That is all you will get from us." She motioned to her blood in the snow. "Tell him to leave us alone."

An odd tightening in Selia's abdomen took her breath. It felt as though a large hand had wrapped around her and squeezed. Gasping, she fell onto her knees in the snow. The raven cawed and flew away.

A shiver traveled down her spine as the pain passed. Was this a warning from Odin? Would he hurt the babe? Had she put her child in danger by refusing the sacrifice? Selia's fear bit thick and dark, and it threatened to overwhelm her for a moment.

No. Hrefna had warned her as she progressed in her confinement she would suffer pains from time to time. This was nothing more than that. Selia took a deep breath, forcing the fear away, and headed for home.

Alrik returned from his short journey early the next morning. Selia was still in bed, half asleep, when she heard him close the bedchamber door. He undressed, then climbed into bed. He lay still, not touching her, and she rolled over to look at him.

"Alrik," she mumbled. "You were gone all night."

"I stayed at Ketill's," he replied.

"How is Bolli?"

"I don't think he will lose his foot after all. But . . ." he trailed off and shook his head. "It isn't good. None of it is good."

Selia examined him closely. Alrik looked thin and exhausted. He hadn't slept well since he had come home, other than when he drank himself into a stupor. The tragedy had aged him, and all of his typical bravado had disappeared. Would he ever be the same again after this devastating loss?

"I'm sorry," she fretted. "I should not have asked you to stay. If you had left when you wanted to, none of this would have happened."

Alrik brooded and didn't answer. Her heart sank. He did blame her then.

But he continued on as though she hadn't spoken. "I asked Ketill to take Olaf's place as my right hand man, and he refused."

Ketill had lost his eldest son in the storm. His youngest son might never walk again. And his middle son had a permanently disfigured face at the hands of the Hersir during their spring trip. Could the man be blamed for hesitating to take Alrik up on his offer?

"Perhaps he needs time to think about it," she suggested. "Maybe it is too soon to ask."

Alrik didn't answer, but only stared up at the rafters, silent and pensive. He finally drifted off into a fitful sleep.

Selia lay next to him until the sun's rays penetrated through the smoke hole. Even in his sleep his face had a worried, pinched expression. His grief over the deaths of his men, and the uncertainty of whether or not the war band would stay together, covered him like a shroud.

She dressed quickly and slipped from the room. Hallveig would want to hand Geirr over to her soon. The house was deserted as she went out the kitchen door on her way to the privy. Every time she stepped outside, she tried to avert her eyes from the wreckage of the ship. It sat at the dock, as broken and forlorn as a ghost ship. But she saw a flash of color from the corner of her eye and turned to see a figure sitting at the dock.

Hrefna.

She approached the woman, calling her name softly so she wouldn't startle her. Hrefna turned, her eyes hollow and ringed with purple. "Hello, my dear," she said in a flat voice as Selia sat down.

She slipped her hand into Hrefna's and squeezed it. The woman's fingers were icy cold. "How long have you been out here?"

Hrefna blinked. "I'm not quite sure. Before dawn."

"You are going to freeze to death," Selia chastised. She removed her cloak and put it around the woman's shoulders. "Come inside and I will make you something to eat."

Hrefna didn't answer, studying the ship instead. "It's odd, isn't it, how we make small decisions, not knowing which one will be our last. I keep looking at the ship and wondering where Olaf was standing when the wave took him. I wonder if he moved at the last moment, or if he was simply in the wrong spot all along." Her eyes traced along the ship's crushed railing. "Did he go under right away, or did he struggle? Did he call for help? Did he try to swim back to the ship?"

Selia shivered. "No good will come from those thoughts."

The woman nodded, not taking her eyes from the ship. "I know, child."

What could she say that would be of any comfort? There was nothing. Olaf was gone, his body lost to the sea. Selia leaned close to put her arms around Alrik's aunt. "Come inside. Olaf would not want you to suffer like this."

Hrefna sighed but didn't make a move to rise. "I've been with Olaf since I was fourteen."

"Yes." Selia didn't know what else to say.

"I'm not sure how to live now. What will I do without him? What use am I?"

"You are of use to me. You are of use to Alrik, and Ingrid, and Geirr. We all need you."

Hrefna gave her a feeble smile. "I'm glad you came back to Alrik, child," she murmured after a moment. "He wouldn't survive this without you."

Selia averted her gaze. "I wish I could help him," she whispered. "I do not know what to do. He does not answer when I speak to him. He is—lost." Olaf had been like a father to Alrik. The man had understood him. He had accepted him. Now Olaf was gone, Ulfrik was gone, and maybe Ketill as well. Alrik was all alone.

"Yes. He is. But that doesn't mean he can't be found. Just be patient."

"Alrik said he stayed at Ketill's last night. He said he asked Ketill to be his right hand man but he refused. The men are turning on him, I think."

Hrefna pursed her lips in thought. "Ketill is angry. They all are, the loss is too fresh. But Alrik is right. Without a right-hand to side with him and speak for him when he's not there, the men will continue to fragment."

Selia's stomach knotted. What happened when a war band fragmented? Would the curse of Ragnarr rear its ugly head once again?

"Did Alrik say anything about Ingrid?" Hrefna asked.

Ingrid was staying at Ketill's to help care for her cousin Bolli. But Selia knew Alrik would not have inquired about Ingrid's wellbeing. He barely noticed her existence. So why would Hrefna ask her this now? "No," she replied, studying the woman.

Hrefna hesitated, then whispered, "Ingrid is with child. Ainnileas is the father."

A nauseating sense of shifting overwhelmed Selia, as though the earth had given way beneath her. The rushing sound of her blood pounded in her ears. *No.* No, it couldn't be. The girl was lying.

"Ingrid denied being with child," Selia managed to choke out. She could barely breathe.

Hrefna shook her head. "Sometimes, early on, there is a little blood. And since Ingrid is barely more than a child herself, how would she know? I finally guessed myself."

"No!" Selia cried. Alrik had already asserted he would never allow his daughter to marry Ainnileas. So, in the reasoning of the Finngalls, the only appropriate way to save face would be to kill him. A vision of the gold lion's head in their bedchamber arose in her mind, the trophy the Hersir had collected from the man who had disrespected him. The crushing weight on her chest intensified.

She stood, clenching her fists at her sides. "We have to do something, Hrefna. Alrik will kill him!" She did a desperate calculation in her head. Was Ingrid too far along to take the draught of poison that would expel the child from her womb? She would mix the concoction herself, and force it down the girl's throat if she had to. Anything to save Ainnileas from Alrik's sword.

Hrefna grabbed her wrist to pull her back down. "Hush, child. Lower your voice. I've already thought of a solution. That is why Ingrid is with Bolli."

Later that afternoon there was a knock at the door. Alrik was still in the bedchamber and Hrefna had gone to the barn for a moment, so Selia was alone at the loom while Geirr slept on the bench next to her. She hurried to the door so the knocking wouldn't wake him.

Ketill stood at the door, his appearance awful, as unkempt as she had ever seen him. Hair uncombed, clothes dirty, face haggard and gray; the man looked as though he had aged much since she had seen him last.

Odin had cast his shadow over Ketill's family just as it had Alrik's. Selia opened the door for him. "Alrik is asleep," she whispered. "And Hrefna is in the barn."

"That's just as well." He stepped inside. "It's you I want to speak with."

"Me?" Selia swallowed. What could Ketill want with her?

He looked around the room. "Are we alone? No thralls?"

She nodded.

"Do you know about Ingrid?"

"Yes."

"Alrik will kill your brother, you know that."

Geirr began to fuss in his sleep and Selia went to him. Her hand was shaking as she rubbed the babe's back. "I know," she whispered. Was that what Ketill had come all the way to tell her?

He watched her intently. "I've half a mind to let him do it. You and your brother have been nothing but trouble. You especially—I have never seen Ulfrik in such a state as he's in over you."

Ketill wasn't going to help them. "Just go away, then," Selia hissed. "Why are you here—to see me suffer?"

"I loved your mother," Ketill said after a moment. "I would have married her. I would have freed her and made her my wife. But she always refused. She said she could never marry a Vikinger after what we had done to her. So I kept her in thrall to me instead. I'm not proud of that."

Selia continued to rub Geirr's back but held her thoughts to herself. Of course her mother had turned down Ketill's offer of marriage. It would be impossible for the woman to clench her spite with both hands if she had allowed herself any modicum of happiness.

Ketill regarded her sternly. "Whatever I do now I do for Grainne and for Ingrid. Not for you, and not for your brother. Do you understand?"

She gave him a sharp look. "So you will let Bolli marry Ingrid?"

"Yes. The girl is my blood and I will not see her shamed. Bolli will claim the babe as his. I will speak to Alrik and settle the matter. If he wants me for his right-hand man, he will give Ingrid to my son."

Selia's body sagged in relief as her tears spilled over. "Thank you, Ketill."

He held his hand up to silence her. "No, do not thank me. Understand the gift of your brother's life is only for Grainne. Not for you. From this moment forth I wash my hands of your troublesome family. My debt to your mother has been paid."

Chapter 10

The seasons shifted again and the darkness of winter descended over the farmstead. Eithne's stories of a Finngall land of ice and endless night finally rang true. A brief appearance of the sun, little more than a frosty twilight. A tease of morning that never fully arrived. The near-constant darkness was unsettling, and Selia craved the return of summer.

Surprisingly, Alrik had agreed to the marriage of Bolli and Ingrid without an argument, and so Hrefna had begun the preparations for a quick wedding. Winter was the wrong season for a marriage, but it could not be helped in this case. Ingrid's child would be born in the spring. A winter wedding was necessary to avoid a bastard birth.

Bolli was still unable to sit a horse. But to be brought to the Hersir's farmstead in a sleigh, like a woman, would have been unthinkable. To be carried through the snow and into the house, a further emasculation. So Hrefna decreed the family would travel to Ketill's house for the wedding to take place there.

And so in the icy darkness of a midwinter morning, the thralls loaded Ingrid's substantial dowry onto a sleigh. They added food and supplies for the wedding feast until the sleigh groaned under the weight. Once the packing was complete, Selia and Hrefna climbed into the sleigh.

Two male thralls sat up front to guide the horses, with Keir between them. Ostensibly, she was being brought along to help Ketill's thralls prepare and serve the food. But since Selia was heavy with child, she knew Hrefna felt it didn't hurt to have another knowledgeable female along in case the babe decided to come at Ketill's farmstead.

The woods were bitterly cold, enough to draw the moisture from Selia's eyes and nose, and make each breath a painful choke that burned her lungs. She was dressed in her warmest gown as well as a heavy wool and fur overcoat that Hrefna had made for her, with her blue cloak over all. Her legs were encased in thick wool stockings, her boots were stuffed with straw, and she had a fur muff for her hands. Selia felt like a tick about to burst, but even with all the layers she was still freezing.

Once she had settled in the sleigh, Alrik tucked several large furs around her, grumbling all the while about Selia's willful nature and innate stubbornness. She did her best to ignore him. Hrefna had warned that her nephew's foul moods increased during the winter darkness, and the amount of ale he drank only exacerbated his short temper.

Alrik had wanted her to stay home for the sake of the babe, but Selia had argued and pleaded with him until he had finally given in. She had not been away from the farmstead in ages. She had almost two full moons remaining until the babe was born, and faced a long, monotonous winter at home. It was unfair to force her to stay behind at the farmstead with Geirr and the thralls while everyone traveled on an exciting journey. Why should Alrik and Hrefna enjoy themselves at Ingrid's wedding while Selia was penned in by the walls of the longhouse, listening to the wolves howl in the darkness outside?

She shivered as Alrik tucked the furs around her. "You are an obstinate woman, Selia," he groused. "Too pig-headed for your own good. If you weren't carrying my child I would put you over my knee."

She smiled at him through her chattering teeth. If she wasn't carrying his child he wouldn't be trying to force her to stay home and miss the wedding. "I will be fine, Alrik. You will see."

Hrefna waved him away with an impatient hand. "Enough. Stop fussing like a mother hen," she said, which only made Alrik's expression darken. "You're going to be late to your own daughter's wedding."

Hrefna had been adrift since the death of Olaf. A woman who needed to be needed, without the sense of purpose she obtained as Olaf's wife, she was lost. Although Selia had done her best to step in as the mistress of the house, it was obvious she couldn't fill the hole vacated by such a strong woman as Hrefna. Only when her nephew had agreed to the marriage of Bolli and Ingrid had she begun to show some interest in life again. The planning of a wedding was just too tempting to resist.

Selia was certain Hrefna's wellbeing was the real reason Alrik had agreed to the marriage. He wanted Ketill as his right-hand man, to be sure, but he wanted his aunt's happiness even more.

Alrik mounted his horse, glaring down at Hrefna and Selia. He'd flung a heavy overcoat on under his cloak as well, made of black wool and leather with fur trim, and wore a fur hat that extended over his ears. He sat tall and proud on his magnificent stallion, his lips and cheeks as red as his cloak from the cold. He looked the part of the Hersir again—handsome and virile, a man in command. She met his blue eyes and couldn't suppress a grin.

As his horse danced in the snow and snorted out a stream of frosty breath, Alrik pursed his lips at Selia. "Only a fool smiles when it is this cold," he informed her. "It will be a long journey. We'll see if you're still smiling when we get there."

The trip to Ketill's would have normally been an easy one by horse, but the weather and the heavily-laden sleigh added to their traveling time. Even through the furs, the bitter wind bit at Selia's face and froze the tears it drew from her eyes.

The sun made its brief appearance and she was able to at least enjoy the scenery for a while. The watery dawn rose over the blanket of white, cold and austere. The branches of the black trees overhead creaked in the wind as the traveling party picked their way through snowdrifts in search of high ground.

A wolf howled in the distance, causing the hackles to rise on Selia's neck. She shuddered and Hrefna patted her thigh reassuringly under the furs. "Not long now, child."

As the sun began to set, they crested a hill and Selia finally saw Ketill's house below. She had been to his farmstead only once before, when they returned from Ireland, but had never been inside the dwelling. The farmstead consisted of a small longhouse, about the size of Ulfrik's, with a few dilapidated outbuildings behind it. It didn't look overly welcoming, but nevertheless was shelter from the cold.

Alrik dismounted, then helped Hrefna and Selia from the sleigh. He left the unpacking to the thralls and escorted the women to the door, just as it was thrown open by a female slave carrying a slop bucket. The woman stopped in surprise. Her eyes lingered on Selia for a moment before she lowered her gaze to the ground.

"They have arrived," the slave called within. She stepped aside and held the door open, and they entered Ketill's house.

Alrik ducked through the doorway, but even fully inside the longhouse, he could barely stand up straight. The rafters were just above his head. Arranged much as Ulfrik's house had been, it boasted one narrow room with benches on both sides and a large hearth in the middle. At the far end of the room was the smaller cooking hearth, near which was set up a loom and a table.

A crowd of people already congregated inside; Ketill, Skagi, Bolli, Ingrid, and even Bjorn the blacksmith. There were two thralls in addition to the woman who had just gone outside, both males. They looked similar enough to be father and son.

With the three thralls the traveling party had brought along with them, there would be more than a dozen people packed into this modest dwelling. None of the outbuildings on the farmstead looked to be slave quarters, so apparently Ketill's thralls slept in the main house. Selia politely refrained from counting the benches to see if there would be enough room for everyone to sleep.

"Hersir." Ketill approached Alrik. "I'm glad to see you made it safely through the snow." He clasped Alrik's arm, then bent to kiss Hrefna on the cheek. To Selia he gave only a closed-lipped smile. "I'm surprised you let her make the trip," he said to Alrik over her head.

Alrik frowned. "Yes. Let's hope my son isn't born in a snowbank."

Selia turned to the hearth, where Bolli reclined on a bench and Ingrid sat next to him. They were whispering about something. Selia pulled her hands from her fur muff to warm them at the fire. Ingrid scowled at her, but Selia ignored the hateful girl and instead focused her attention on Bolli. It was his willingness to marry his cousin that had in all likelihood saved Ainnileas' life, after all.

"Bolli," she began, "Alrik told me you are able to walk again."

The boy faced her, wincing a bit. "Yes," he nodded. I've been using a cane. It is a little easier."

She smiled. "I am so happy you are all right."

Ingrid's scowl deepened. "Just because he can walk doesn't mean he can fight," she snapped. "Or are you too stupid to know that?"

Selia refused to be baited. The girl was angry, and with good reason. She carried the child of a man she loved but couldn't wed, and was being prodded into a marriage she didn't want as a result. And it couldn't help matters that Ingrid was reminded of Ainnileas every time she looked at Selia.

Ingrid was wearing a new gown, cut a bit loose so her condition wasn't obvious. But her breasts were fuller, her lips were fuller, and the color was high in her cheeks. She wouldn't be able to hide her belly for much longer, and she was too far along to be able to marry an unsuspecting man and trick him into thinking the babe was his. Bolli was her only option. The girl should stop her ranting and be grateful she had someone who was willing to marry her at all.

The child in Selia's belly kicked, hard, and she had to sit down on one of the benches to catch her breath. Selia grew suddenly hot, and she pulled off the cloak and overcoat and fanned herself with her hand.

Ingrid snorted. "You've gotten very fat. I suppose we'll need to lock the pantry or we'll have nothing left."

Selia gritted her teeth. There was only so much she could take. She opened her mouth to respond just as Hrefna came over. "My dear." The woman embraced Ingrid. "You look lovely. Is that a new gown?"

Selia chimed in. "Yes, Ingrid, it does look new. Have your other gowns grown too small already?"

"Bitch," Ingrid mouthed at Selia around her aunt's head. Selia merely bared her teeth in a mockery of a smile.

Hrefna took Ingrid's hand and led her behind the curtain that had been erected along the far side of the longhouse. The girl needed to finish her wedding preparations. Selia settled in more comfortably next to Bolli. He was a handsome boy who must have favored his mother more than he did Ketill. He had wavy brown hair and blue-gray eyes, and only the faintest trace of a moustache. He looked very young, and very nervous.

How must Bolli be feeling about this marriage? Eydis, Ingrid's mother, had been Ketill's half-sister, the product of their father's second marriage after Ketill's mother had died. Although Ingrid and Bolli weren't quite full cousins, they nevertheless had the blood of a common grandfather flowing through their veins. They were as close as brother and sister. The prospect of joining as husband and wife could not be appealing for either of them.

"Bolli." She met the boy's gaze directly. "Thank you."

Bolli flushed, looking a bit uncomfortable. "It's all right. I do care for her."

Before Selia could say any more, the sound of a drum filled the room. One of the thralls, the younger male, sat on a bench across the hearth and held the drum in his crossed legs. His hands moved expertly as his head nodded in time. The beat grew louder, quickening Selia's pulse.

The slave made eye contact with Bolli and smiled. Bolli sat up, grunting with the effort, and shook his head at him. "No, Hakon," he said. He seemed annoyed, and a little embarrassed. The interaction reminded Selia of how Ainnileas always began a tune on his whistle and then expected her to sing.

The behavior of Ketill's slaves had struck her as very relaxed and informal, nothing like the demeanor of Alrik's slaves. The Hersir's thralls did their best to stay in the shadows and not be noticed. They looked terrified whenever he spoke directly to them. But these three slaves of Ketill's appeared almost as though they were part of his family. And until very recently, this little family had included a fourth slave. *Grainne.*

Hakon shrugged and looked over at Bjorn, as the beat of his hands on the drum intensified. Bjorn was tapping his toes as he stood in conversation with Alrik and Ketill. The blacksmith hesitated for a moment, then Ketill laughed and pushed him forward. Bjorn finally nodded at the boy with a smile.

Bjorn and the slave boy began to sing at the same time. Bjorn's deep voice and the thrall's higher tone complemented each other's beautifully. They followed each other note for note, the only difference in the pitch. Selia sat spellbound as she listened. She had never heard anything quite like it.

The song told the story of an eager bridegroom and a shy young bride, and the ridiculous lengths the bridegroom had to take to finally coax the bride into the wedding bed.

The words to the song were quite bawdy, and Selia blushed as she met Alrik's gaze across the room. His eyes twinkled at her as he laughed and stomped his foot to the song. She hadn't seen him look this relaxed and happy in quite some time, and her heart contracted in her chest as she watched him. Maybe he would be all right, after all.

The drumming came faster as they neared the end of the song. The slave was flushed with exertion as he drummed and sang. He was a handsome lad, thrall or not, with wheat colored hair cropped close to his head, and a pleasing bone structure. He was slight of build, with slim, elegant hands and no facial hair, but nevertheless appeared to be a bit older than Bolli.

The song ended with a whoop. The Finngalls clapped and stomped, calling for more. The thrall laughed as he launched into another song, with a less intense beat. Selia again turned to finish her conversation with Bolli.

But she stopped as she saw the boy's pale face. There was an indescribable expression on his features, a mixture of anger, sorrow, and . . . shame. Why was he so upset? Had the words of the song embarrassed him? No, his troubled appearance seemed more to do with the slave boy than the song itself.

She observed him covertly. The emotion on Bolli's face, coupled with the strange interaction between him and the thrall when the boy started to drum, almost seemed as though the two were lovers. Selia had heard of such things, of course, but only in the way of village boys slinging insults at each other.

When newly-wed and traveling on the dragonship, it had become apparent that children were not the only ones who exchanged these types of insults. One night when the men were drinking heavily, the slurs had gone too far. One man had drawn his weapon on another, and Alrik was forced to intervene.

Ulfrik had been hesitant to translate these ugly terms when she'd asked for an explanation. Apparently, to the Finngalls, there was no greater dishonor than for a man to serve in the female role when lust existed between two men.

Selia felt a flush creeping over her face as realization dawned on her. Bolli loved the slave boy. Not in a depraved way such as the sniggers on the ship suggested, but in the way of any person loving another. Everything made much more sense now: Hrefna's idea that Bolli and Ingrid should marry, the boy's ready acceptance of a marriage to his cousin carrying another man's babe, and Ketill's willingness for his son to raise a child not his own. For even though the child wasn't Bolli's, it did at least carry Ketill's bloodline through Eydis and Ingrid. Close enough, perhaps, to even bear a resemblance to that side of the family and convince a casual observer that Bolli was indeed the father.

So that was why Ketill had been so quick to agree to this wedding.

As though sensing her scrutiny, Bolli turned to Selia. They exchanged a long look that told her suspicions were correct; he didn't want this marriage any more than Ingrid did. He loved another, just as Ingrid did.

Bolli closed his eyes and leaned his head back against the wall, escaping with his mind as he was unable to do with his body.

Ingrid and Hrefna emerged from behind the curtain a little while later. Ingrid wore the same gown, but her skin was scrubbed clean and her hair had been combed. Hrefna had dressed Ingrid's hair very simply, with two small plaits at the temples joined at the back of her head, the rest of her hair hanging free down her back. She wore an elaborate headdress consisting of strands of wheat woven into braids and knots. The bridal crown was supposed to be trimmed with flowers, but since the winter wedding didn't allow for that, Hrefna had improvised by trimming it with silk cording. Selia thought it lovely.

"We are ready," Hrefna said to the group, and to Selia's surprise everyone began to don their overcoats and cloaks. Apparently the wedding was to take place outside.

Bolli swallowed. He drew in a deep breath and smiled at Ingrid. The boy stood up with some difficulty, gripping his cane, and his father approached him. Ketill had a long, wrapped parcel in his hands.

"I never thought you would be the first of my sons to marry." Ketill addressed Bolli formally as he unwrapped the parcel. It was a sword, recently polished, and it gleamed in the firelight. "The sword of your grandfather, to be kept in trust for your son."

Ketill made eye contact with Selia, a long, slow blink, before turning away. He wanted to be sure she understood the significance of this.

At the naming ceremony when Geirr was born, Alrik claimed the child as his own and presented him with the sword of Geirr Jorulfson. Selia could only hope that Ingrid's babe was a girl. Then, at least, Ainnileas' son wouldn't be given this heirloom sword from Ketill's dead father. Maybe the sword could be used instead for Skagi's son, if any woman could ever be convinced to marry him. Selia kept her eyes to the floor as Ketill fastened the sword around Bolli's waist.

Bjorn had a similarly-wrapped parcel as well, which he untied and handed to Alrik. It too was a sword, new and beautifully worked, and the crowd murmured in appreciation as Alrik unsheathed it and held its lustrous length before him. He tested the sword's weight and examined the blade, then nodded down at Bjorn.

"Well done," Alrik praised. Bjorn smiled, as pleased as a mother whose child had just been complimented.

Bolli gripped his cane as he hobbled to the door. Even though Ketill held his other arm, each step was labored and uncertain, and his face looked pinched from the pain.

The thralls had cleared a path through the snow that led to a copse of fir trees near the house. Torches had been erected and placed along the path to light the way. The intention must have been for the trees to block the weather, but they did precious little against the bitter wind. The small wedding party huddled in the trees, shivering, as the female thrall led a sow into the clearing by a rope.

Alrik stepped forward, waiting silently until all eyes turned to him. He stood tall and formidable, and he studied both Ingrid and Bolli in turn, with a look on his face that would strike fear into the hearts of battle-hardened men. Hrefna hadn't told him of Ingrid's condition, but Alrik was no fool; surely he suspected something. Quick winter weddings weren't planned without good reason.

"We are here to call witness to the marriage of my daughter Ingrid, to Bolli, son of Ketill, grandson of Bruni. The dowry and the bride-price have been exchanged and all business has been settled to satisfaction." Alrik turned to Hrefna. "Proceed, Hrefna Erlandsdottir."

Hrefna stepped forward. She took the sow from the slave and handed the woman an ornately carved wooden cup. The placid sow shifted in the snow on its small black hooves and studied the wedding guests.

"My friends," Hrefna said. "Each god holds one beast sacred above all others. The sow is sacred to Freyja. It is in her honor that we offer up the blood of this beast so that Bolli and Ingrid's marriage shall be blessed with prosperity, fertility, and happiness."

Hrefna moved quickly. She straddled the sow between her legs and held the rope taut as the animal began to squeal and struggle. With a swift motion, she pulled her dagger from her belt and slit the sow's throat. The thrall moved in with the cup to catch the spurting blood. The sow sank to its knees, and Hrefna lowered the body to the ground as the animal's blood darkened the blanket of snow beneath it.

Queasy at the blood, Selia averted her eyes. The scene reminded her too much of the murder of Father Coinniach. Surely the priest's death had not been planned by Alrik all along as a sacrifice to bless their union, as the sow was meant to bless Bolli and Ingrid's? Selia studied Alrik's face but his expression was stony.

With the sow dead at her feet, Hrefna held the cup high. "Bolli and Ingrid, the joining of husband and wife is a sacred union and not one to enter into lightly. We pray the gods see fit to bless your marriage, to open Ingrid's womb to bear Bolli many strong and healthy children, and to give Bolli the vigor to provide for his wife and family and to protect them from harm."

Hrefna dipped a small bundle of tied fur twigs into the cup of blood. She tapped it lightly three times on the side of the cup, then, to Selia's surprise, she flicked the bundle in the direction of the wedding party. A fine spray of blood hit Selia's face. "May the blessing of the gods rain upon you, and know they show favor to those who honor them and offer sacrifice."

Selia shivered and refrained from wiping the blood away. Hrefna then nodded to Bolli. The boy looked very wan, and Ketill stood close as Bolli unsheathed his grandfather's sword.

"Ingrid Alriksdottir," Bolli said, his young voice cracking a bit. He cleared his throat and continued. "It is with reverence that I offer you the sword of my ancestors. I charge you with the task of keeping this sword in trust for my future son, and for his son after him. Will you accept this sacred duty of a wife?"

Ingrid's nervous gaze met Bolli's. She at least had enough sense to feel guilty about pawning off her bastard child on her cousin. "I will," she said in a quiet voice. Ingrid took the sword from Bolli and passed it to Hrefna. Ingrid then turned to Alrik, who handed her the new sword.

Alrik narrowed his eyes at Bolli. "Bolli Ketilson," Alrik said, "I offer you this sword, forged new in a spirit of trust and unity. By taking up this sword, the responsibility of my daughter's protection and care is transferred from father to husband. Will you accept this sacred duty?"

"I will," Bolli said. Ingrid laid the gleaming sword in his hands.

"Then speak your vows," Alrik commanded.

Bolli looked to Ketill, who pulled a ring from the pouch at his waist and carefully placed it on the tip of Bolli's new sword. Bolli turned back to Ingrid. He gripped his cane with one hand and with the other offered her the ring, dangling from the sword. It seemed odd to offer a ring in such a way— almost an implied threat should the wedding oath be broken.

Ingrid looked sick as she put the ring on her finger.

But Bolli smiled at her. "Before the gods and these witnesses, I, Bolli Ketilson, take you, Ingrid Alriksdottir, as my wife."

Ingrid now trembled. Selia had never seen her so uncertain. The girl stared at Bolli, and Bolli nodded to her in encouragement. Ingrid drew in her breath and spoke in a small, hesitant voice. "Before the gods and these witnesses, I, Ingrid Alriksdottir, take you, Bolli Ketilson, as my husband."

"It is done," Alrik said with a curt nod. The wedding party erupted into cheers.

Thankfully, they began to move back toward the house. Selia was so cold she could barely feel her toes. It was slow going, however, as Bolli led the way, hampered by his lame foot. It was obvious he was exhausted as he hobbled toward the door.

When he reached the threshold, Bolli turned to Ingrid and held out his arm for her. His face was waxy pale and he looked as though he was about to faint. Ingrid took Bolli's arm and put it around her shoulder, and wrapped her other arm around Bolli's waist.

Bolli took in a deep breath as he looked down at the lip of the threshold. "Welcome to my home, wife," he said to Ingrid in a shaky voice. He led with his good leg, leaning heavily on the cane and on Ingrid, but as he tried to bring his crippled foot over the threshold it caught on the raised lip and Bolli stumbled forward ever so slightly. Ingrid held him with both arms around his waist to keep him from falling, and they stepped through the door and into the house.

A hush fell over the wedding party. This Finngall threshold ritual was apparently of extreme importance—Selia remembered how Ingrid had tried to make her stumble as Alrik had led her through the doorway the first time she had entered his house. For the bride to stumble was an ill omen.

Selia could only assume that the stumble of the groom couldn't portend any better. She looked at Hrefna but the woman wouldn't meet her eyes.

Chapter 11

The wedding festivities lasted well into the evening, with a sense of forced merriment in the house, as though the guests were attempting to erase the bad luck incurred with Bolli's stumble. Alrik had brought a cask of wine left from the battle at sea, and it flowed freely. Ingrid and Bolli drank a sweet concoction made of ale and honey, which they were instructed by Hrefna to quaff together for a full cycle of the moon.

Selia was tired and had a backache from the long ride in the sleigh. The babe was restless and had unfortunately decided to bang its head against her bladder for most of the wedding ceremony. Alrik had forbade her to use the outside privy unless someone accompanied her, because the harsh winter made the wolves bold. For the convenience of the wedding, a bucket had been placed behind the curtain in the far corner of the dwelling, but Selia was reluctant to use the bucket in a house packed with drunken men. She would wait until she could stand no more.

She made herself as comfortable as possible on one of the benches and sipped at her wine as she watched the interaction of the wedding guests. Alrik and Ketill were deep in conversation. They matched each other in their quest for the oblivion they could only find at the bottom of the wine barrel, and kept Kier scrambling to refill their cups.

Skagi and Bjorn sat a bit apart from the others. Bjorn looked animated as he only did when talking weapons, and indeed he moved his hands in the air as if describing the beauty of a sword to Skagi. Selia was always loath to look directly at Skagi. His face had healed from the beating inflicted by Alrik in the spring, but his nose would be permanently crooked and he had no teeth on one side of his jaw. Skagi held his mouth in an odd way when speaking as though trying to hide his lack of teeth. He had never been handsome even before the beating, but now the odds of him finding a wife were abysmal.

Ingrid and Bolli sat together, heads bent close, whispering to each other. Bolli's face had more color in it now as he drank the bridal ale and laughed with his new wife. Selia studied them. Although their marriage was a ruse, it was obvious they cared for each other very much. Many a good marriage had begun with much less than that, according to Hrefna. And Bolli was kind and even-tempered. He would make a good father for Ingrid's child. *Ainnileas' child.*

Selia would never see her brother again, but that wound was eased a bit at the thought of the babe growing in Ingrid's belly. Selia would have something of Ainnileas, at least.

The marriage of Ingrid and Bolli had been a clever solution, and Hrefna had chosen wisely. She must have been privy to Bolli's secret. Did everyone know? Bolli and the slave boy, Hakon, hadn't even looked at each other since their strange interaction earlier. Still, an unspoken connection seemed to link them, as if each knew where the other was in the room. But perhaps that was Selia's imagination after guessing the nature of their relationship.

Hrefna was in the kitchen area with Ketill's female thrall, whom Selia had heard Ketill call Aslaug. She was Hakon's mother. The thrall had butchered the sow and was now cooking it, and the smell wafting over from that side of the house was delicious. Hrefna looked more content than Selia had seen her since the death of Olaf. She fussed over the cooking pot, wanting the spices just right, and waved Aslaug away.

The child in Selia's belly shifted again, and she could take no more. It was either the slop bucket behind the curtain or the privy outside. Selia looked over at the curtain, and just at that moment a drunken Bjorn came stumbling out from behind it, laughing as he fastened his breeches. No, Selia would take her chances outside with the wolves.

She crossed to Hrefna and whispered, "I must go out," motioning below her belly.

Hrefna thought for a moment and then called, "Aslaug, fetch your cloak."

Aslaug nodded and donned the garment, lifting one of the torches that burned from urns along the wall. "This way, Mistress," she said to Selia.

Selia put on her cloak as well and followed Aslaug out the door. It had started to snow again. The night air was very cold, and burned her lungs, but it felt good to take a deep breath after the smoky air of the house. A path had been cleared from the house to the privy, some distance away, but the fresh snow was quickly covering it.

"Take my arm, Mistress," Aslaug said. "It may be slick."

Selia did as instructed, but Aslaug gazed at her for a moment. "What is it?" Selia asked as they began to walk.

Aslaug shook her head. "Forgive me, Mistress. I shouldn't stare. But Grainne was my friend and she spoke of you often. It seems so strange to see you now. You are as beautiful as she said you were."

Selia stopped. "She spoke of me?"

"Yes. Of you and your brother. She used to cry at night when she first came here. She thought you were dead. She was so happy to know you had survived."

"Oh." Selia wasn't sure further mention of Grainne was a good idea. "You have been here a long time."

They began to walk toward the privy. "I was born here," Aslaug replied. "But my mother was Irish, so I knew a bit of what Grainne was saying." She was silent for a moment. "I do miss her. Did she go home after all? To Ireland?"

"Yes. She went with my brother."

Aslaug smiled. "Well. That is good, then."

This woman was Grainne's friend, probably her only confidant. If anyone knew what was in Grainne's heart, it would be Aslaug. Giving in to her curiosity, Selia stopped again and turned to the woman. "Did my mother ever say anything about . . ." She paused, unsure how to ask the question that had plagued her for so long. "About why she thought it was my fault my father died?"

Aslaug averted her eyes. "Yes. She did. Her mind was very troubled by it."

"Please tell me." Selia was shivering, and her bladder felt ready to rupture, but she couldn't move until she heard what the thrall had to say.

"Grainne said you were very small when you were born. Too small to live. You were barely breathing and couldn't suckle properly. Your father was distraught and he took you out of the house the night you were born. Grainne feared he was going to expose you, to end your suffering. But later when he returned with you, she said you were like a different child."

"What did he do?"

"He took you to a cunning woman. She cast a spell."

"A spell?" Selia faltered.

"Yes. A spell to make you strong. And Grainne always thought that was what brought the ill luck to your father. It was a punishment from the White Christ."

Selia shook her head. Of course it went against God's word to work magic, but as spells went, this one seemed relatively benign. "How could that be bad, making a babe strong?"

Aslaug frowned. "Because there is no such thing as something from nothing. Summer doesn't come without winter. Morning falls to night. To make strength, it must be taken from something else. From whatever your strength was drawn, Grainne thought it was unnatural. And your father paid the price."

Selia shuddered. Maybe Grainne wasn't as mad as she'd at first believed. Perhaps Selia was brimming with dark magic after all. Hadn't she always had an attraction to Finngalls and their heathen ways, even as a child? Hadn't she married a Finngall Hersir, and loved him even after learning the evil deeds he had committed? Hadn't she prayed to a heathen god to ensure her husband's safe return and nearly slaughtered an animal in that god's name?

Selia's knees felt as though they would give out from under her. "Can the spell be broken?"

Aslaug shook her head. "I don't know. I'm not a cunning woman. As I said before, Grainne thought you were dead until just recently, so there was never any reason for her to talk about breaking the spell. The damage had been done. Your father was dead."

Selia's thoughts remained unsettled as the evening wore on. The wedding guests drank and laughed, Hakon played his drum, and the men sang and stomped their feet. The noise in Ketill's small house was overwhelming. The thralls served the wedding feast, and although the sow smelled delicious, Selia had no appetite. She wanted nothing more than to go home and sleep in her own bed. But unfortunately they wouldn't leave until tomorrow. And with the way Alrik was drinking it seemed unlikely they would get an early start.

The conversation with Aslaug played over and over in Selia's mind. Could the story be believed? It was obvious Grainne believed it, and had convinced Aslaug. But Grainne's memory of that night might not be accurate. The woman had given birth to twins, had most likely been exhausted and in pain, then upset when one of the infants proved sickly. Could she be blamed if her memory of the night was faulty?

Grainne had spent half her life obsessing over the death of Faolan, to the point where she became consumed by it and had slipped into madness. The more probable events of the night of Selia's birth was one where her father had taken her out of the house and gone to a priest for last rites, and the prayers had revived her.

No, the story of a dark spell worked by a cunning woman was most likely the product of Grainne's unbalanced mind. Grainne had lost her husband in a Finngall raid, but so had countless other Irish wives. Would those wives blame their husbands' deaths on a spell? Of course they wouldn't. They would place the blame where it was due, on the Finngalls.

The party finally reached the point where the bedding of the bride needed to take place. The wedding guests laughed as Ingrid and Bolli stumbled off to the farthest bench. They climbed in, both flushed red, and Bjorn followed them over. As the only freeborn man at the wedding who was not related to either the bride or the groom, it was his responsibility to ensure the marriage was consummated.

Bjorn was very drunk. He winked at them and pulled the curtain closed. "Get on with it now," he called to them through the curtain.

Selia raised her eyebrows at this. Her own wedding night had been terrifying in its own right. But thankfully it hadn't included a roomful of people listening in.

She looked over at Alrik, laughing at something Ketill had said, and watched him for a moment. He was beautiful, with his hair glittering in the torchlight, and his cheeks flushed with the wine. He smiled and Selia found herself blinking back tears. Alrik had been so sad since he had returned from the fall trip. The deaths of his men, especially Olaf, had nearly destroyed him. It was good to see him laugh and enjoy himself.

Maybe this renewed alliance with Ketill would bring Alrik back into the good graces of the surviving members of his war band. Maybe Selia would get her husband back, instead of this shell of a man who sometimes seemed to be looking through her when she spoke to him.

When Alrik burned bright, as he did now, Selia could feel his overpowering pull even from across the room. Whatever radiated from him—power, heat, vigor—it was an attraction that drew her in like a moth to the flame. Selia couldn't resist it even if she wanted to. If Grainne was right, and Selia was under some sort of a wicked spell, could it have made her fall in love with Alrik? Or would that have happened regardless?

There was a rustling behind the bed curtain, then Bolli and Ingrid peeked out, giggling and sheepish. "It is done!" Bjorn shouted. Clapping and cheers arose from the wedding party. Selia clapped as well, but studied Bjorn. Had the cousins actually consummated their marriage, or only pretended to? Bjorn could very well be in on the entire ruse. He was like a second father to both Bolli and Ingrid. It could be that Bolli's apprenticeship with Bjorn had been set up by Ketill to deny his son easy access to Hakon.

The drumming had stopped some time ago. She looked around the room for Hakon but he was nowhere to be found. He must have slipped outside unnoticed, preferring to freeze than to be present for the bedding of the bride.

Chapter 12

Selia stood at the looms with Hrefna as the wind howled outside the longhouse. Another storm had hit shortly after they returned from Ingrid and Bolli's wedding, and the snow had continued to fall almost without interruption. The wind blew the drifts in swirling fury, until they stacked halfway up the outside walls of the longhouse. Each morning the thralls had to dig the snow away from the doors so they could get outside. It seemed that spring would never come.

She stopped working for a moment and leaned back to stretch. Her belly was enormous, bigger than she ever imagined was possible. She pushed the bulge down with her hands as if she could make more room for her lungs. It was no use. She hadn't been able to take a deep breath in so long.

The weight of the child put an unbearable strain on Selia's back. She was tired, she was grouchy, and her fingers were so swollen she was barely able to weave. Hrefna continued on with her own work, her weaving perfect as usual. Selia scowled at her.

Hrefna gave her a sympathetic look. "It's all right, my dear. Go rest if you like. I'll keep an eye on Geirr."

The babe was sleeping in the cradle Bjorn had made. No one had had the heart to ask Alrik to do it after he returned from the fall trip, so Hrefna had finally just asked the blacksmith. They would be in need of another cradle, soon, but Alrik hadn't seemed interested in working on it. One would think the anticipation of the birth of his child would give Alrik something to focus on, other than the ale vat.

Selia looked toward the bedchamber where Alrik slept. He stayed in there most of the time, sleeping and drinking. Hrefna said he would come out of his melancholy with the arrival of spring. Selia could go in there now and lie with him, but sometimes that made things worse. Alrik preferred to be alone.

Geirr stirred in the cradle and cried out. Selia went over and peered down at the babe, and Geirr broke into a toothless grin. He kicked his chubby legs and raised his arms up to her, squealing in infant delight.

Selia laughed. "All right, little boy," she chided him in Irish. "I see very well you're awake." She hefted him up— no small feat, as he had grown huge on Hallveig's milk— and the babe snuggled into her shoulder.

Selia breathed in his sweet smell and kissed the top of his fuzzy head. She had grown to love this child, and indeed couldn't imagine loving her own child any more than she did Geirr. How could she have known she would feel a mother's love for her stepson?

Just at that moment, something shifted uncomfortably inside of her, followed by a sudden feeling of unbearable pressure. Selia nearly dropped the babe. There was a sensation—or maybe a sound—of something popping, then a hot gush of water down her leg.

Was Geirr urinating on her? Selia held him at arms' length but it was clear he was dry. Was she urinating on herself? The water was definitely coming from her. "Hrefna!" Selia shouted in confusion.

Hrefna rushed over, gasping as she saw the puddle at Selia's feet. Taking Geirr, she yelled over her shoulder for Keir, who was working in the kitchen.

"What is happening, Hrefna?" Try as she might, Selia couldn't keep the panic at bay. It was hard to not feel fright when it was so obvious Hrefna was panicking.

"The babe is coming, child."

"No, no. It is too soon," Selia argued.

Keir hurried to them, wiping her hands on a rag. "Yes, Mistress?" she said to Hrefna.

"Find Hallveig and have her take Geirr. Then come back immediately and help me prepare for the babe. It is coming."

Keir's eyes grew wide. She nodded and ran for the door.

"No, Hrefna," Selia protested. She stomped her foot for emphasis. "The babe is not coming. It is not time."

Hrefna gave her a stern look. "Selia. That water you're standing in came from the sac around the child. Once it is broken the child will be born. There is nothing else to be done."

Selia stared at Hrefna as the words sank in. It was coming. She was having a babe, right now. A vision of Muirin arose in her mind, screaming, eyes wild with pain, as Geirr was ripped from her body. And another vision of Muirin, cold and still on a bed of bloody straw as her dead eyes stared into nothingness.

Selia began to shake as the room spun around her. She wasn't ready. She was supposed to have more time to prepare. What if she couldn't do it? What if Hrefna had to rip her apart to get the child out? What if she died tonight?

"Breathe, my girl," Hrefna urged. She gripped Selia's arm to keep her from falling. "Sit here on this bench. Lie down if you feel faint. I'm going to wake Alrik."

Hrefna hurried off with Geirr in her arms. Selia sank to the bench and shivered. Her shoes and part of her gown were wet, and cold. Maybe she should change her clothes. No, Muirin had been naked when she gave birth. Surely Selia wouldn't be expected to squat down on the floor like an animal, naked and exposed?

A sudden, intense spasm in her back took her breath. Selia gripped the edge of the bench until the spasm passed, as quickly as it had come. It reminded her of the pains she had felt when she had nearly bled the child out in the woods. It seemed so long ago.

This was real. It was happening.

The bedchamber door opened and Alrik staggered out, with Hrefna behind him. Disheveled and bleary-eyed, still a look of worry creased his face. He knew the child was coming too early.

Alrik knelt in front of Selia. His big hand was gentle as he smoothed a lock of hair away from her face. Selia met his gaze and her tears welled over. "I cannot do this, Alrik."

He shushed her. "You can. You can and you will."

"I do not want to die like Muirin!"

Alrik scowled. "Do not speak of such things. You are strong, Selia. You are unbreakable."

Selia threw her arms around him and buried her face in his neck. He smelled like the bottom of the ale vat, but she didn't care. If Alrik's child killed her, this would be the last time she would be with him.

Her tears fell in earnest now. "I love you," she sobbed.

The sob turned to a scream as another pain hit her, and her fingers dug into Alrik's shoulders. Alrik held her tightly. "Do something, Hrefna," he begged. The fear in his voice made Selia cry harder.

Hrefna was brisk. "Selia Niallsdottir, you could cry an ocean of tears and it wouldn't stop that babe from coming. There is no sense in wasting your energy on worry." She thrust Geirr into Alrik's arms. "Hold your son," she ordered. "Hallveig will be here soon to take him. I need to get Selia out of those wet clothes."

Selia sniffled as Hrefna led her into the bedchamber, then handed her a clean shift and instructed her to put it on. She pulled a bale of straw into the middle of the room and cut the binding. The straw had been placed in the corner some time ago, just for this purpose, and had been there for so long Selia had stopped noticing it. Hrefna fluffed it out onto the floor and laid a blanket on top.

Another pain came and Selia doubled over, gripping the bed. This one seemed to last longer, radiating from her back to her belly, and she was panting as it finally passed.

Hrefna frowned. "Those are coming fast. Get into the bed and let me check you."

Selia did as instructed. Hrefna's probing fingers were uncomfortable and Selia flinched and tried to pull away. But Hrefna's other hand pressed on her belly, feeling for the position of the babe. Hrefna's face was grim as she finally withdrew her hand.

"This isn't going to take long, child," she said. "You are nearly ready."

"What?" Selia cried. How could this be? Muirin's labor had seemed endless. Yet Selia's first pain had come on fast. "Is something wrong?"

Another pain slammed into her. Selia screamed and drew her legs up toward her chest. It didn't help. The pain lasted a long time, and as it crested Selia could do nothing but whimper. Just when she thought she could take no more, it finally passed.

An awful restlessness enveloped her. She needed to move. No, not just move—she needed to run away. Her body had betrayed her and she needed to get away from it. It wasn't supposed to happen like this. She was supposed to have more time. The next pain hit hard and Selia wailed. They were coming one right after the other, with no time in between to even catch her breath.

"Help me, Hrefna! Make it stop," Selia sobbed. Hrefna looked confused and Selia realized she had spoken in Irish.

Keir rushed into the room and stopped short as she saw Selia. Hrefna snapped at her. "Don't just stand there, girl, help me get her onto the floor."

The women each took hold of one of Selia's arms and led her toward the bed of straw. Another pain hit and Selia stumbled down onto her hands and knees. She rocked back and forth, and a sound came out of her mouth that started as a scream and ended in a grunt. Why, oh why was this so awful? All women had to pay the price for Eve's original sin, but this seemed too much. She could not bear it. What had she done to deserve this additional punishment? "No!" Selia again spoke in Irish. "I don't want to do this!"

Selia felt Hrefna lift the back of her shift up higher on her hips to keep it out of the way. Her hand paused for a moment, and her voice was strangely calm as she finally spoke. "Selia. I can see the babe's head. You must not push until I tell you to or you will rip. Do you understand?"

Selia wailed. *Rip.* Just like Muirin. Hrefna knew there was no way she could get this child out without tearing Selia apart. Her worst fears had been confirmed.

The vise around her midsection squeezed again, pushing on its own as if it would expel the babe from her body with no regard for Hrefna's warning. "Don't push!" Hrefna cried.

She wasn't pushing. The child was propelling itself out, forcing its way through her flesh. Selia felt as if her hipbones would snap. A primal, animalistic sound came from her lungs that horrified her almost as much as the child trying to burst from her. She had completely lost control of her body.

"No, no, no, no, *no*!" Selia screamed as she was torn in two. She leaned into Keir, panting, as the pain passed.

"The head is out," Hrefna said. "But the shoulders are large—"

The vise clamped down again. It pushed and squeezed, trying to force the babe out, but nothing happened. Her body was blocking it. She was too small; her hips were caging the child in. The pain grew intolerable and Selia screamed as every part of her mind and body focused on releasing the child from her. "*Pull it out.* Pull it out, Hrefna! I can't do this!"

She had spoken in Irish and Keir had to translate for Hrefna. Hrefna cursed and stood up. "Help me get her into a squat, Keir," she directed. "Quickly!"

Selia moaned as they shifted her. She squatted, hips stretched wide, with Keir in front and Hrefna behind. Selia sobbed as she felt the pain coming again. "Make it stop," she begged.

Keir put a hand on Selia's face and looked directly into her eyes, as she never had done before. She spoke to Selia in Irish. "Mistress, it is almost over. One more push and the child will be born."

The vise squeezed and Selia bore down. White-hot pain exploded through her loins as Hrefna manipulated the babe's shoulders. A sensation of unbearable pressure, of bone grinding against bone, forced a scream from Selia's throat as she pushed with every ounce of strength she had.

Suddenly the babe expelled from her body. Selia sobbed with relief as she sank into the straw. It was over.

The child let loose a lusty cry and Hrefna laughed. "It is a boy."

Selia raised her head wearily as Hrefna wrapped the child in a blanket. "Is he all right?" He had been born so quickly, and too early at that.

"Yes," Hrefna said. "A bit small, but otherwise perfect." The child wailed again and Hrefna gazed down at him with approval. "And he has a good set of healthy lungs."

"Let me hold him."

"You're not finished yet, child. You must deliver the afterbirth and then we must stitch you up."

But Selia crawled over to Hrefna and pulled the edge of the blanket down. The babe was very small, only half the size Geirr had been. He had a dark shock of hair, matted to his head with a bloody fluid. Selia opened the blanket all the way and examined his skinny limbs and his tiny penis. The babe screamed in fury at the cold, but Selia smiled. He was intact. He was perfect. She had given Alrik a healthy child. She had given him a son.

And she had survived.

Selia woke some time later, in the bed, warm and dry in a fresh shift. Hrefna had given her some tea before she stitched her up and it must have made her fall asleep.

She sat up, wincing. It felt as though there was a hot iron between her legs. Where was the babe? She patted the blankets, suddenly terrified that he had been in the bed with her and she had smothered him. "Hrefna?" she called out.

There was no answer. The house was quiet. Had something happened? The stories Eithne had told of Finngalls taking their children to a wolf den for inspection flooded Selia's mind. Surely those stories had been fabricated. No one had taken Geirr away to be suckled by a she-wolf after he had been born. It was only a silly story.

God forbid, had the child died? Had Odin demanded his blood sacrifice after all? An irrational terror overtook her. "Hrefna!" Selia cried.

Again there was no answer, but Selia heard the faint wail of the child from another room. He was alive. She flung the blankets aside and hobbled to the door.

Hallveig was nursing Geirr in the main room. "Where is my babe?" Selia demanded.

"In the kitchen, Mistress," Hallveig said. "But you should not be out of bed."

Selia shuffled to the kitchen. Hrefna and Keir were huddled around the worktable as the babe howled. "What are you doing?" she asked, pushing her way in. The child lay on the table and Hrefna washed him with a basin of water and a rag.

"You should be resting," Hrefna admonished. She finished the final rinse and wrapped the babe in a clean blanket. He continued to fuss and Hrefna made soothing sounds at him.

"He needs to nurse," Selia said.

"Hallveig can nurse him the first time, if you like. You need to get your strength back."

"*No*," Selia insisted. "I will feed him. I am his mother."

Hrefna studied her. "Well, of course you are, my dear. As soon as Alrik gets back to perform the naming ceremony, you can feed him. All right?"

Finngalls and their ceremonies. "Where is Alrik now?"

"He went to make a sacrifice."

Alrik came in the kitchen door, carrying a dead lamb. Its head wobbled above the gaping wound where its throat had been slit. Alrik frowned when he saw Selia, and laid the lamb on the floor. "Why are you out of bed?" He strode over and scooped her up into his arms. Selia didn't protest as he carried her back to the bedchamber.

Alrik laid her down and pulled the covers over her. He stared at her for a moment with his intense blue gaze. "You did it, little one," he said finally. "But I had no doubt you would." Alrik's hand was gentle as he touched her face.

Selia smiled at him. Alrik had been so distant since his return. He always seemed far away even when he was in the same room with her. But now, her husband was fully present, focused on his family. Selia nuzzled into his hand, reluctant to break the spell.

"I thought I would name him after your father," Alrik continued. "What was his name?"

Selia gave him a puzzled look. Alrik knew her father's name. "Niall," she said.

"No. Your real father."

Selia's eyes grew wide. Finngalls were very superstitious about the names they gave their children. Great care was given to select the name of an individual, typically a deceased family member, whose characteristics they wanted to live on in their children. For this reason Selia was certain there would never be another Ragnarr in Alrik's bloodline.

She had fully expected Alrik to name the child Olaf. Or maybe even Jorulf, after Alrik's older brother. The thought of Alrik naming his son after a man he had killed on a long ago raid had never crossed Selia's mind.

"Faolan," Selia said hesitantly.

"Faolan. Faolan," Alrik repeated. His Norse accent clipped the vowels and Selia had to say the name several more times before Alrik got it right.

"What does the name mean?" Alrik asked.

Selia shivered involuntarily as the meaning dawned on her. "It means 'wolf,'" she said.

Any Norse name with the root 'ulf' also meant wolf. The name had had special meaning for Ragnarr, as the wolf gave a warrior strength and cunning in battle. Two of his sons, Jorulf and Ulfrik, carried the essence of the wolf in their names.

Alrik pondered this for a moment, and nodded. "Faolan. It is a good name—a warrior's name. Faolan Alrikson will be a man to be reckoned with."

Chapter 13

883 AD

Selia made her way through the crowd of the gathering. Hrefna was still feeling poorly and had needed her help supervising the meal preparation, but what had begun as a quick inspection in the kitchen had turned into a longer ordeal when one of the thralls burned her arm and required a salve. Selia hadn't seen Geirr or Faolan lately.

The kitchen had been hot and overcrowded, and Selia was glad to be outside. The summer morning was balmy, the sky a crisp shade of pale blue and the water a darker shade that sparkled in the sunshine. The breeze felt cool against Selia's flushed cheeks and damp curls. She heard a clatter up ahead of metal against wood and turned toward the noise. Alrik would most likely be there, sword sparring. And with any luck the boys would be with him.

Alrik was standing in a crowd of men waiting to fight the victor. Two men were fighting and the others cheered them on. No one had ever beaten Alrik in this contest, so to keep it fair the men fought each other and then Alrik fought the last champion. That man would lose to Alrik, but would have the satisfaction of knowing he had bested the rest of the men.

Selia walked up to Alrik and studied him for a moment as the breeze blew his hair back from his face. He watched the fight intently, with a gleam in his eyes and a slight smile on his lips. Selia had made him a new shirt for the gathering, and his body was so tense with excitement that the material strained against the muscles of his powerful torso. She never tired of looking at him.

"Alrik." She spoke quietly.

He looked down at her and smiled. That smile could still make her heart flutter in her chest. "Did you come to see me win?"

"Yes," Selia replied. "But the boys will want to watch, too. Have you seen them?"

Alrik turned back to the contest. "No."

Selia bit her lip. Geirr was easily distracted and prone to mischief. And Faolan could be quick-tempered when anyone got his dander up. She hated that they were alone, completely unsupervised.

Alrik glanced at her when she didn't answer.

"They're fine," he scowled. "Stop coddling them."

Finngall children grew up fast, and the boys were now much too old to be babied. Geirr would be seven and was nearly as tall as Selia. She'd had this argument with Alrik many times before, and Selia did her best to avoid it. But the last time she had ignored her instincts, Geirr had fallen through the ice and nearly drowned. Before that he had jumped from the roof of the barn and knocked out two of his front teeth.

Geirr had needed constant supervision from the moment he learned to crawl. There was a scar on his thigh from pulling over a kettle of scalding water on himself when he was a toddler. He still walked with a slight limp, and Hrefna rubbed salve into the scar often to keep it from tightening. For Selia, it was a permanent reminder of what could happen if she let her guard down.

It infuriated Alrik that the child refused to listen. According to Alrik, Geirr deserved what he got. Eventually he would learn to be less impulsive. But Selia couldn't count on that happening anytime soon. And Faolan wasn't much better. Not as reckless as his brother, he nevertheless required nearly as much supervision. Faolan found it incredibly irritating to be responsible for stopping Geirr from doing bodily harm to himself, and so was apt to simply tackle his brother and wrestle him to the ground instead of trying to reason with him. The boys fought frequently, and the fights had ended in bloodshed more than once.

Selia watched them like a hawk and only truly relaxed when they were asleep. But Alrik was jealous of the time Selia spent with the boys since it gave her less time to spend with him. He was still so like a large child himself when it came to his need for her. In that respect not much had changed.

Her anxiety increased as Alrik's frown deepened. He would be angry if she left now. Yet he turned away with a dismissive expression. "Go. Find your little nurslings."

Selia sighed. He could be so exasperating. But it wouldn't look well to get into an argument about the boys in front of Alrik's men. This would have to wait until later. As she turned to go, a thrall child ran up to them, out of breath. He stood before Alrik and lowered his head in deference.

"Master," he panted, "Geirr asked me to come get you. Faolan . . ." He paused to catch his breath.

Selia grabbed the boy by the shoulders. "What?" she demanded. "What about Faolan?"

"Geirr said to get his father." The slave boy swallowed. "No one else can stop it."

Selia sprinted down the hill in the direction the thrall had indicated. She heard a clamor of young voices and followed them to the beach and around to a rocky cove. In a small clearing in the brush just off the cove, a half-dozen boys surrounded what appeared to be a fight. Selia couldn't see over the boys' heads to see who was fighting but she knew it was Faolan. He might not be near as large as his brother but the boy had a quick temper. Sinewy and strong, he frequently bested Geirr when their arguments came to blows.

"Faolan, stop! You're going to kill him!"

Selia recognized Geirr's voice. She ran around to the other side of the mob of boys and grabbed his arm, and his body sagged in relief to see her.

Geirr swiped at his bloody nose with his forearm. "Did you bring Father?"

"He's coming."

Alrik strode through the brush and shoved aside the crowd of boys. He snatched Faolan up by the scruff of his neck. Faolan howled like an animal and his wild eyes rolled back in his head. He flailed his small, bloody fists in the air, screaming in rage.

"Faolan!" Alrik bellowed, shaking him a bit. "Stop!"

In his fury, Faolan didn't seem to hear his father at all. Alrik carried the boy, kicking and snarling, to the edge of the water and tossed him in. Faolan went under and came up with a sputter. He got his feet beneath him and tried to run back toward the boy lying on the ground. Alrik grabbed him again and tucked Faolan's small body under his arm as he struggled anew.

"Find out whose boy that is," he snapped at Selia. "I'll be back." He carried Faolan down the beach, away from the house and the gathering crowd.

A cold sweat enveloped her shaking body as she knelt by the boy. He was unconscious, but alive—Selia could hear him breathing wetly through the blood in his mouth. He looked to be older than her boys, ten or twelve summers perhaps. His face was a mangled mess and a few of his front teeth were broken off. Geirr's missing front teeth had been first teeth, at least. This boy was old enough for his to be permanent.

"Does anyone know who he is?" Selia asked the group of boys.

They shifted and looked at one another. No one spoke. Selia gave Geirr a hard look and he finally responded. "His name is Audunn. He came with Eysteinn Refsson."

Selia recognized the name. Eysteinn Refsson was married to the daughter of one of Alrik's men. Alrik had once turned him down for his war band, as the man had a reputation for spreading discord and conflict wherever he went. This boy was most likely fostering with him.

"What happened?" Selia asked. "Why were they fighting?"

Geirr wouldn't meet her gaze. "I will tell you later," he said in a quiet voice.

"No." Selia regarded him sternly. "Tell me now."

A couple of the boys snickered nervously. Geirr scowled at them and turned back to Selia. "Audunn said no one would ever follow me if Father made me Hersir. That's what Eysteinn told him. Because I am a thrall."

Selia raised her eyebrows at this. "That's why your brother was fighting?" This type of insult had been flung at Geirr before. It seemed odd that Faolan's reaction would be so extreme.

Geirr flushed and looked at the ground. He finally spoke in Irish. "He said you were an Irish whore who bedded Father's brother. He said you don't even know who Faolan's father is."

Selia felt as though she had been punched in the stomach. The blood pounded in her ears, churning hard like a stormy sea. *No.* How could this be happening, now? No one knew about the kiss Ulfrik took from her, so very long ago. Selia hadn't told anyone. Surely Ulfrik would not have spoken of it, and thus put Selia's safety in jeopardy.

No one knew—this was just another blind insult, slung by a jealous man with nothing better to do than spread gossip. Only Selia's reaction would tell anyone if the charge held any truth.

Her gaze took in the group of boys. They all watched her intently.

She drew herself to her full height and addressed them in her best *wife-of-the-Hersir* voice. "Audunn has greatly insulted the Hersir with this vile accusation." Selia gestured to the boy on the ground. "Faolan Alrikson was right to defend his father's honor. This boy should count himself lucky he only lost his teeth."

The body language of the group of boys changed immediately. The air of excitement dissipated as they realized the significance of Audunn's taunts. It was not just an insult to Selia, but more importantly, to Alrik. The Hersir.

Selia frowned fiercely. "There will come a time when each of you will want to join Alrik Ragnarson's war band. Alrik only accepts the most loyal and brave men. He does not accept cowards or gossipmongers. The fact that none of you stood in defense of the Hersir does not bode well to gain his favor. This slur will be remembered, mark my words."

The boys hung their heads and glanced at each other with uncertainty. Only Geirr kept his eyes on her. Selia looked at her son. "Geirr Alrikson, upon manhood you will be Hersir. Would you accept any of these boys into your war band?"

Geirr puffed his chest out and crossed his arms. At six he was a strikingly handsome boy, with Muirin's green eyes and hair like pale honey, but with the angular cheekbones and full mouth of Alrik and Ulfrik. Tall and broad-shouldered like both the sons of Ragnarr, his young body held the promise of their powerful musculature as he grew. He gazed around at the group in all his golden glory, as though already Hersir.

A drop of blood ran from Geirr's nose, but like a true warrior, he ignored it. "Only Bausi and Fuldarr," he said after a moment. "They are loyal and I trust them. The rest, no."

Bausi and Fuldarr were both older than Geirr, but looked at him in awe, nodding. The remaining boys squirmed where they stood. Selia regarded them coldly. "If any of you want a place in this war band, I suggest you rethink your loyalties. Go, now."

They ran off into the brush and Selia turned back to Geirr and the other two. "Take this boy away before Alrik returns," she instructed Bausi and Fuldarr. "Tell his foster father what happened. I imagine he will want to be far from this farmstead when Alrik learns of the insult."

The two bigger boys lifted the injured child by the arms and half-dragged, half-carried him back toward the beach. Geirr stood quiet and solemn until the boys had gone. Then he threw his arms around Selia and nestled into her neck.

"I'm sorry, *Mamai*," he whispered.

Selia stroked his blond head. She had taught her sons her native language, and they had both used the Irish term of endearment for 'mother' when they were small. But they rarely called her *Mamai* anymore—the fact that Geirr did so now told her how upsetting this incident had been to him. For all his cocky performance of a moment ago, he was still a child.

"I know," she reassured. She held him at arm's length and tilted his head back to examine his nose. It didn't appear to be broken, at least. "Who hit you?"

Geirr wouldn't meet her gaze. Finally he admitted, "Faolan."

Selia stilled. "Faolan?"

"Not on purpose. Don't be angry with him."

The familiar gnawing anxiety started up in Selia's belly. She took a deep breath and pushed the worrisome thoughts away. Faolan was a Finngall; of course he was rough and aggressive at times. What Finngall boy wasn't? There didn't have to be anything ominous about him having a quick temper.

There was a rustle in the brush as first Alrik then Faolan appeared in the clearing. Faolan looked pale and tired, his clothing and his black curls still sodden from his dip in the sea. Selia restrained herself from rushing over to him.

"Where is the boy?" Alrik asked, scowling at the spot where the child's blood darkened the ground.

"I sent him back to his foster father. Eysteinn Refsson," Selia replied.

Alrik's frown deepened. "I will have to speak with Brunn about his son-in-law. Or better yet, I'll pay a visit to him myself." Alrik turned to Geirr and looked down his nose at the boy. "You can't have your brother do your fighting for you, Geirr. If you expect those boys to follow you, you must show you are deserving of their respect. Next time take care of the situation yourself."

Geirr swallowed, his eyes downcast. "Yes, Father," he acquiesced.

Selia studied Faolan. He met her gaze, his face so like Alrik's it was unnerving at times. All he had gotten from Selia was her dark hair. Faolan's bright blue eyes were framed with Selia's black lashes, making the color of his irises even more intense. He blinked at Selia and looked away.

Obviously Faolan had only told Alrik half of the truth. What would Alrik do if he learned what the boy's foster father had said about Selia and Ulfrik?

Chapter 14

At dusk, Selia went in to check on Hrefna. The preparations for the gathering had drained the woman. Most nights she'd taken to her bed early in the evening, and encouraged Alrik to continue the festivities without her. Hrefna was also having a difficult time without her daughter Kolgrima, who had not come to the gathering. Her own daughter Bergdis was heavy with her second child and Kolgrima had gone to be with her for the summer. Hrefna missed her terribly.

Selia stood in the doorway of Hrefna's room. "Are you awake?"

Hrefna turned over and gave Selia a wan smile. "Yes, my dear. Come in."

Selia shut the door behind her and sat on the edge of the bed. Alrik's aunt had aged quickly after Olaf died. Grief lined her face and stole the vibrancy of her beautiful hair. It held more gray than red now, reminding Selia of fabric that hadn't taken the dye evenly.

The winter had been a harsh one for Alrik's farmstead. Four thralls had died from a coughing sickness. Hrefna had succumbed to the illness as well and still hadn't quite fully recovered. Her breathing became labored with the slightest exertion and her skin had an unhealthy bluish tint to it. Hrefna had tried to pace herself at the gathering, but it seemed to Selia she needed to rest for longer and longer periods.

Thankfully this was the last of the gathering. The horde would leave tomorrow and things could go back to normal. Hrefna could focus on regaining her health.

"How are the boys?" Hrefna asked.

"They're fine. I made them go to bed," Selia replied.

The boys slept in the main room. All the women and children were bedding down in there as well, so Geirr and Faolan had been sharing a bench during the gathering. Selia had shut their curtain and given them both a stern warning to stay put and go to sleep.

"And what of the boy Faolan was fighting with?"

"He left with Eysteinn. I'm sure they didn't want to remain and wait for Alrik to hear of what was said."

Hrefna nodded. "Still, it seems strange Faolan would overreact about someone slinging insults at Geirr. It's not as though it hasn't happened before."

Selia kept her face impassive. "Just one time too many, I suppose."

"Yes," Hrefna agreed, but her eyes held steady on Selia. The woman was clever enough to know Selia was hiding something.

Now was not the time to tell Hrefna about the second insult. She had guessed Ulfrik's feelings for Selia long ago, and had suspected something had happened between them when Selia was apart from Alrik. To discuss this with Hrefna now would only raise her suspicions again.

Besides, there was something else more pressing in Selia's mind. A question she had wanted to ask Hrefna for some time but hadn't had the nerve to. Now was as good a time as any.

"Hrefna," she said in a hesitant voice, "do you think there is something wrong with Faolan?"

"Something wrong?"

"Yes." Selia paused and wiped her palms on her gown. "Do you think . . . do you think Faolan is like Alrik?" She couldn't even use the word *berserker* in the same sentence with her son's name.

Hrefna lay silently, and Selia's heart sank. "He is like his father in many ways," Hrefna murmured at last. "But in other ways he is like you. I have witnessed gentleness in that boy I never saw from Alrik as a child."

Selia swallowed painfully. "When he was fighting, he had the look of Alrik when in a fury. It frightened me."

Hrefna nodded and patted Selia's hand. "I did not know Alrik when he was as young as Faolan. But what I understand of Ragnarr tells me he would have encouraged viciousness in his sons. And my poor sister was powerless to stand up to him. What Faolan has that Alrik didn't have is a mother who can teach him there is more to being a man than fighting."

Later, Selia lay in her bedchamber, sleepless. Some of the women and children hadn't yet retired and there was a constant, low murmur of voices and occasional laughter from the main room. A babe cried as a couple of overwrought children argued.

The men were all still outside. Alrik hadn't come to bed until very late every night of the gathering, smelling strongly of ale.

Noises from the main room poured in for a moment as the door opened and shut quickly. Faolan stood with his back to the wood, looking sheepish.

Selia sat up. "What's wrong?"

"I can't sleep."

She threw the covers back and Faolan climbed in the bed with her. He lay on Alrik's pillow facing Selia, and reached for a lock of her hair. He curled it around his finger, over and over, as he had done since he was small and still at the breast.

The memory caused Selia's breath to catch in her throat. It had been so much easier when warm milk and a cuddle could make everything right again in Faolan's world.

Selia gazed at her son. Such a beautiful child, with his black curls and vivid blue eyes. His body was small and thin, and reminded Selia somewhat of how Ainnileas had been built as a child. But where Ainnileas' thinness had held a delicate, almost frail quality, Faolan's body was ropy and tight with coiled muscle. Like a tiny warrior.

Ainnileas had whiled away his youth avoiding strenuous labor whenever possible, but Faolan and Geirr spent much time wrestling and sparring with each other. It was hard to tell whether Faolan's body would eventually take after that of Alrik rather than Ainnileas when he grew into a man.

"I'm sorry," Faolan burst out, obviously miserable.

Selia squeezed his hand. "I know you're sorry, Faolan. But that boy didn't deserve to lose his teeth."

Faolan's lip quivered. "But what he said about you—"

"There will always be boys who say things you don't like. Those boys will grow into men who say things you don't like. Will you knock all of their teeth out?"

"Yes," Faolan asserted. "If they call my mother a whore I will knock all of their teeth out." His eyes flashed fierce and blue as if imagining the fight in his mind's eye.

Selia couldn't suppress a laugh and she pulled Faolan closer. His hair still smelled of seawater as she kissed the top of his head. She would have to make sure he bathed tomorrow when everyone left.

"My little Faolan," she whispered. "Thank you for protecting my honor. Those boys will think twice about sullying my good name ever again."

Selia had meant it as a joke but Faolan didn't laugh. He looked up at her with a serious expression. "Why does Father never talk about his brother?"

"Hmm." Selia kept her face unreadable. "They had a dispute, long ago. And Ulfrik left."

Faolan pondered this. "What was the dispute about?"

"Many things, but partly about me. Ulfrik and I were friends. He taught me to speak Norse when I first came here. But your father didn't like us spending time together."

"Oh," Faolan said. "Because he was jealous."

"Yes."

"Father is always jealous."

Selia nodded. "That is why it's better he doesn't hear about what Eysteinn Refsson said. None of it is true, of course, but it is best he doesn't know. I'm glad you didn't tell him."

Faolan snuggled into Selia's shoulder. "Don't worry, Mother. I won't tell him."

Selia woke near dawn with Alrik's hands on her body. The candle had gone out and the room was in darkness. "Wait," Selia whispered. "Faolan is here."

"No," Alrik said as he lifted Selia's shift over her head. "Not anymore." His hands were steady and his words weren't slurred. So he hadn't drunk himself into a stupor tonight.

Alrik's silky hair fell around Selia's face as he leaned down to claim her mouth, and she curved her arms around his neck as she returned the kiss. Yet something in Alrik's manner struck her as odd. He seemed troubled.

What could be wrong?

He slid his hand up her thigh and over her belly, then stopped at her breast and brushed his thumb across her nipple in a slow circle. Taking hold of her hair, he tugged her head back and worked his way down her neck with kisses. "My turn," he said, as he took her nipple into his mouth.

Alrik had not argued with Hrefna's assertion that Selia's first child should be her last. In fact he had seemed somewhat relieved when Selia agreed to take Hrefna's tea to prevent his seed from taking hold in her womb again. He had been resentful of the time Selia spent with the boys when they were small, but especially selfish of Faolan's constant demand for her body. Alrik had wanted Selia to allow Hallveig to be wet nurse to Faolan alongside of Geirr, but Selia had refused.

It had been one of the few times Selia flatly challenged Alrik's authority. Faolan was her son, and she would be the one to feed him. How could Alrik not understand there was no greater satisfaction for a woman than to see her child grow plump and healthy on her own milk? But to Alrik, it only meant Selia was choosing someone else over him. The act of disobedience did not settle well with him and he hadn't let her forget it.

Now Selia twined her fingers into Alrik's hair as he nuzzled. Although pleasant, his slow and disciplined enjoyment of her body was unusual. Nothing like the typical intensity of his lovemaking. Something definitely bothered him.

"What's wrong, Alrik?" she whispered into the darkness.

"Nothing," he mumbled into her breast, but stopped what he was doing. "So you want it rough, then, little one?"

A shiver went through Selia at his words. Even after all this time, she still craved him with the same passion she had in the beginning.

Unquestionably, Alrik was a maddening individual. There were times he pushed her so far with his selfish and fickle behavior, she wondered if she had made the right choice to stay in Norway. But none of that had ever dampened her desire for him. She wanted Alrik as much as ever.

Selia ran her hands over his broad back, feeling the heavy muscles under his skin. She wiggled beneath him until they were face to face again. "You know what I want." Her voice throbbed with desire.

Even in the almost complete dark of the room, Selia could see the flash of Alrik's teeth as he smiled. He made a noise that was half-laugh, half-growl as his mouth came down on hers again, possessive this time, demanding. He slid one arm under her shoulders and gripped the base of her skull with just enough force to hold her head still. Alrik plundered her mouth as he would soon plunder her body, and when he finally broke the kiss Selia gasped for air.

She moaned, needing him desperately, but he wouldn't let her move. At last he parted her legs with his knee and sheathed himself inside her, claiming what was his.

He thrust hard, still holding her by the back of the neck. Alrik always enjoyed pinning her down, and whenever he did so Selia was reminded of the way a male animal would bite the neck of a female to hold her still during copulation. She cried out now as her body shattered around him in a release so intense she drifted off into the darkness for a moment.

Alrik finished with a groan, panting above her, and his grip on her skull finally relaxed.

Dazed and satisfied, Selia pushed Alrik's hair away from his eyes. She smiled at him but he didn't return the smile. The pale light of dawn snaked through the smoke hole and Selia could see from the expression on his face that something was still troubling him. She rose up to kiss his cheek. "You're upset. Tell me what's wrong."

Alrik rolled to the side and lay next to her. He sighed. "I've been thinking about what that boy said. The one Faolan was fighting with."

Selia went still. Surely he hadn't heard the ugly slur? She studied him, looking for any sign of jealousy or suspicion, but there was nothing. He looked troubled but not angry.

Alrik continued. "Geirr is the wrong choice for Hersir, Selia. He is too reckless and foolhardy to lead a war band. A Hersir holds the lives of many men in his hands. How can I expect Geirr to do that when he can't even be responsible for himself?"

His unsettled expression had nothing to do with her and Ulfrik. A sense of impending doom crept through Selia's soul like the shadow of a storm on a clear summer afternoon. "I do not understand," she whispered.

"Faolan is a better choice for Hersir. You know this. He is a natural leader, and a true warrior. He has the wolf in him. I've sensed it before but now I know it for truth." Alrik paused for a moment before turning to Selia with a look of defiance on his face. "I marked him myself tonight. With the men to witness."

The dark shadow within her breast intensified and threatened to suffocate her. Selia grabbed Alrik by the shoulder. "What do you mean, you 'marked him?' What did you do to my son?" she choked out.

He shook her off. "He is my son too, woman, and you would do well to remember it." Alrik raised his chin and looked down his nose at Selia with the sneering expression he used whenever he wanted to be sure his audience knew who was in charge. He struck the tattoo on his chest, just over his heart. "I marked him."

Selia gasped. The berserker tattoo. Alrik had put it on Faolan just as Ragnarr had marked Alrik. From father to son, the sign of the shape shifter would live on.

An unholy fury coursed through Selia's veins and she attempted to slap Alrik, but he caught her wrist before her hand hit his face.

"You would raise your hand to me?" he hissed.

Selia tried to hit him with her other hand, but he caught that one as well. He held her by both wrists as she struggled against him. "My son is not a berserker!" she spat at him. "I will never forgive you for this!"

"It is done." Alrik pushed her away. "Faolan Alrikson will be Hersir."

Clenching her teeth until they ached, Selia clambered from the bed, dressed, and ran from the room. She picked her way through the mass of bodies on the floor and crossed to the bench Faolan and Geirr were sharing. Alrik must have crept in and taken Faolan from Selia's bed, then returned the child to his bench after the evil deed had been committed upon him.

She drew the curtain back and watched the boys as they slumbered. They were so beautiful when they were asleep, so peaceful.

When her boys became men, a longship full of Vikingers would cross the sea, Faolan at the helm, bringing terror and destruction to unsuspecting villages, raping and plundering, killing anyone who got in his way. He would tear families apart. Irish children asleep in their beds would wake with Faolan's sword through their bellies.

Selia shivered. It had been horrible enough to imagine Geirr as the future Hersir. She had come to love the boy as though he were her own child, and in return he loved her as a mother, not a stepmother. Geirr of course knew Selia hadn't given birth to him. He knew his mother had been a slave and had died when he was born.

But that mother was only a ghost, and Selia was real and warm and alive. In Geirr's young heart, Selia was his mother. His unwavering devotion rivaled Faolan's.

Selia still struggled with the bargain she had struck with Muirin, to claim Geirr as Alrik's son and make him the future Hersir. How could she have known she would come to love the boy as much as she loved Faolan?

But the past couldn't be changed. And knowing she had at least saved one of her children from a future as a Vikinger was some comfort, albeit small.

But Alrik had taken even that from her. Now both of Selia's sons would sail across the sea on twice-annual raids. And eventually, Faolan would be the man giving the order to kill.

She should have known this would happen. Whenever Alrik tried to show the boys some sort of fighting skill, Faolan would focus intently, watching every move of Alrik's body, and then practice it to perfection. Geirr would start by watching his father, but eventually lose interest and instead focus on something else entirely.

If Geirr's attention targeted a flock of birds flying in the sky, or a woolly worm crawling along a nearby branch, Alrik would erupt with fury.

Geirr's lack of concentration frustrated his father beyond measure, who frequently claimed the boy was untrainable—a simpleton. But Selia had always protected her children from Alrik's rages. More than once she had stepped in between

Geirr and his father when she felt Alrik's anger approach a dangerous level. This interference in what he saw as his parental right to discipline his sons was never received well, and had caused friction between them.

But what Alrik didn't seem to understand was that for all Geirr's seeming inattention, he actually grasped the skill being taught, often before Faolan did. For whenever Selia watched the boys sparring, Geirr's lithe young body eased effortlessly into the drill. He moved like a dancer, strong and nimble, and even the scar on his leg couldn't make him falter.

Faolan needed, and craved, the constant practice and repetition. Geirr did not. The movements seemed as natural to him as breathing.

Faolan stirred and rolled onto his side. The blanket slipped a bit, revealing the fresh marking on a reddened area of his chest. The tattoo was smallish but its lines flowed crisp and dark. As Faolan grew, the mark would fade and stretch out over his breast just as Alrik's had.

Selia stared at the despised symbol, a choking bile rising in her throat. What was done could not be undone. Her son had been marked for life as a shape-shifter. A berserker. But having the tattoo would not make Faolan like Alrik.

I will find a way to stop that from happening.

She pulled the blanket up around her son's small shoulder and drew the curtain closed.

Chapter 15

The farm returned to its normal rhythms with the departure of the guests. Selia was not on speaking terms with Alrik, however, and as expected he had gone away to avoid another argument with her. As soon as he left, Selia sent a thrall to inform Ingrid that it was safe to come for a visit.

The birth of Ingrid's daughter Eydis had been a difficult one, the babe sickly and small. Ingrid had kept the fragile child secluded and had allowed no visitors other than Hrefna.

It had infuriated Selia to be prevented from seeing Ainnileas' daughter. Her own flesh and blood. Ingrid was selfish and cruel for doing so. But for Selia to insist on seeing the child would only draw suspicion. Everyone knew there was no love lost between her and Ingrid, so why would Selia have reason to visit her stepdaughter?

Hrefna brought back frequent news of Ingrid and little Eydis, but it wasn't until Hrefna became ill that Selia learned the real reason for Ingrid's reluctance to have visitors to Ketill's farmstead. With Hrefna's inability to travel in her weakened condition, out of frustration Ingrid finally sent word to Selia. The next time Alrik left the farmstead, she would come for a visit.

The hatred between Ingrid and her father ran deep, but even for her this seemed extreme. Selia could only shrug it off. Ingrid was as stubborn and unforgiving as Alrik himself, and there was no point in arguing with either of them. So when Alrik had gone hunting with the first thaw of spring, Selia sent for her stepdaughter.

Selia's first opportunity to meet Eydis occurred late that afternoon, right after Alrik left. Ainnileas' daughter was a tiny slip of a child, much smaller than Geirr and Faolan, though the children had all been born fairly close together. The shy little girl had clung to her mother's skirts, with her eyes lowered and her face partially hidden from view by the hood of her cloak. But when they entered Hrefna's chamber to visit, Eydis ran to her great-aunt without hesitation.

It was then that Selia got a good look at Eydis, and she had nearly fainted in shock. Eydis' hair, a beautiful red-gold, glittered over her shoulders like a glorious sunset. It had been the hair color of Hrefna's sister—Alrik's mother—and a color common to the Finngalls in general.

But little Eydis' face looked nothing like that of the Finngalls. Her face was all Ainnileas. And Selia.

The big gray eyes, the arched brows, the curve of the chin, the smile, even the manner in which she held her head. Selia had watched as Eydis stroked Hrefna's cheek with a hand that was shaped exactly like her own, and her stomach lurched in apprehension.

Mouth agape, Selia had turned to Ingrid, who watched for Selia's reaction with defiance on her face. "I see why you haven't come for a visit," she whispered shakily.

Ingrid's expression revealed a similar concern. "It's becoming more difficult as she gets older. I have to hide her from anyone who has ever met you. Or your brother." The last was flung with resentment.

Though she understood, the accusation smarted, and Selia had swallowed painfully. The child's face was an announcement to the world of who had fathered her. If Alrik ever met his granddaughter, or spoke with anyone who could put the obvious pieces together, Ainnileas was as good as dead.

"What about Bolli? And Ketill?"

"They love her as their own. But they see the danger and so they keep my secret."

A peal of laughter had erupted from the little girl as she sat on the bed with Hrefna. Selia sucked in her breath. *She even laughs like Ainnileas.* "What are you going to do?"

"I will keep her hidden, as I always have. Ketill says when it is time for her to marry he will find a man who lives far from here." Ingrid's voice had trembled at that.

To keep Ainnileas safe, she would have to send her daughter away to live with strangers. By law, she could be married at the age of twelve, just six summers from now. There would be a strong probability the girl would never see her family again.

Regardless of the discord between Selia and Ingrid, there was little Eydis to think of. Selia had laid her hand on her stepdaughter's arm and squeezed reassuringly. "I will help you any way I can, Ingrid."

Ingrid and Eydis arrived after the crowd of the gathering had cleared and Selia sent word that Alrik was gone. He had decided to journey to Bjorgvin to visit with Gudrun, no doubt as good a reason as any he could think of to get away from the farmstead and Selia's icy glare.

Unlike most women, Ingrid and Eydis traveled alone, which did not surprise Selia. Ingrid was crafty, strong, and as deadly with a dagger as any man. Anyone foolish enough to come upon Ingrid with wicked intentions might not live long enough to regret it.

Selia was returning from the dairy as they appeared over the ridge. Eydis had her own diminutive pony, and she trotted along behind her mother's horse. The morning sun glinted bright in the little girl's hair and her cloak stirred in the breeze. She held the reins expertly in her tiny hands and Selia couldn't help but smile.

Ainnileas was a terrible horseman, and preferred the wagon to the saddle. Selia herself had never ridden a horse without Alrik holding on to her, always fearing she would fall if one of her spells came upon her. Little Eydis was already a better horsewoman than Selia and Ainnileas put together.

Selia met them at the barn and lifted Eydis from the saddle. Just touching Ainnileas' daughter sent a thrill of happiness up her spine. She put her arms around the child and breathed in the scent of warm sunshine in her hair.

Eydis returned the hug. After her initial shyness, the girl recognized a kindred spirit in Selia, and they had spent a good deal of time together at Ingrid's last visit. Selia and Eydis enjoyed many things Ingrid felt was a foolish waste of time. Hair plaiting into intricate knots was a particular favorite, and Selia had worked Eydis' gold-fire locks into a magnificent pattern of braids.

"Will you fix my hair again, Selia?" Eydis asked, smiling up at her.

"Of course. You will look like a princess when I'm finished with you."

Selia and Ingrid walked together toward the farmhouse with Eydis skipping ahead of them. "How is Hrefna?" Ingrid asked.

"She's tired from the gathering. She hasn't been out of bed."

Ingrid grunted but didn't respond otherwise. There was a shout from the beach as the two boys noticed them. They ran up to greet them, making as much racket as possible along the way. Eydis stopped her skipping and watched them, looking a bit guarded. She still wasn't accustomed to the rough ways of her kin.

The boys reached them, laughing and out of breath. "Hello, sister," Geirr said to Ingrid, and Faolan giggled.

"Hello, niece," he said to Eydis.

Ingrid shook her head at them. When the boys had met Ingrid and Eydis for the first time this past spring, Selia had a difficult time explaining to them this grown woman was their sister and they were both therefore uncle to her child, Eydis. Geirr and Faolan thought this tremendously funny.

"Hello, boys," Ingrid said. "Have you been fishing?"

The boys were barefoot and soaking wet from the knee down. "How did you know?" Geirr wondered.

Ingrid gave a sideways glance to Eydis as if to imply that Geirr was not so bright. Eydis pulled at Ingrid's hand with excitement. "Can I go fishing, Mother?"

Ingrid glanced to the docks where one of the thralls waited for the boys to return. Both Geirr and Faolan were excellent swimmers, but Selia wouldn't let them go out on the boat alone.

"No." Ingrid moved Eydis back behind her. "Not now."

Eydis nodded and raised the hood of her cloak, knowing better than to argue. Selia's heart ached for the little girl. Did she understand the danger of her face? Had Ingrid told her? If one of the thralls got a good look at Eydis, how long would it take for the rumor to spread that Bolli was not her father? Most of the thralls currently on the farmstead had been here the summer Ainnileas had come, and would remember how besotted Ingrid had been over him. A quick calculation would prove the truth of Eydis' parentage.

Hrefna and Selia had told the boys Ingrid and Alrik didn't like each other, and he would be very angry if he knew Ingrid had visited. Under no circumstances were they to tell Alrik of the visits or of the fact that they had met Eydis. They both had nodded solemnly and vowed to keep the secret.

Geirr and Faolan had seen Alrik at his wild-eyed worst. They had no desire to bring that wrath down upon their newfound sister and niece.

The breeze picked up suddenly, whipping the women's gowns around their ankles and Eydis' hair over her face as a few fat raindrops splattered on the ground. The sky grew dark over the water and thunder rumbled in the distance.

Selia frowned as the clouds moved in. A storm was coming, and fast. Ingrid and Eydis were lucky they had made it to the farmstead in time. "No fishing, boys."

"But Mother—"

"No." Selia gestured firmly. "In the house, now."

A bolt of lightning struck the water. Eydis clung to her mother's skirts and the boys snickered nervously. Selia gave them a push and they all hurried toward the house. The raindrops came down a bit faster, still warm, then suddenly the heavens opened up a deluge that quickly turned cold. They ran through the rain and into the house, and Selia slammed the door on the storm. The boys laughed and shook themselves like dogs, flinging water everywhere.

Keir came in from the kitchen and looked from one to another of them as they dripped puddles on the floor. She moved toward the hearth to stir the coals.

Ingrid pulled Eydis behind her. "Go back to the kitchen," she ordered.

Selia huffed impatiently. "It's Keir. She can be trusted."

"No," Ingrid insisted, waiving Keir away. "Go on."

"I'm sorry, Keir," Selia said to the slave. "I'll call for you if we need anything."

"Yes, Mistress," Keir replied. She lowered her gaze and left the room.

"That was very rude, Ingrid," Selia remonstrated when the slave had left. "You hurt her feelings."

Ingrid uttered a dismissive laugh. "She's a thrall."

Selia bristled. In a strange way, she and Keir had bonded during Faolan's birth. Keir was a kind and loyal woman. Ingrid was nervous about anyone seeing Eydis, and rightly so, but that didn't excuse her discourtesy.

"You stir up the fire, then," she snapped. "I'll get dry clothes for the children." Selia rummaged through the boys' chest of clothing. She pulled out outfits for both of them, as well as one of Faolan's tunics for Eydis while her gown was drying.

The boys stripped naked and began a game of chase around the hearth. Laughing, Faolan darted one way then quickly another, causing Geirr to over-correct and stumble. Faolan pounced on him and they wrestled on the floor. Eydis gaped at the boys in prim disapproval.

"Enough!" Selia cried. She grabbed Faolan by the back of his hair and pulled him away from his brother. "We have guests."

Faolan twisted away, still laughing. Selia shoved the dry clothing at him. "Both of you go into my bedchamber and get dressed, now."

Geirr leapt from the floor, flaunted his buttocks at his brother, and ran into the bedchamber. Faolan shouted and followed after him. They slammed the door and Selia turned back to Ingrid and Eydis with a sigh. "I'm sorry. They're not used to having little girls around."

But something had changed, for Ingrid's face drained of color. She stared at Selia for a long moment before handing Eydis the tunic and pushing her toward Hrefna's bedchamber. "Go see if Hrefna is awake. And change your clothes while you're in there."

Ingrid watched her daughter skip away and then rounded on Selia angrily. "I cannot believe you let my father mark Faolan."

"Let him?" Selia sputtered. "I didn't let him! Alrik only told me after it was done."

"You let him do anything. He almost killed you and you still came back to him. But I would think you'd have more sense than to let him mark your child like that—"

"*Ingrid.*" Selia had fast grown frustrated. "I told you I didn't let him. And Alrik is mistaken. Faolan is not a berserker. He lost his temper and got into a fight with another boy, but that does not mean he is a berserker. I will find a way to make Alrik understand. That tattoo means nothing."

"Is that what you think it is? The badge of a berserker?"

Selia paused. "Well, yes."

Ingrid regarded her as though she were dim-witted. "You really are a stupid girl, aren't you? That tattoo is a shadow spell, meant only for great warriors. Whoever bears the mark will be able to draw forth Odin's power during battle. He will have the strength and the cunning of the wolf. But a man who is too weak to bear the mark will die. Only a true berserker can attempt it, since the wolf is already in his nature. But even some of them will be unable to survive the weight of the spell. They will slip into madness. Like Ragnarr."

Selia sat down hard on one of the benches, heaviness in her chest, a constriction that made it difficult to breathe. This was so much worse than she could have ever imagined.

What had Alrik done? Why would he dedicate his son to Odin, a god who had brought him only misery? Odin deserved nothing more from this family. *Nothing.*

Selia remembered the rabbit she had refrained from killing in Odin's name. In her mind's eye she saw the raven cawing at her from the branch, and the squeezing pressure around her belly that came next, as though it had laid claim to her babe. To Faolan. The tightness in her chest felt like that now; the evil claws of Odin's raven.

Odin had won. The sacrifice had been made after all.

Selia burst into tears.

Stony-faced, Ingrid watched her cry. "You are a simpering fool," she sneered. "You had a chance to escape my father and you didn't take it. If you had left, he would have killed himself with drink and I could have been with Ainnileas. You are a stupid, spineless woman and now you have the nerve to cry about it? You deserve everything you've gotten, Selia, and if anyone feels sorry for you then they are as foolish as you."

Selia cried harder. "I hate you, Ingrid!" she choked out. "I'm glad my brother left you."

Ingrid's laugh held bitterness. "I will find him again once Eydis is married. I will leave and I will find Ainnileas. We'll be together and there won't be anything you can do to stop it. And you can stay here and rot with your mad husband."

Suddenly the door flew open and hit the wall behind it hard enough to make both women jump. Ingrid leapt to her feet, startled, as Alrik stormed into the room.

He ripped off his soaking cape and flung it to the floor. His gaze landed on Selia and Ingrid, and his expression froze Selia's blood in her veins. Such fury on Alrik's face . . . had one of the thralls caught a glimpse of Eydis and told Alrik?

Ingrid inched toward Hrefna's bedchamber door, but Alrik wasn't interested in his daughter. He strode to Selia, massive and menacing, and she cowered as he leaned over her with his fists clenched at his sides.

Selia gasped at the wildness in his eyes. Alrik was frequently angry with her but he had always held himself back, probably in fear of the ring. But this was different. An air of malevolence surrounded him, directed squarely at Selia. The beast was furious and it wanted to hurt her.

"What did you do, Selia? You thought you could lie down with my brother and I wouldn't find out?"

Selia shrank as small as possible. "I don't know of what you speak—"

Alrik picked her up by the shoulders and shoved her against the wall. "I spoke with a man in Bjorgvin who used to sail with Gunnar One-Eye. He told me everything."

"He told you nothing!" Selia cried, squirming. "Because there is nothing to tell!"

"You're lying!" Alrik roared, shaking her. "Otherwise you would have told me Gunnar's men came here when I was gone. You kept it from me because you were guilty!"

"No!"

The boys ran from the bedchamber and stared, open-mouthed, at the sight of their father holding her against the wall. "Let go of her!" Geirr shouted. He lunged at Alrik and tried to push him away from Selia, but Alrik turned on the child with a snarl. He swiped at Geirr like a cat swatting a mouse. Geirr ducked but Alrik's hand caught his ear and knocked the boy several feet across the room.

Selia screamed. "Stop!"

"Alrik, no!" Hrefna cried. She stood in the bedchamber doorway, breathless, holding on to the wall for support. Two bright spots of color had appeared in her ashy cheeks. Little Eydis clung to her in terror. Hrefna beckoned to Geirr and he crawled over to her.

Alrik paused at the appearance of Hrefna. He gawked at her for a moment, then blinked down at Eydis, taking in the face, so like that of his wife. He dropped Selia and she crumpled to her knees.

"You," he sputtered, turning on Ingrid, "you thought you could hide your whoring from me?" The full scope of the situation hit home as it became clear Alrik realized the extent of his family's treachery. He glared at Hrefna and then back down at Selia. "All of you hid this from me? You thought I wouldn't find out, that you could keep me from killing your white-livered brother?"

"Alrik, please—"

He laughed harshly and stood tall over Selia. "Know that I will kill him, Selia. Know that Ainnileas will suffer greatly before he begs for death."

Selia sagged against the wall and let out a keening wail. Faolan darted between them, quick as a flash of lightning, and pulled out his father's dagger from where it hung from his belt. "Get away from my mother," he cried, gripping the dagger in front of him.

Alrik narrowed his eyes at his son, clenching his jaw hard. "Put that dagger down or I will break your fingers, boy."

Faolan didn't move. Alrik's hand flashed out and he grabbed the child by the scruff of his neck before he could dart away. With Faolan kicking and screaming, Alrik disarmed him and sheathed the dagger back in his belt.

Alrik studied the boy closely. He looked over at Geirr, then back to Faolan, and finally turned to Selia. His face was livid. "They're probably both Ulfrik's bastards," he spat. "You hid your whoring just as Ingrid did."

Selia grabbed hold of Alrik's arm. "No," she cried. "Faolan is your son. Let him go!"

"Why would I believe you? Your mouth is rotten with lies. And now the little bastard pulls a dagger on me—what more proof do I need?" Alrik shook Faolan hard, and a cry escaped the child's lips.

Cold fury coursed through Selia's veins. She squeezed in between Alrik's body and Faolan, then shoved at Alrik with all her strength. "I wish he wasn't your son!" Selia shouted. "You are a terrible father! I wish I had left with Ulfrik when I had the chance!"

Alrik gawped, dumbstruck, and dropped Faolan. The room was deathly quiet and for a long moment all that could be heard was the storm raging outside.

Then Alrik snapped and released a howl of rage that echoed through the room. Grabbing Selia by the hair, he dragged her toward their bedchamber. Faolan looked panicked and made a move to go after them.

"No!" Selia cried. "Go with Ingrid!" Alrik pulled her through the doorway and Selia twisted around and locked her gaze with Ingrid's. "Take them away from here," she begged.

Alrik slammed the door and bolted it shut. He strode to his chest where he kept his weapons, then released Selia. She watched in horror as he drew out his axe. Alrik was going to kill her. And he was between her and the door— there was no other way out.

"Alrik, no—"

Hrefna pounded to get in. "Alrik! Open the door!"

Alrik raised the axe over his head. Every muscle in her body coiled tight as she prepared to dart away. If she was quick enough maybe she could get around him and make it out the door.

But Alrik turned and brought the axe down hard on the chest that held all of Selia's possessions. Screaming in fury, he smashed it until it splintered into pieces, then proceeded to destroy everything that spilled out—her clothing, jewelry; her toiletry items. Once everything she owned was ruined, he whirled to the bed, slamming the axe down on the mattress, over and over, until feathers filled the air and floated over the floor. The frenzy of destruction continued as Alrik attacked the wooden posts of the bed.

He was so enraged it was as though he had forgotten Selia was even in the room. She inched toward the door and when his back was turned, she unbolted it and slipped outside.

Hrefna leaned against the wall, sobbing and gasping for air, as pale as death. "Oh my child," she wheezed when she saw Selia. "I thought he had killed you!"

Selia's eyes flashed around the room. "Where are the boys?"

"Ingrid took them."

She nodded in relief and pulled the woman toward the front door. "We have to flee, now."

Hrefna stumbled and held back. "No. I can't," she panted. "I can't make it. You go and I will keep him from following you."

"Hrefna—"

The clatter from the bedchamber intensified. Hrefna grabbed Selia's arm and locked eyes with her. "Selia. Go now. He won't hurt me."

"I won't leave you!"

With a surprising strength given her illness, Hrefna dragged Selia to the front door and pushed her out into the rain. She slipped in the mud and fell on her backside. Hrefna slammed the door shut and Selia heard her bolt the latch.

"Go!" Hrefna yelled from inside.

Selia stared despairingly at the door, torn between making sure her children were safe, and protecting Hrefna. Alrik's madness was in full force but Hrefna knew enough to keep out of his way. If the woman bolted herself in her bedchamber she could wait Alrik out until he exhausted himself. Of all of them, Hrefna was the only one able to reason with him.

Where would Ingrid have gone with Eydis and the boys? Selia ran to the barn to see if they had taken the horses. Ingrid and Eydis' mounts were still stabled. Ketill's longhouse was too far away for them to have traveled on foot. They had either gone into the woods to hide or had sought shelter at Bjorn's.

Eydis' fear of storms meant it was more likely Ingrid had taken the children to Bjorn.

Selia made her decision and ran.

Chapter 16

She arrived at Bjorn's small farmstead, soaking wet and covered in mud, and pounded on the door. "Bjorn!" she cried. "It's Selia. Please let me in!"

The door opened and Geirr and Faolan threw themselves into her arms. "*Mamai*," Geirr choked out, "I thought he would kill you."

"Where is Hrefna?" Ingrid demanded. She had a dagger in her hand and only sheathed it when she saw Selia was alone. Ingrid pulled Selia and the boys into the house and shut the door.

"She wouldn't come."

"What?" Ingrid looked as though she would strike her. "You left her there with him?"

"She wouldn't come, Ingrid! There was nothing I could do."

"If anything happens to her I will kill you myself."

Selia turned her back on Ingrid and surveyed the room. There was no one else there other than Ingrid and the children. Bjorn's family and thralls were conspicuously absent although there was a pot of stew bubbling at the hearth. "Where is everyone?"

"Bjorn left to get Ketill and Bolli. I told him my father had gone completely mad and probably killed you."

"Where is his family?"

"They went with him in the wagon. He wasn't going to leave them here if my father came after us."

Selia's heart sank. "No," she whispered. "I need the wagon. We have to get to Ulfrik's house."

Ingrid scowled. "It's a bit late to run to your lover. He has long lived elsewhere."

Selia averted her gaze and took a breath to steady herself. The time had finally come; her life with Alrik was over. Somehow she had always known it would happen, had always known his volatile nature would eventually push her to choose between her safety and her love for him. But once the words were said they couldn't be unsaid.

"I'm leaving Alrik. And there is something at Ulfrik's house I need."

Alrik had destroyed all of her jewelry save for the necklace she was wearing and her carved silver ring. How much would those be worth if she sold them? Not enough to buy passage out of Norway for her and the boys. She needed to get to the beach at Ulfrik's house and dig up the bride price. But how to travel there without a wagon? And how to gain Bjorgvin without Alrik finding them first?

Selia could feel tears burning at the back of her eyes again, and she blinked them away.

Ingrid studied Selia as though assessing her intentions. "If you're leaving, we're coming with you."

Selia's narrowed eyes took in her stepdaughter; the face that was so like Alrik's. She despised Ingrid with a passion. Only for Eydis' sake would she consider taking her along. And Ingrid knew that.

But Ingrid was nearly as big as a man and expert with a dagger. Plus she could saddle a horse.

Both Geirr and Faolan were excellent riders but neither boy had strength enough to tighten the saddle. If Selia allowed Ingrid to come, she could saddle Bjorn's other horses and Selia could double up with Faolan or Geirr. They could ride to Ulfrik's house to dig up the bride price and then from there go to Bjorgvin to buy passage on the first ship sailing out of the harbor in the morning. With any luck they would be gone before Alrik even knew where to look for them.

Whether Selia liked it or not, she needed Ingrid. She gritted her teeth. "All right. But we leave now."

They rode through the woods toward Ulfrik's house, avoiding the ridge that Alrik typically took. As purple twilight descended upon the forest, the rain turned to a drizzle, soaking them to the bone.

Miserably cold, Selia rode behind Geirr on one of Bjorn's horses and clung to him, both in an attempt to stay astride the animal as well as to keep Geirr warm. He was shivering so badly Selia feared he would fall.

Ingrid rode Bjorn's largest horse, with Eydis in front of her and Faolan behind. None of the children had their cloaks and Eydis was barefoot. In their haste to get away from Alrik, Ingrid hadn't let Eydis retrieve her wet shoes from Hrefna's bedchamber.

Selia was pensive as they rode. The brief sense of relief she had felt with her decision to leave had dissipated when the stark reality of their current situation hit her.

They'd flee for their lives. Two women and three children with no supplies other than what they had quickly snatched from Bjorn's pantries. Her boys were trying to be brave but Selia could sense their fear. And they were right to be afraid, for it was as though the rule Alrik had always abided by had suddenly been torn away. His fury was now directed at Selia and at them.

Alrik had snapped just as his father had before him. He had lost control and terrorized his family in a way that was very personal, very real. The boys had seen him at his worst and knew to avoid him when he was angry, but Alrik's rage had never been directed at them as intensely. Selia had always been able to deflect it from them. Alrik would typically stomp off and gather himself, sometimes staying away for a bit if necessary.

But this was different.

This was a harsh reminder that Selia had married a berserker. A dangerous man whom she had seen kill in the blink of an eye. And his hands had been on her children.

There could be only one outcome to these events. Selia would divorce Alrik and save her boys from the fate of Jorulf Ragnarson.

Hadn't Selia always known, somehow, that this would happen? Hadn't she always known at some point she would be forced to make a choice between Alrik and her own safety, and that of her children? Ulfrik had presented her with the opportunity to leave and Selia hadn't taken it. She had stayed with Alrik even after learning what kind of man he was. She had stayed with him knowing the restless beast would eventually turn on her.

She'd fooled herself into believing she could help Alrik—could save him somehow. Instead she had nearly gotten them all killed.

Why hadn't I been more prepared?

She'd have been wise to dig up the bride price from Ulfrik's house and move it somewhere closer. She should have kept cloaks and supplies at the ready. But somehow, to prepare for Alrik's inevitable breakdown would have been an admission of defeat. An admission that Selia could not, after all, stop Alrik from turning into Ragnarr.

And what of poor Hrefna? She was so fragile now. Who would take care of her? Selia wanted to believe Alrik wouldn't hurt his aunt, the closest thing he had to a mother. But how could she know for sure? How could Selia live with herself knowing she had left Hrefna behind?

There was a sound of hoof beats in the distance. Selia stilled and listened. A solitary rider was approaching. Her heart hammered in her ears and she motioned Ingrid and Geirr to turn deeper into the woods, off the path completely. They hid in a dark thicket of trees but the sound of the hoof beats intensified. There was a shrill whinny from Alrik's horse as it reared up behind them. Geirr's body tensed tight in preparation to defend his mother, and Selia felt his hand move to unsheathe his dagger.

"Selia," Alrik called. His voice was angry and hard but not out of control as it had been before. "Where do you think you're going?"

Selia wrapped her hand around Geirr's to hide the dagger. She willed herself to stay strong. "We're leaving. Don't try to stop us."

"I do not give you permission to leave. Go back to the house, now."

Selia confronted him, her teeth chattering in fear and cold. "I'm finished, Alrik. I will not have you hurt my children."

In the wet undergrowth the horse pranced beneath Alrik's big body. Selia saw his jaw clench. The leather of his saddle creaked as he leaned directly into her face, his blue eyes boring into hers.

"Selia. You will go home now."

"No." She took a deep breath to brace herself. "I divorce you, Alrik."

For several long seconds he stared at her, and she cringed to see a flicker of panic in his eyes. This would not end well. Alrik's hand whipped through the air and snatched her from the horse, and Selia screamed as she was pulled onto his saddle.

The boys flew into an uproar, shouting and flashing their daggers, as Eydis burst into tears.

Alrik turned the horse and galloped away.

He pushed the horse for speed over the wet ground, much too fast for safety, back in the direction of Bjorn's house. Selia tried to twist around to reason with him but Alrik's heavy arm held her tight against his chest. The wind rushed through her ears and she couldn't tell if Ingrid and the children were following them.

Would Ingrid have enough sense to use this opportunity to escape and take the boys with her? The thought of never seeing her children again rent Selia's very soul from her body.

But they would be safe. They would be alive. And Faolan wouldn't be given over to Odin like some bloody sacrifice.

Alrik reared the horse to a stop at Bjorn's farmstead. He dismounted and dragged Selia by the arm toward the blacksmith's stable.

Selia had never been inside the building where Bjorn worked. It was nearly the size of Bjorn's house, with a large fire pit in the middle surrounded by several work tables. Other tables against the walls held the raw material he used. Metal rings and utensils of various sizes hung from hooks on the wall.

Selia's stomach gnawed with anxiety as she stumbled within the entrance. "Why are we here?" she choked out to Alrik. But he ignored the question and pulled her to the furthest corner of the room, away from the doorway. He pushed her to her knees with a look of contempt.

The fire was still hot. Bjorn must have been working when Ingrid had arrived with the children. Alrik picked a small slug of iron from one of the tables and dropped it into the fire. Selia eyed him warily. What did he mean to do? She searched for something she could use as a weapon. There was nothing sharp nearby, but the table next to her held several hefty blocks of metal. Selia grabbed one when Alrik's back was turned and hid it in the folds of her gown.

The door flew open and Bjorn, Ketill, and Bolli charged inside. They took in the sight of Alrik at the forge and Selia cowering in the corner. Alrik turned on them with a snarl.

"Oath breakers, every one of you. I should run the lot of you through and be done with it."

"What are you talking about?" Ketill asked.

"Your 'granddaughter,'" Alrik spat. "No one thought

to tell me she had been sired by a spineless Irishman? You thought you could keep this from your Hersir?"

Ketill stepped forward. The look on his face was as defiant as Selia had ever seen it. "Alrik. Ingrid is my niece— the only living child of my dead sister. I will not see her hurt. Her child has the blood of my father in her veins, whether sired by Bolli or not."

"That matters nothing! You hid Ingrid's whoring from me."

"The child looked enough like Bolli early on. There was nothing to hide. And when I realized the truth, I cared for the girl too much for it to matter."

Alrik's face darkened. "Then you are a fool. And your son is an even bigger fool."

Bolli approached Alrik. His foot had healed as well as could be expected, but he still walked with a noticeable limp. "Where are they? What have you done with them?"

Alrik laughed. "I've done nothing with them. They were leaving you. They probably continued on, so you should consider yourself lucky to be rid of them."

Bolli looked visibly shaken. Ketill nodded in Selia's direction. "And what are you doing with her?"

Alrik turned back to study Selia. His face seemed lit with some evil purpose, and Selia shrank back against the wall as she gripped the hunk of metal. "I'm going to show her what happens to those who defy me."

Yanking one of the metal rings from the wall, he advanced on Selia. She stared at it, dumbstruck, as the ugly realization set in. It was a slave collar. And Alrik was about to put it on her.

Selia cried out and darted around him as he reached for her. She ran over to the group of men. "Help me," Selia begged Ketill.

"I can't," he said, shaking his head. He looked very sad. "I'm sorry."

Selia heard Alrik's footsteps behind her. In a panic she threw her arms around Ketill's neck and held on. "Have you heard from Ulfrik?" she whispered into his ear.

Alrik grabbed her and tore her away from Ketill. Selia met Ketill's gaze, imploring him with her eyes. Ulfrik had said if Selia ever wanted to leave, all she need do was go to Ketill and he would get word to him. Ulfrik would help her with no expectation of anything in return.

But would Ketill remember the code Ulfrik had told him so long ago? And if he remembered, would he even care? Ketill had told Selia he was only willing to allow Bolli to claim Ingrid's child for the sake of Grainne, the woman he loved. He didn't care if Selia died and had even stated it would be easier on all of them if she had.

Ketill stared at Selia for a long moment, then gave a small, almost imperceptible nod.

Selia's relief was short lived as Alrik pulled her toward the fire. "No!" she shouted at him. "You cannot do this, Alrik. I am your wife!"

He turned on her with a snarl. "You are my wife no longer. You divorced me. I told your father I would have you as my wife or my thrall. So now you will be my thrall."

Selia screamed and tried to hit him with the hunk of metal, but Alrik blocked the attack. He jerked the metal from her hand and threw it aside. Then he bent her face first over the work table closest to the fire, pinning her down by her head.

Alrik ripped the jeweled necklace from her throat and slung it into the fire. "Bjorn," he barked. "Unless you want to see her burned, come and help me."

Selia writhed frantically but couldn't move. She reached behind her and dug into his hand with her fingernails; his grip didn't loosen. "Alrik, stop!" she begged. "I'm sorry—I didn't mean what I said!"

Alrik only growled harshly as he slapped the cold metal collar around her neck. Bjorn retrieved the iron slug from the fire with a pair of tongs, and Selia's eyes grew large as she saw it. A rivet to secure the collar around her neck that could only be broken by a chisel struck with great force very close to the head, as Bjorn had done when Muirin had been freed.

Removing a collar from a living thrall was a difficult business, requiring a sure aim and a steady hand. Most collars were only removed after death.

Selia bucked wildly, fighting with the strength of terror. Alrik leaned close to her face and met her gaze. The flames of the fire flickered in his eyes as he spoke, and made him look like a madman.

"Hold still, little thrall. Unless you want an ugly scar."

Stilling in defeat, Selia took a shuddering breath and closed her eyes. Alrik turned the collar upon her neck, heat radiating from the rivet as Bjorn put it through the ends of the collar and bent it around upon itself. Selia flinched as cold water was poured over the rivet to cool it.

There was a sudden rush of wind as the door to the blacksmith's stable opened again. Selia heard a child's cry of indignation that she recognized as Faolan's. Alrik released her head and Selia stumbled away from the table. The rivet was still hot and she screamed as it touched her. She held the collar away from her skin as best she could, sniffling in pain and humiliation.

Faolan and Geirr rushed to Selia. Furious tears flowed down Geirr's cheeks but Faolan was quiet. He examined the slave collar around his mother's neck and the blister that was forming on her collarbone. His face grew dark and the color of his eyes intensified as it did whenever he was enraged, just as Alrik's always had. Selia had the strange sense she was not looking at the face of a young child, but instead at the man her son would eventually become.

Faolan's body vibrated with fury as he spun to Alrik. He locked eyes with his father and spoke with the searing conviction of one casting a curse. "I will kill you for this, Alrik Ragnarson. Know this truth as you know your own name."

Selia stared at her son. Geirr could pull off the tone of a miniature Hersir when necessary, but Faolan had never needed to and so had never tried. To hear the words of a warlord come out of Faolan's childish mouth felt eerie and thick with portent. Selia shivered.

Alrik erupted with a cry of outrage. He rushed at Faolan and backhanded him with enough force that the child left his feet with the impact. Selia screamed as her son's small body flew through the air and thudded against the wall.

Faolan landed in a heap on the floor, as still as death.

Chapter 17

Selia's misery continued as Faolan slowly recovered. He drifted in and out of consciousness, and when he did open his eyes they were dim and unfocused. Once his little body had thrashed about on the bed, and Selia and Hrefna had to hold him down to keep him from falling to the floor. His eyes had rolled back in his head as his body continued to twitch under their hands.

Selia had been certain Faolan would die, and she vowed to the heavens to kill Alrik if her worst fear did come to pass. She would kill him in his sleep; draw a blade across his throat and watch him bleed out. His men would avenge the murder of their Hersir, of course, but Selia would die knowing she had avenged her son.

But Faolan grew stronger, until it became clear he would live. He was still very weak and was only able to sit up in the bed for short periods. He had no memory of the events leading up to his injury, and once he could talk he repeatedly asked Selia why she was wearing a slave collar.

Selia didn't know how to answer him. And even when she did answer, he didn't remember her response for long. He would awaken later and ask her again.

Alrik had taken to sleeping on one of the curtained benches in the main room since his own bed was ruined. He barely spoke to anyone, least of all to Selia. She and the boys slept with Hrefna, still terribly weak herself. Yet she seemed to pull herself together at the knowledge that Selia needed her help.

Not even Hrefna had been able to get through to Alrik and convince him it was not within his rights to put a slave collar on his wife as a punishment for threatening divorce. Hrefna realized, finally, that Alrik had slipped into Ragnarr's madness and might never return. Selia told Hrefna of her plan to escape with Ulfrik, and Hrefna was in agreement that she should go.

"You must leave with us when Ulfrik comes," Selia whispered to her as they lay in the bed. Faolan slept between them and Geirr was curled at the foot of the bed.

A single candle burned on the table, but it didn't offer enough light for Selia to see Hrefna's face clearly. They'd had this conversation several times before and Hrefna always avoided giving Selia a definite answer.

"My dear," the woman sighed. "This is my home. The only person I know in Ireland is Dagrun, and I'm not even sure if she's still alive. And more to the point, I'm too old to sneak off into the night. I would only slow you down."

"You would not," Selia argued. "And we won't stay in Ireland. Ulfrik said Ireland would be the first place Alrik would look for us. As soon as we warn Ainnileas we will go somewhere else. Anywhere you like."

"Be that as it may, I'm still too old to hide out in a foreign land, Ireland or no."

"Hrefna—"

"I will die in the land of my birth," Hrefna vowed with conviction. "I will help you when the time comes, but I will not go with you."

Selia swallowed the tears building in the back of her throat, and her voice wavered as she pleaded, "The boys need you. I need you."

Hrefna reached around Faolan's sleeping form and clasped Selia's hand. "My dear. I love you like a daughter—you know this to be true. I love these boys as though they were my own as well. When you leave you will have each other. You will have Ulfrik and perhaps Ainnileas to protect you. Alrik has no one left but me now. No one to care for him. I am his mother because there is no one else. I cannot abandon him any more than you can abandon your children."

Selia pulled her hand away. "He is a grown man. Not a child. And he almost killed Faolan."

Hrefna sighed. "You will realize your children never stop being your children, no matter their age. And no matter what wickedness they have committed. A mother's love does not falter, although I sometimes wish it could."

The next morning a rider came to the farmstead; a thrall, by the looks of his rough clothing and cropped hair. As Selia met him at the door she recognized Hakon from Ketill's farmstead.

Her anxiety rose as she stepped back to let him enter. Did he have troubling information about Ingrid? Or, God forbid, Eydis?

"Hello, Mistress," Hakon said. His eyes took in the sight of the collar around her neck but he didn't appear surprised. It would seem news traveled fast about how Alrik Ragnarson had humiliated his wife when she tried to divorce him.

Selia was not permitted to speak to anyone other than Hrefna or the boys unless Alrik was present. He had brought all the thralls on the farmstead together and warned them that anyone caught in conversation with Selia would be killed immediately, without question. Obviously Hakon hadn't heard about this further injustice or he wouldn't have spoken to her.

Selia motioned for Hakon to follow her and she led him over to the bench where Alrik slept. It was late in the morning but he had drunk himself into a stupor the night before.

"Alrik," she said loudly, throwing open the curtain. "Wake up."

He snorted and rolled onto his side. Selia leaned over to shout in his ear. "Alrik!"

He sat up, sputtering in fury, glaring at Selia and then Hakon, who took a hasty step backward.

"This thrall has come from Ketill's. I do not know what he wants since you have forbidden me to speak to anyone outside of your presence." She turned to Hakon. "Now that the Hersir is awake you can tell us your news."

Hakon hung his head in apprehension. "Master. I am sorry to inform you, my master Ketill Brunason is dead."

Selia gasped and her knees nearly gave out from under her. No. *No.* How could Ketill be dead? She needed him—he was the only one who could send for Ulfrik. The only one who could help get her children to safety. It all had hinged on him. What was she going to do now?

Alrik swung his legs around to sit on the edge of the bench. As Hakon's words sank in, the muscle in Alrik's jaw twitched. "How?" he finally asked.

"On the road. He had planned a trip to Bjorgvin so we didn't expect him back soon. But he had been gone for some time, so Bolli went to see why he was taking so long to return. He found Master Ketill's body. His horse was dead as well, nearby. It must have gone lame and thrown him."

A rush of unbearable frustration shot through Selia's veins. It was all she could do to keep from screaming. It seemed even in death, Ketill Brunason would continue to spite her. Had he gone to Bjorgvin to get word to Ulfrik? Had he fulfilled his promise?

Perhaps he had done what he had set out to do, and now Ulfrik was on his way to rescue her. Or perhaps Ketill had died on the way to Bjorgvin before he had a chance to speak to anyone.

She sank to the edge of the bench and dropped her head in her hands. She could not contain a sob.

Alrik raised his eyebrows. "I didn't know you cared so deeply for Ketill Brunason."

What to say that wouldn't raise Alrik's suspicions? "I know he loved Eydis as his own." Selia sniffled. "Who will protect her from you now?"

"If I wanted to kill that child I would have already done it."

Hakon's eyes grew large. "The funeral is soon." He shifted from one foot to the other. "Master Skagi bade me return immediately after I delivered the news. May I take my leave?"

"You may." Alrik waved him away. "Find Keir and tell her to give you food and supplies to take back with you for the funeral. I will come along shortly."

"Yes, Master." Hakon appeared relieved.

"Wait," Alrik called as Hakon turned to leave. His chin jutted and his eyes narrowed in the Hersir expression Selia knew so well. "Tell Bolli Ketilson this will not postpone our fall trip. If he is ready to prove his loyalty to me, I am in need of a new right-hand man. Tell him to ponder this until I see him."

Hakon bowed and hurried out the door.

Alrik turned back to Selia. He studied her, taking in her disheveled appearance. Selia had been so distraught over Faolan, she had given no attention to her hair or clothing. And Alrik had smashed her comb anyway.

He seemed to focus on the slave collar around her neck for a moment, then he looked away and scrubbed his hands through his hair in the way he did whenever he was upset. He seemed almost contrite.

"How is Faolan?" he asked.

Selia kept her face impassive. "He is as well as can be expected after being thrown across the room by his father."

"Any father disrespected in such a manner would have done the same."

Selia felt it pointless to respond. It was true every father had the right to discipline his children in the way he saw fit. The behavior of a man's children reflected upon him directly, and children who were disrespectful or out of control were seen as an indication the father was lacking in some way.

Many men were heavy handed with their families for this reason. Selia had seen children, both Irish and Norse, hit by their parents with fists and switches. Niall had never hit her or Ainnileas, but his disciplinary choices were unusual.

The difference in Alrik's methods lay in his reputation as a berserker. When his rage overtook him, he lost control in a way other men did not. A lesson in discipline could easily turn into Alrik doing his children great bodily harm. How could the man not see that?

Alrik caught Selia's wrist and drew her to him. He wrapped his arms around her and buried his face in her hair. Selia held herself stiffly until Alrik finally pulled back.

"I did not mean to hurt him, Selia," he murmured. "I'm sorry. I want everything to go back to the way it was."

"Then take this off." She fingered the collar.

"Not quite yet. I don't think you've learned your lesson."

"I have learned my lesson. I am your wife and I love you. Take it off."

He eyed her closely. "You say you love me. But how can I believe you? You were going to leave—you said you wished you had left with Ulfrik. An Oath Breaker. The same Oath Breaker it was rumored bedded you when Gunnar One-Eye's men were here."

"You believed a vile rumor spread by someone you met in Bjorgvin. I was angry you accepted the word of a stranger over that of your own wife. Can you blame me? But I'm sorry now, Alrik. I'm sorry for what I said. I never would have left you."

Alrik lifted the collar as though to test its weight. His voice grew hard. "There was a time I wouldn't have kept you here if you didn't love me. There was a time I wouldn't have forced you to stay." He hooked his finger under the collar and tugged Selia toward him until her face was inches from his. Alrik's eyes grew flinty. "But that time is over, Selia.

Whether you love me or you hate me, I will not let you go. You are mine and no one else will ever have you."

Selia gulped, praying he would not see her fear. "I understand. Please take the collar off."

His gaze searched hers. "Not yet. When I return from the fall trip we will see how contrite you are. After you've been my thrall for a time, perhaps you'll be more inclined to be my wife again."

Selia hurried back to the bedchamber. Hrefna and Faolan were sleeping, and Geirr was sitting on the floor playing with a pile of rocks and sticks meant to represent a war band on a raid. He and Faolan had invented this game over the long winter, and it proved useful to keep the boys quiet whenever it was impossible to send them outside.

She knelt beside him. "Geirr, I need your help with something very important. I would do it myself but I can't."

Geirr smiled in expectation and dropped the rocks. "What is it, Mother?"

"There is a thrall outside, a man named Hakon. He is talking to Keir but he will be leaving soon. I need you to speak with him without anyone else hearing. And you must tell him exactly what I say."

Chapter 18

Bleary-eyed, Selia sat near the hearth with her sewing. It was late in the evening, but with only a few more stitches the project would be complete. Everything would be ready tonight as long as Hakon had indeed followed her instructions. But surely he had. Of all people, Hakon would have a vested interest in Selia's plan.

Keir came in from the kitchen, startling Selia into dropping the needle. She had thought everyone had already gone to bed. She crumpled the sewing in her lap.

"Mistress," Keir said. "Let me stir the fire for you." Now that Alrik had gone to Ketill's funeral, Keir had resumed speaking to Selia. She was the only one who had, for the rest were still terrified of the Hersir even when absent from the farmstead.

Selia shook her head. "It's all right, Keir, I will keep the fire going. I need to finish this. Go on to bed." Keir lowered her gaze but didn't leave. Selia studied her. "Is there something else?"

Keir swallowed. "Mistress Hrefna told me your plans. I am fearful for your safety and I wished to tell you safe journey."

"Oh," Selia breathed. It was not surprising Hrefna had confided in Keir. Since Hrefna's illness, Keir had taken over much of the responsibilities of the farmstead as well as helping Selia care for Hrefna and the boys. She had proven herself to be loyal and trustworthy. Selia would miss her very much. "Keir," Selia began hesitantly, "would you . . . would you consider coming with us?"

Keir fell silent for long moments. "I am honored you would ask," she whispered. "But Mistress Hrefna will need someone to assist her after you're gone. I will stay. And I will pray for your safety and happiness."

Selia rose from the hearth and put her arms around Keir. Other than during Faolan's birth, they had never touched. Keir stiffened for a moment before relaxing into the embrace. "You are a good woman, Keir. I will never forget you," Selia vowed. "I will pray for your safety and happiness as well."

At the soft sound of the front door opening, Keir stepped away from Selia and lowered her head as Ingrid and Eydis entered the room.

"What is she doing here?" Ingrid hissed.

Selia replied tersely, "Keir knows. And she can be trusted. You certainly took your time, Ingrid."

"I had to wait until everyone was asleep, didn't I? Sigrun was very talkative tonight." Ingrid gestured with impatience as she mentioned Bjorn's wife. "I should have brought some of Hrefna's special tea for her."

As part of the plan, Ingrid was to cry and carry on when Alrik arrived at Ketill's farmstead. She was to refuse to be in the same house with him and finally storm off with Eydis to stay at Bjorn's. This would not be seen as out of the ordinary for anyone who knew how Ingrid despised her father. And Alrik would be eager to have her leave. Ingrid's tantrums were an embarrassment to him.

"Well. Let's hope she doesn't rise early and discover you're gone."

"No, she'll think I went back for the funeral. I told her I would, even if it meant I had to see my father."

Selia nodded and folded up the sewing project that was not quite finished. The breeches weren't hemmed properly, but she could make do. It was time to leave.

They entered Hrefna's bedchamber and Selia opened one of the storage chests. She lifted out several of Hrefna's gowns to get to the satchel at the bottom. It held a pair of

Geirr's old shoes, a small dagger, a hand shovel, a pair of scissors, food, and two flasks of water. She added the clothing she had been sewing to the satchel and tied it closed.

Hrefna and the boys were asleep. Ingrid roused Hrefna to say goodbye, and Hrefna sat up in the bed and held Ingrid and Eydis for a long time. She whispered something in Ingrid's ear and Ingrid nodded.

Selia woke the boys and handed them their shoes and cloaks. They would not be cold and wet this time. They dressed quickly and then Hrefna pulled them close. "Be strong now, boys. You must take care of your mother. And Eydis." Hrefna turned to Ingrid with a sad smile. "But I think your sister can take care of herself."

The boys nodded, both blinking back tears. Selia's heart contracted at the sight of them trying to be so brave. Hrefna was a grandmother to them. And if all went well with Selia's plan, they would never see her again.

Selia sat on the edge of the bed and clung to Hrefna's neck. She had spoken her goodbyes already, but there was something else that needed to be said. "I do understand how you love him, Hrefna. I understand why you're staying with him. And I'm grateful to you for it. It would be harder for me to leave if I knew he would have no one."

Only Hrefna understood the tragedy of loving someone who was damaged beyond repair. Selia had gone through so much to be with Alrik. She had stayed with him despite much turmoil and heartache. Truth be told, she was only leaving for the sake of the children. If not for the threat to the boys' safety, Selia would again try to smooth things over with Alrik, knowing he would eventually come to his senses. He would forgive her and their lives would go back to the way they once were. For a while it would be good between them. The good times between the bad were made all the more precious because Selia never knew how long they would last.

She had lived for those times.

But the image of Alrik slinging Faolan across the room was burned indelibly into Selia's mind. It had taken a near-tragedy for her to gather enough courage to leave. She was foolish to love a man like Alrik, but not foolish enough to allow him to hurt her children.

Hrefna hugged her one last time. "Safe journey, dear child," she whispered to Selia. "I will take care of him."

The boat slipped silently through the dark water. The moon was high and lit up the cove as Ingrid steered toward the beach at Ulfrik's house. Geirr jumped out and pulled the small boat onto the shore.

Selia hurried to the spot where Ulfrik had indicated she should dig. Her bride price was buried there. Her eyes traveled over the rock and her throat tightened, remembering the events of that fateful afternoon.

More than once Selia had wondered what their lives would be like if she had left her husband. Ulfrik was so different than Alrik in every way, it seemed, except in his desire for her. Ulfrik claimed to love Selia as he had no other woman. Would she have been content as Ulfrik's wife? Would she have grown to love him?

Selia cared for Ulfrik a great deal. They understood each other. At one time, Selia had felt closer to Ulfrik than she had to anyone, other than perhaps Ainnileas. But the intense, overwhelming, irrational *need* she felt for Alrik was not an emotion she had ever felt for anyone else.

That was 'love.' Wasn't it?

Selia knelt to dig. It was hard work and slow going, and after a while Ingrid snatched the shovel from her and began to dig herself. As the hole got progressively deeper, Selia's anxiety grew. What if the bride price wasn't here? What would they do?

"It's not here, Selia," Ingrid snapped. She pushed her sweaty hair away from her face with her forearm. "If it was ever here at all."

"Of course it's here. Ulfrik said so. We just need to dig deeper."

"No. The tide washed it away. Or maybe Ulfrik grew tired of waiting for you and he came back and dug it up himself. Maybe he used it to buy a new little Irish girl."

Selia hadn't told Ingrid the details of the reason the bride price was buried in this spot, but she'd had to reveal enough of the story so Ingrid understood how important it was to go to Ulfrik's house first. Ingrid only knew Ulfrik had wanted to marry Selia but she had refused him. Ingrid was still smarting that not one, but two men had desired Selia. All the while Ainnileas had left Ingrid in Norway and sailed away.

The bride price had to be there. Without it the rest of their plan was futile—only the bag of silver would buy them passage out of Norway. Selia took the shovel from Ingrid and resumed digging. "He would have buried it deep so the tide wouldn't get it."

Selia dug furiously, becoming more and more apprehensive, as Ingrid and the children watched. It had to be there. *It had to be there.* There was no other way to keep Geirr and Faolan safe.

The shovel hit something that resisted the metal blade. Cloth. *A bag.* Selia cried out and used her hands to scoop the sandy dirt away from the bag. The cloth was rotten from being in the ground for so long, and as she lifted it the seam gave way and the silver spilled out into the moonlight.

"Oh," Selia gasped. There were so many little nuggets of hack-silver. Enough to buy passage anywhere they wanted to go in the world, with plenty left over to start a new life and live comfortably. Ulfrik had buried a fortune and walked away from it, all on the off-chance that Selia would need it to escape.

Selia's heart hitched in her chest. She had treated him so badly.

They painstakingly picked up every piece of silver and laid them all in a pile on top of the bag. Selia had sewn little pockets into the interior of the boys' clothing, and Ingrid had done so as well to her skirts and Eydis' gown. They divided out the silver and put some into each of the children's pockets and tied them shut. Selia would have to carry Ingrid's portion until later tonight after the next step of the plan.

She returned to the satchel she had brought and pulled out the clothing and Geirr's old shoes. Behind a rock Selia changed into the new outfit, then stuffed the folded parcel containing her old garments into the hole. Gown, shift, cloak, and shoes. After a moment's hesitation, Selia removed her ring and dropped that in, too.

Ingrid made a move to reach into the hole. "We can sell that, you know."

Selia grabbed her hand. "No. We have plenty of silver. Leave it."

Ingrid didn't argue further. Selia started to push the dirt back in and heard Ingrid snickering behind her. Selia gritted her teeth at the sound. She had always found her stepdaughter's laugh grating.

"Wait. Don't cover the hole yet—I think you're forgetting something." Ingrid rummaged through the satchel and pulled out the pair of shears.

Selia's mouth went dry and she nodded. Her hand went up to finger her hair one last time. It was dressed very simply in one long plait down her back. The tip reached well past the swell of her buttocks. Other than an occasional trim, Selia's hair had never been cut.

She sat before Ingrid and steeled herself. The boys knelt beside her and each took one of her hands for comfort.

Ingrid gripped the plait and began to cut. Each snip of the shears pulled Selia's head back for a moment and then released it as a chunk of hair was cut. Finally Ingrid made one last snip and Selia's head was free.

With shaking hands, Selia reached up to feel it. Ingrid had cut off the plait at the nape of her neck, and the ends of her hair felt odd and bristly. The boys stared at her, both looking as though they were about to cry. Eydis stood in horror and gripped her own hair as if to assure herself it was intact. Ingrid swung Selia's rope of hair like a tail, then dropped it into the hole. She was obviously enjoying this. Selia turned away and started to rise.

"Not yet." Ingrid pushed Selia back down. "It's not short enough."

Ingrid began to snip in earnest now. She worked quickly, grabbing handfuls of hair and cutting each clump off very close to Selia's head. Tufts of black curls drifted down onto Selia's lap and she closed her eyes so she wouldn't have to look at them. Selia's hair had always given her a feeling of security—the thick curls had hidden the dent in her skull. Was Ingrid clipping her bald? Was that really necessary?

Finally Ingrid stopped cutting and sat back to examine her work. "There," she said. "It's done. You look hideous."

Selia touched her head and gasped. Ingrid had shorn her nearly to the scalp. Her head felt cold and bare. Exposed. The sensation was distressing, somehow more naked than actual nudity.

But Ingrid wasn't finished just yet. She picked up a clump of dirt and began to rub it all over Selia—on her face, her hands, and her clothing. Ingrid screwed up her face and studied her.

Selia averted her gaze. "Do I look like a boy now?"

Ingrid frowned. "No," she said finally. "Your eyelashes are too long."

"I'm not going to let you cut my eyelashes!"

"Then it was pointless to cut your hair. You still look like a woman."

Selia pondered the fate of Eydis, of her boys. Their safety depended on her passing as a male thrall. She would be infinitely more conspicuous traveling as a woman than as a boy. A woman with uncut hair, fine clothing, and a slave collar would be recognized immediately as a bed-thrall. An exquisite slave only the wealthiest Finngalls could afford, whose sole purpose was to appease her master's lusts. So the disguise had been essential to the plan.

If Selia hadn't cut her hair and dressed in boy's clothing, she would have been at the mercy of every man's desire during the trip across the sea. It was a crime to rape a free woman but not a thrall. Selia suspected this was the reason Alrik decided to leave the slave collar on until he returned from his fall trip. He knew how foolhardy it would be for her to try to escape with it on, and he knew it would be impossible for Selia to remove the collar without risking death or disfigurement.

The collar had given Alrik a false sense of security. He hadn't realized it afforded Selia a unique opportunity for a traveling disguise.

It was imperative that Selia pass as a boy. The eyelashes had to go. Selia turned back to Ingrid.

"Cut them."

Chapter 19

The blisters on Selia's hands had broken and now the dampness on the oars felt more like blood than seawater. The pain was excruciating. But she couldn't allow herself to focus on it—they still had more work ahead of them. They had returned to Alrik's farmstead for the final step in the escape plan.

She was in one of the small boats with Eydis, and the boys were in the other. Ingrid had attached the dragonship to the boats with ropes and they were attempting to drag it out of the bay. They had tried, unsuccessfully, to row the dragonship itself. After struggling with it, they had decided to try to drag it out of the harbor instead. It was moving, now, but slowly.

As soon as Alrik realized they were gone he would gather the men together and head to Bjorgvin in the dragonship. He was clever enough to know Selia and Ingrid wouldn't hide in Norway, but would instead travel to Ireland to warn Ainnileas his life was in danger. And to do that they would need to go to Bjorgvin to buy passage. Selia was certain Alrik wouldn't travel to Bjorgvin by horseback. He would go by water in case they had already made their escape, to be better equipped to pursue them.

So it was vital Alrik not have access to his ship. Burning it would be easier but the flames would alert the thralls. They were so fearful of Alrik, one of them would ride to Ketill's farmstead to let him know what happened. And that would reduce the time Selia had to get out of Norway. So the plan was to drag the ship into the open water, unfurl the sails, and hope it ended up somewhere far away.

Ingrid had stripped down to her shift and was in the dragonship, attempting to steer it. Although she claimed to know what she was doing, it was obvious she had overestimated her abilities. The ship listed hard, scraping into Selia's boat, and Selia cried out and gripped the sides for a moment. Stupid Ingrid. She knew Selia couldn't swim.

Faolan's anxious voice could be heard in the darkness, from the other boat. "Are you all right, Mother?"

"Yes. Be careful, boys."

Ingrid leaned over the rail of the ship and called out to them in a rough whisper, "Untie the boats and move out of the way. I'm going to try to raise the sail."

Selia's hands felt clumsy and numb as she struggled to untie the rope. Eydis helped her with small, nimble fingers, and finally the rope was free. The boys untied their own boat and rowed over to Selia and Eydis. Balancing carefully, each stepped into Selia's boat, and Geirr took the oars from her.

Faolan's face looked wan in the moonlight. He had helped Geirr with the other boat and it had obviously been too much exertion for him. Selia brushed his hair out of his eyes and Faolan caught sight of her hand. "*Mamai*, you're bleeding!"

Selia examined the raw skin of her palms and gave Faolan a rueful smile. "It's all right. I'll have to toughen them up or no one will believe I'm a thrall."

There was a flapping sound as the sail unfurled and caught the wind. The dragonship began to move through the cleft in the cliffs and toward the open sea. It was moving too fast for Geirr to keep up, so Selia took one of the oars from him and they both rowed the boat after the dragonship. Each pull of the oar was agonizing but Selia bit her lip to keep quiet. If she showed any sign of pain Faolan would insist on helping.

Suddenly a long, white hand gripped the side of the boat, and Ingrid's smiling face peered up at them from the water.

She was enjoying herself. "There it goes," she said with satisfaction. Her eyes followed the dragonship as it sailed away. "Let's hope the sea smashes it to bits."

Selia and Ingrid took turns rowing all night. Eydis curled into a ball on the floor of the boat and went to sleep. Finally Faolan and Geirr nodded off as well. Ingrid had brought an extra shift, knowing there was a distinct possibility of her having to swim tonight. She tore her wet shift into strips, and she and Selia tied the strips around their hands so they could continue rowing.

Selia had been to Bjorgvin twice with Alrik since their marriage, once for a funeral and once for the wedding of Gudrun's son. But they had gone on horseback so she didn't know the way by boat. Ingrid claimed if they just stayed near land they would eventually end up in Bjorgvin, but dawn had come and gone with no sign of the city. Should it be taking this long? Selia was exhausted and in pain, and if she didn't need Ingrid for the rest of the journey she would have kicked her overboard.

At last they rounded a massive cliff overhang and came upon Bjorgvin. Selia stopped rowing for a moment and gazed at the sight, smiling. The city seemed to nearly sparkle in the early morning light. Or perhaps she was just so relieved to finally arrive, her mind was playing tricks on her.

The docks were bustling. Dozens of ships lined the harbor and hundreds of people hastened along with purpose, hauling cargo onto some ships and off others. Huge nets of fish were being dumped into carts and transported up through the winding streets of Bjorgvin on their way to the market. Shouts and calls could be heard above the general din of the harbor.

Selia's grin widened as she saw the number of ships docked. Surely one of them would be leaving for Dubhlinn this morning. Their luck had held, after all.

"Stop smiling like that," Ingrid snapped. "You're supposed to be a thrall. And a simpleton."

"You said I'm not supposed to talk. Now I can't even smile?"

With a voice obviously female, her Norse still carried the lilt of her native language. To further the disguise, Ingrid had decided Selia should not speak for the entire journey. And they would use the now-obvious dent in her skull as the excuse for her muteness.

"No." Ingrid retorted. "You can't. Thralls don't smile." They pulled up to one of the unused docks and Ingrid tied the boat to it. She smoothed the tangles out of her hair with her fingers and turned to Selia. "How do I look?"

Ingrid's pale blond hair flowed over her shoulders, glorious even after her swim in the ocean. The color was high in her cheeks and her eyes flashed with excitement. The loose tresses made her look younger than twenty-two, but her face was that of a strong and confident woman. She was the perfect female version of Alrik, and every man on the dock would notice her.

Which was why they had to leave quickly. This morning, if possible. The longer they stayed in Bjorgvin the greater the likelihood of being noticed by someone who knew Alrik Ragnarson. Someone who would be able to tell Alrik exactly what ship they had left on.

"You look beautiful. Be careful someone doesn't try to carry you off. We can't do this without you."

Ingrid smirked, but it was obvious she felt pleased to be so necessary. "Don't fret, thrall-boy. I'll find a ship for us and be right back."

Ingrid was gone for a worrisome time. The gnawing anxiety in Selia's belly returned and she watched the docks with furtive glances when the children weren't looking. They were restless and hungry, so Selia got out the bundle of food she had packed and gave them hunks of bread and cheese. With full bellies, Faolan and Eydis settled into the bottom of the boat and went back to sleep. Geirr stayed alert, seated next to Selia.

"It will be all right, *Mamai*," he assured her as Selia studied the harbor once again. Geirr took her hand. "Everything will be all right. We will go to Ireland and we will find your brother. And your hair will grow back."

Selia's eyes grew misty. "You are a good boy, Geirr. I am so proud of how brave you are." She withdrew her hand. "But you must remember I'm a thrall now. Not your mother. Ingrid is your mother until we get to Dubhlinn. We will all be in danger if anyone learns the truth."

Geirr's lip trembled and he nodded. Selia felt as though her heart would break. She couldn't even comfort her own son.

Suddenly Ingrid stomped up and climbed back into the boat. She sat in silence for a moment, clearly upset, glaring at the expanse of water as though too disgusted to speak.

"Well?" Selia asked. "What took you so long?"

Ingrid huffed out a breath. "All these ships," she groused, waving her hand across the water for dramatic effect, "are *fishing boats*."

"Why does that matter?"

"It matters because fishing boats do not sail to Ireland. They catch fish and they sell it at market. In Bjorgvin."

Selia studied the harbor. There were numerous fishing boats, to be sure, but others that looked different—more like Alrik's dragonship. "Ingrid," she said, growing impatient, "they're not all fishing boats. There is a longship. And there is another one."

"Yes, Selia. I'm not a fool. But those ships have returned from their journey and aren't leaving again. Only one ship soon leaves for Dubhlinn."

Selia's anger began to rise. "Why didn't you just say so? Did you buy passage?"

"I did."

"Let's go, then." Selia began to pack their remaining supplies back into the satchel. Truly, if she made it to Ireland without killing Ingrid it would be a miracle. As usual, the girl was being purposely difficult just for the sake of getting a rise out of her.

Ingrid reached for her arm and the look on her face made Selia pause. Ingrid swallowed. "We're going to Ireland on Gunnar One-Eye's ship."

Selia gawped, open-mouthed. She tried to speak and nothing came out but a stutter. Had Ingrid gone completely mad? The girl knew who Gunnar One-Eye was. She knew the long and sordid history between Gunnar and Alrik. She knew Gunnar had met Selia when he had come to the farmstead long ago and Hrefna had given them shelter from a storm.

How could Ingrid possibly think it was a good idea to travel to Ireland on a ship full of ruthless pirates, whose leader would relish the chance to obtain his revenge against Alrik Ragnarson? Would not torturing and killing Alrik's family be suitable revenge? Or selling them all into slavery?

Unless there was something Ingrid wasn't saying.

A spark of hope flickered in Selia's heart. "Please tell me Ulfrik is still sailing with Gunnar," she breathed.

"No. Of course not—I would have told you that. Your lover is gone, Selia. He's not going to help us."

Selia had to restrain herself from slapping Ingrid. "Then you have lost your mind! I'm not putting my children on a ship with Gunnar One-Eye! How long do you think it will take him to realize who we are? Go right now and get our silver back. We will find another ship!"

Ingrid shook her head. "Did you not hear me when I said there is no other ship? We're lucky to even get passage with Gunnar. He planned to leave at dawn but one of his men was missing and they had to find him."

"No," Selia argued. "It won't work. They will discover who we are and kill us all."

"The only one of us they've met is you. And you weren't a little thrall boy then, were you?"

"You look like Alrik, Ingrid! How do you plan to explain that?"

"I already have. I told Gunnar my mother is Dagrun Ragnarsdottir and my father is Elfrad Audunarson. Dagrun's husband. There is no love lost between Elfrad and my father."

"What do you mean?"

"They had a falling out. Before I was born. Hrefna told me they hate each other. So I am now Alrik Ragnarson's niece, not his daughter. Gunnar asked me about Alrik and I said I had never met him and never intended to. I told him I was embarrassed to name him as uncle and that my father had threatened to kill him if he ever set foot in his house again. So Gunnar has no reason to take his revenge against us. Why would he hurt us when we hate his enemy as much as he does?"

At Selia's silence Ingrid added, "I told Gunnar I was a widow and was traveling with my three children and a thrall to my father's house in Dubhlinn. I have paid Gunnar half and told him my father Elfrad will pay him the remainder when we arrive safely. So everything will be fine, you will see."

"How do you know Gunnar or Einarr Drengsson won't recognize me?"

"You're a thrall, Selia—they won't even notice you. Who notices a thrall?"

Selia felt sick. She and her children were about to board a warship led by her husband's greatest enemy. A man who would take untold delight in throwing them all into the sea and sailing away. Or worse, even, than that, for there were things far more heinous than killing. Selia had heard when raiding, Gunnar slaughtered everyone except the most beautiful women and children. There were depraved men who bought slave children, both boys and girls, with the intention of using them to fulfill their baser desires. Hadn't Muirin been sold to a brothel when she was still a child?

Three small faces stared at Selia, waiting for her decision. So innocent, and so beautiful. The thought of any harm coming to them was a knife in Selia's belly. But if they didn't go with Gunnar now they might not get another chance. Alrik could already be on his way to Bjorgvin, looking for them. This was it, then. There was no other choice.

Selia took a deep breath. "All right. We haven't any more options. But we all need to be on our guard—one slip and we're dead." Selia turned to the children. "Listen carefully. You must not look at me or speak to me for the remainder of the journey. Ingrid is your mother and I am only a thrall. And we must think of new names for all three of you."

"Why?" Faolan asked.

"Because Gunnar Klaufason is very clever." Selia looked over at Ingrid. "Did Gunnar ask you your husband's name?"

"No."

"He will. So think of a name and the details of where you lived. You must memorize it, all of you, and answer without hesitation. Or he will know you're lying."

Chapter 20

Gunnar's ship loomed large at the dock as they approached. It held forty men, only ten more than Alrik's ship, but it was nearly twice as big. The more room for transporting its human cargo to market, apparently.

Selia fought back a wave of nausea as they stopped in front of the ship. Her heart pounded, her throat dried up, and her hands shook with apprehension. She remained several steps behind Ingrid and the children and kept her head lowered in the typical submissive posture of a thrall.

"Ahh. My lady," a familiar voice drawled. Selia barely contained a shudder as she recognized the voice belonging to Einarr Drengsson. "Gunnar told me you were boarding with us but he neglected to tell me your name."

"Inga Elfradsdottir," Ingrid replied.

"And your mother is Dagrun Ragnarsdottir, am I correct?"

"You are."

"Then I am delighted to inform you we are cousins," Einarr said in his most charming voice. "I am Einarr Drengsson."

"Is that so?" Ingrid asked, keeping her voice firm and matter-of-fact. Selia had warned her to watch out for him. "I do not recognize the name."

Selia could see Einarr's deep bow even with her head lowered. "It is so. We are distant cousins, but cousins nonetheless."

Ingrid stepped closer to him. "In that case, cousin Einarr, I would like to ask you to keep us under your protection for the duration of the trip." Ingrid dropped her voice and put her hand on Einarr's arm. "Some of these men appear a bit unsavory. I would like to return to my father with my honor intact."

"Of course! Of course, dear cousin. You and your children will arrive in Dubhlinn unmolested. You have my word."

Ingrid beckoned for the children and they stepped forward. "Children, meet your cousin Einarr Drengsson. We are under his protection. Einarr, these are my sons Gisi and Fasti, and my daughter Edda."

"What lovely children. Beautiful."

"Thank you. Where shall I have the boy put our things?"

"We've got a corner for you, over here. Come with me, boy," Einarr called to Selia over his shoulder.

"Hakon can hear you but he doesn't speak," Ingrid said to Einarr as Selia stepped on to the ship. Of course Ingrid had chosen the name of Bolli's lover to be Selia's moniker for the remainder of the journey. Selia had thought to protest but didn't bother. It was as good a name as any.

Selia could see Ingrid make a motion up by her head, as if indicating the skull injury to Einarr. Selia froze as she felt Einarr come close and bend over her. Einarr made a disgusted noise in the back of his throat as he examined the divot in her skull. "Was it a horse?"

"Yes," Ingrid laughed. "The boy was too stupid to get out of the way, I suppose."

Einarr joined in her amusement as he strode to the spot that would be their home for the duration of the journey. Selia's heart sank. It was just big enough for the five of them to lie down comfortably, but not much else. There was no tent set up for them as Alrik had erected for Selia on the trip to Norway. No place to hide from prying eyes. No place to relieve her bladder in privacy. No place to hold her children in the night and tell them she loved them.

Selia would be completely exposed during the journey, with no possibility of a respite from her disguise.

She set the pack down on the planks of the ship and blinked back tears. The overwhelming need to cross herself and pray for protection was a bit surprising. Selia hadn't prayed since the awful incident with the rabbit after Alrik had returned from his ill-omened fall trip so long ago. It seemed wrong to pray, after that.

Better to just do nothing than to ask for forgiveness for such a sin. As though by not praying she could postpone the inevitable punishment she would receive. What would God do to a Christian who had dabbled in heathenism?

There was a ruckus as two men boarded the ship carrying another man between them. The man was drunk, clearly unhappy about being dragged onto the ship so early in the morning. There were shouts and laughter from the others, and someone threw a hunk of bread at the drunken man. "Where was he?" a man called out.

"In the brothel. Where else?" one of the men carrying him answered. "It was his wife who told me where to find him."

This elicited another round of laughter from the crew, but no one seemed surprised. They dropped the man onto the deck and Selia was able to get a quick look at him. He wasn't recognizable as one of Gunnar's men, and her heart lightened a bit.

Gunnar had a reputation of being a hard man to sail for. His crew might very well have changed. It could be many of the men were recent additions to the war band and weren't with Gunnar the night his crew had stayed at Alrik's farmstead.

A pair of heavy boots came into Selia's line of sight and continued toward the drunken man. The boots stopped and a man knelt beside him. *Gunnar*. He spoke softly but his words were carried by the wind.

"We waited for you, Brudd. We lost precious time and favorable winds searching for your worthless hide. If you weren't married to my sister I would slit your throat now and feed you to the fish. But that doesn't mean I won't do it on the return trip and tell her you died in battle."

No one laughed. The threat was a real one, not a joke. The man Brudd started to grunt a reply but another man shook him into silence. Gunnar stood up. His voice was deceptively calm as he spoke again. "Sober up, Brudd. And sleep with one eye open. You know I always do."

Selia stared at the night sky, sleepless and uncomfortable. Her bladder was full to bursting and the rocking of the ship made it unbearable. But worst of all, she could not stop thinking of Alrik.

He would know she was gone by now, of course. And he would be furious she had taken his ship. What would he do? Go to Bjorgvin and charter another ship, most likely. He could easily be gaining on them.

As afraid as she was of Alrik finding them, there was a part of Selia that missed him terribly. Not the crazed, wild-eyed Alrik who had hurt the children and put a slave collar on her. Selia missed the other side of Alrik, the side that smiled at the boys' antics and bantered with Hrefna at supper. The side that pulled Selia to him in the night and held her in his protective embrace; made her body shatter with pleasure.

For all the bad times in her marriage to Alrik, there had always been enough good to even it out. That balance had been irrevocably tipped, but Selia still mourned the loss of what she had. Those good memories seemed all the more precious now. There would never be any more.

Selia lay a few feet from Ingrid and the children. It was maddening to not be able to touch the boys, to whisper to them she loved them and was proud of them for being so brave. They had been reserved and observant in a way that made Selia both thankful and sad. Even Geirr, normally so restless, sat quietly with Faolan and Eydis. Both boys watched the men on the ship as though sizing them up and considering the best defense if anyone chose to attack.

It seemed to Selia her children had grown up overnight.

Babies no longer, they now acted like miniature men who were prepared to protect the women in their charge.

The boys were asleep now, lying with Eydis and Ingrid between them. They were doing exactly as Selia had instructed. So why did she feel as though her heart had been ripped out of her chest?

Little Eydis had cried herself to sleep, muffling her tears in her cloak. Out of all of them it was she who was the most confused. Her life had been sheltered and uneventful until very recently. Now her grandfather was dead and she had left behind a father who loved her. Eydis missed Bolli terribly.

Ingrid had told her of her true parentage just last night and the news was still raw. Why would Eydis want to cross an ocean to find a father who was not only a stranger but a foreigner, when she had a perfectly good father right here in Norway? Even the knowledge Selia was in fact her aunt by blood didn't raise Eydis' spirits. In an odd way it almost seemed to make her dislike Selia. The little girl just wanted to go home and forget all this had happened.

An intense wave of nausea hit Selia and she breathed through her nose until it passed. She hated sleeping on the ship. She needed to keep her eyes on the horizon, which was impossible to do once she closed her eyes. The nausea would be unrelenting until they reached the coast. The Finngalls slept on land whenever possible, but this first leg of the journey would necessitate the crew to sleep on the ship.

Which had brought about a very uncomfortable realization for Selia. She was on a ship full of men, with no tent for privacy and—for a while at least—no nightly reprieve of land. How exactly was she expected to relieve her bladder? Ingrid and Eydis could wrap their long cloaks around them and squat down onto the bucket supplied for that purpose. The boys could untie their breeches and release their stream over the side. What was Selia supposed to do? Wet herself?

The men slept in shifts so there was no possibility of using the bucket without being noticed. But Selia's bladder felt ready to burst. She needed to think of something.

She sat up, clenching her belly as though she were sick, fumbling about, then pulling herself to her feet she doubled over as if in pain. One of the crew noticed her and called out in a rough whisper. "Boy! In the bucket or over the rail! If you make a mess I'll throw you overboard."

Selia grabbed the bucket and ran with it to the side of the ship. She dry heaved over the rail, loud and long for effect, and then before she could change her mind, untied her breeches and sat on the bucket.

She leaned over again, clutching her belly, rocking back and forth. The man gave her a look of disgust as he turned away. Selia had purposefully made her tunic large and baggy to better hide her woman's body. It came down nearly to her knees and covered her well enough to sit on the bucket.

She nearly cried in relief as she emptied her bladder. But she would need to think of a better plan or she would have no choice but to feign illness until they reached land.

Dawn came early, and Selia squinted into the bright sun. Faolan was also awake and lay quietly next to Ingrid. But he was turned toward Selia, and his lip trembled a bit as he met her stare. Faolan's beautiful eyes shimmered with unshed tears. The color of his irises intensified whenever his emotions were high, and right now they fairly glowed.

Faolan's hand lay close enough to touch, only a few inches away from hers. She could reach out for him. She could pull her son to her breast and hold him close. Selia's own eyes filled with tears as she held herself back. She gazed at Faolan for a moment longer, then rolled away from him.

Oh, to be through with this journey and safely in Ireland.

She would hold her boys and never let them go. Damn Alrik for forcing this fate upon them.

The ship pitched a bit and Selia's belly gave an answering lurch. She breathed through her nose and focused on the horizon, willing the nausea to subside. But it was too late. Selia leapt to her feet and made it to the rail just in time. She vomited violently over the side and then sagged against the rail with her sweaty forehead on her arm. The act of breathing seemed almost too difficult. Had the nausea been this bad last time?

The weather had been fine on Selia's trip from Ireland to Norway, newly wed to Alrik. Now the sea was choppier and caused the ship to pitch harder. That was all. Once she was on land again everything would be all right.

It was frightening to allow herself to contemplate any other possible reason for her illness.

Such as the fact Selia had forgotten to take Hrefna's tea for a time when Faolan was hurt. Alrik had ignored her for the most part, like a petulant child, but his lustful frustration got the better of him once and he had pulled Selia behind his curtained bench when everyone had gone to sleep. Her lack of response angered him, so he had finished quickly and pushed her away without speaking to her. But perhaps the damage had been done.

Running away with three young children was difficult enough. A babe would ruin everything. Selia's plan, after finding Ainnileas and warning him of the threat to his life, was to buy passage to Iceland and settle there with Geirr and Faolan. The Icelandic settlement was young but promising, and many Finngalls who were tired of the poor farming conditions in Norway had decided to seek their fortunes in this untried land.

They couldn't stay in Ireland, as much as Selia wanted to. Alrik would look for her there. They would only stay in her homeland long enough to find Ainnileas.

Ingrid hadn't decided whether she and Eydis would go to Iceland or not—it depended on whether they could talk Ainnileas into coming with them. The possibility that he might already be married by now, with a family of his own, didn't bear contemplating. Ingrid was confident that as soon as Ainnileas saw her again, they would be together. She refused to acknowledge divorce was a foreign concept for Christians.

Selia didn't argue with Ingrid about it. She needed the girl, at least for the first leg of this trip. As soon as Ingrid took her to a blacksmith to have the slave collar removed, Selia would be more than happy to part company with her.

But a babe in her belly would change Selia's plans drastically. Even though they had plenty of silver with which to start a new life, Selia wanted to find work as a servant in Iceland. It would be much easier to hide from Alrik as an ordinary servant than as the lady of a farmstead, living alone with two children. Selia had no doubt she and the boys would be able to find work on a farm in Iceland. They were young and strong, and Selia was an excellent weaver. Her cloth had always been in great demand whenever Alrik took a surplus of it to Bjorgvin.

But would her skills be considered fair enough trade for an extra mouth to feed? Children the age of Faolan and Geirr were seen as an asset on a farm, but younger than that a burden. It would be a dangerous business to travel all the way to Iceland and not be able to find a place to stay. If she were indeed with child, Selia would have to hide her condition as long as possible and hope to make herself invaluable to her new employer before they found out.

The sound of someone else vomiting made Selia raise her head from the rail. Poor Eydis was leaning over into the bucket, heaving through her sobs. The little girl was as green as Selia herself felt. Ingrid woke with a start and went to her. She murmured soothing noises to her daughter and stroked her narrow back.

Selia observed her stepdaughter's nurturing. She had never seen such kindness from Ingrid. For all her rude and callous behavior to nearly everyone else, she was a good mother. Like Alrik, she was capable of gentleness—it just didn't happen often. But Ingrid loved Eydis and treated her well. Thankfully the child had that much. It was more than Selia could say for Alrik's relationship with the boys.

She knelt close to Ingrid and Eydis with her back to the men of the ship, hoping if anyone noticed they would only see a loyal thrall worried about the health of his mistress's daughter. "A tent," she whispered to Ingrid. "Ask them to make a tent for Eydis."

Ingrid frowned but didn't make eye contact with Selia. It was clear she wasn't happy about Selia breaking the rules they had decided upon. Ingrid grabbed Selia's arm and pulled her closer to Eydis. "Stay here with her, Hakon," she said, loud enough to be overheard.

Ingrid looked around at the sleeping men and loosed an impatient sigh when she spotted Gunnar and Einarr, still asleep. She strode to the group of men who were awake. One was Gunnar's son Leif, a boy of twelve or thirteen, who had his father's dark hair and violet eyes but so far had seemed not to share his cruel disposition. Another was Brudd, the man who had been dragged onto the ship the previous morning. Apparently he was taking Gunnar's threat seriously, to sleep with one eye open.

"I need to make a tent of some sort for my daughter," Ingrid stated. "She's very ill and I want to keep her out of the sun. Do you have an extra blanket we could use?"

The boy Leif looked around at the other men, then held out his blanket to Ingrid. Brudd gripped Leif's arm to stop him. The man's craggy face flushed with desire as his gaze scraped over Ingrid from head to toe. "I've got an extra blanket," he said with a slow smile. His hand snaked down to his crotch as he adjusted himself. "What will you give me for it?"

Selia gasped and took a step backward. She put her arm around Eydis and motioned Faolan and Geirr closer to the rail. Ingrid could take care of herself.

From the corner of her eye Selia could see Ingrid draw herself up and cross her arms, just as Alrik always had. Selia couldn't see her stepdaughter's face but she could picture its arrogant expression perfectly.

"I have paid Gunnar Klaufason well for our passage," Ingrid retorted, "and I assumed that would include a blanket for my child. Should I wake Gunnar now and tell him you refused?"

Brudd spat on the deck, then studied Ingrid with the long, irritated stare of a man unaccustomed to dealing with an assertive woman. After a moment he took the blanket from Leif and held it out to her. But as Ingrid reached for it, Brudd grabbed her wrist and pulled her close. He twisted her around so she was forced to sit in his lap, and he held her by both wrists with one of his enormous hands.

Ingrid cried out and struggled against him but she couldn't move. She was strong but Brudd was stronger.

Though Brudd leaned close to her ear and spoke softly, Selia was close enough to hear. "I don't know who you think you are, girl, but it would be a mistake to get on my bad side. If you're nice to me I can be very nice to you." Brudd's hand crept up to fondle Ingrid's breast. "But if not, I can see to it that you get passed around to every man on this ship before we throw you over the side."

Ingrid reared her head back and cracked Brudd in the nose. He screamed and pushed her away as blood gushed over his shirt. "Bitch!" he shouted through his hand. "I'll kill you!"

Ingrid pulled her dagger from her belt and held it at the ready. She smiled at Brudd as he unsuccessfully tried to staunch the bleeding. "If you ever touch me again I'll cut off something very important to you and throw that useless bit of meat over the side."

The entire crew was awake now. A few of the men laughed nervously as they saw Gunnar approaching. He stopped between Brudd and Ingrid. "Brudd, what have you done?" Gunnar's voice was icy calm.

"That little bitch broke my nose!" Brudd bellowed.

Gunnar narrowed his eye at him. "Inga Elfradsdottir has only paid half the price of her passage. Her father will pay us double for her safe return. Now, I have a question for you. Do you think he will pay us anything at all if his daughter is raped?"

"But she disrespected me! And she broke my nose! My shirt is ruined—"

Brudd's words were cut off as Gunnar leaned close to him. There seemed to be a mild struggle between the two men although Selia couldn't see everything. But suddenly Ingrid gasped and jumped back, and Selia saw with horror what Gunnar had done.

A dagger stuck out from Brudd's belly, buried deep. As he looked down at it in surprise, blood bubbled up and flowed from his mouth.

Brudd sank to his knees as Gunnar eyed him dispassionately. "Your shirt is truly ruined, Brudd. And you've made a mess of my ship. Who will I get to clean this up?"

Gunnar dragged Brudd to the rail, leaving a dark trail of blood on the deck. He hefted Brudd's body up by the armpits and leaned him over the side. Brudd struggled momentarily like a hooked fish, then sagged against the rail in exhaustion. The bleeding man's breath came in an irregular rattle as his gaze fixed on the water below.

"Now," Gunnar said in the same calm, eerie voice, "if I pull the dagger out you'll die very quickly. But I don't want you to die quickly—I want you to swim for a while. I want you to live long enough for the sharks to find you. So, do I lose my favorite dagger to the sea, or do I pull it out and show you the mercy of a quick death?"

Gunnar passed his regard over his men. Every eye was upon him and no one made a move to help Brudd. Gunnar's gaze locked with that of his son, as though daring him to step forward. Leif remained motionless. The children cowered next to Selia as Ingrid stood in front of them.

Gunnar's mouth curved in a smile so wicked it chilled Selia to the bone. He turned back to Brudd quickly. With one hand on the scruff of his shirt and the other arm hooked under his knee, he lifted the big man and tossed him into the ocean. He watched Brudd bob on the waves for a moment before facing his men with a shrug.

"I can get another dagger," he said.

Chapter 21

The children stared in horror as the ship sailed away from Brudd's flailing body. Eydis emitted a piercing shriek and her small finger pointed to a fin in the water, moving quickly toward the bleeding man. Ingrid clapped a hand over Eydis' mouth and blocked the child's sight with her body, shushing her hysterical sobs.

The boys' faces were ashen as they looked back and forth between Selia, Ingrid, and the war band of Gunnar's men. Selia wanted to grab her sons and hold them, as Ingrid was holding Eydis, but she could not. She was a thrall. And to be recognized as their mother—Alrik Ragnarson's wife—could mean the difference between arriving safely in Ireland and ending up a shark's meal like Brudd.

Did Ingrid understand now what sort of man Gunnar Klaufason was? Had his actions made it clear enough for her?

Selia collected the blanket from where it lay at Leif's feet and made a makeshift tent with it. She tied two corners on the ship's rail and pulled the other side down, holding it in place with the satchel. The tent was small but it would provide a modicum of privacy where Eydis could rest and Selia could relieve her bladder. That was all she could hope for.

Ingrid climbed inside the tent with Eydis, and the boys stood in front of it as though on guard. Eydis' sobs turned to hiccups after a few moments, and Ingrid called out to bring a flask of water for the child.

As Selia rifled through the satchel, a heavy hand came down on her shoulder. She froze and lowered her head, shaking so hard her teeth chattered.

"Boy," Einarr boomed, "The deck needs to be scrubbed. You can empty out that bucket and use it." Einarr motioned to the bucket Eydis had vomited in. He handed Selia a boar-bristle brush and walked away.

Selia swallowed, staring at the mess she would need to clean. There was a small amount of blood on the deck in the spot where Brudd's nose had been broken, and a much larger puddle where he had been stabbed. The red trail widened where the man had been dragged to the rail, two bloody handprints smearing the place where he had tried to avoid being tossed overboard.

The sight of blood had always turned Selia's stomach. She had nearly fainted when Alrik had been gutted by the boar. Even bandaging the boys' cuts and scrapes made her lightheaded. Geirr and Faolan gaped at her now, knowing how hard this would be for her. But there was no choice but to follow Einarr's orders.

Selia brought the water flask to Ingrid and turned toward the deck.

The tension on the ship dissolved after the death of Brudd. Gunnar and his men seemed to relax, as though the murder had been long anticipated and well received. They laughed and joked with one another and spent most of their time playing dice games.

The boys, tired of the confinement of the ship, crept close to the men and watched their game. They admired Leif greatly, a boy not much older than they were but seemingly accepted by the group of men as an equal. He, for the most part, ignored their attempts to gain his favor.

The sight of her children so near to Gunnar and his men made Selia nervous, yet there was nothing she could do but keep a close eye on them.

Now that the men had a thrall to shoulder some of their work, Selia stayed very busy. She served their meals, poured their ale, and emptied the bucket they used as a privy. Once they reached land she gathered firewood and cleaned the strings of fish they caught. All the while she tried to keep as small and inconspicuous as possible.

How could they be so near to her and not realize she was a woman? The wife of their leader's greatest enemy? But Ingrid had been right, for the disguise of a thrall made her nearly invisible to the men. And even if they did look at her, all they saw was a boy. Selia's hands had grown rough and red with the labor and her skin had tanned from the constant exposure to the sun. She looked no more like a female than Geirr or Faolan did.

Leif was an excellent carver, and he spent a good deal of his free time carving objects out of whale bone. He gave Eydis a small carved bird, exquisite in detail. The boys were jealous that Leif seemed to have taken to Eydis and not to them, but the gift was clearly only meant to keep the child quiet.

Eydis remained ill and stayed in the tent most of the time when they were sailing. Once they reached land she cried every morning when she had to board the ship again. Ingrid kept a close watch on her, and Selia was happy to relieve her whenever she emerged from the tent. This was the only time she could empty her bladder as they sailed. Unfortunately, the need to do so was happening with greater frequency.

There was no deluding herself any longer. She was with child. Exhausted in a way that had nothing to do with the constant hard labor of a thrall, her nausea had not relented. Her breasts hurt, her back hurt, and the various smells associated with a ship of men were nearly unbearable. Whether Selia liked it or not, Alrik had planted his seed inside her and it was taking hold with a vengeance.

She calculated the babe would come in the late spring. If they could sail for Iceland very soon after arriving in Ireland, that would give her time to get settled for the winter and prove her usefulness to her new employer. If this was anything like last time, she would be able to hide her condition through the winter.

Her other option was to try to find a husband. She had already decided to tell her new employer she was widowed—to say she was divorced would only bring up the question of why. There were more men than women in Iceland, so chances were good Selia could locate employment with an unmarried man. Securing his interest in her might prove harder.

There had been a time when half the male population of Baile Átha Cliath had been enamored of her. But Selia had been young and beautiful then, with fine white skin and a cascade of curls down her back. Now she claimed twenty-five summers, well past the prime marrying age. Her skin was sun-reddened, her hands rough and calloused. Her black hair was buried on a remote beach in Norway. Who would want her now, especially when they learned she was with child?

The thought of marrying again was frightening in and of itself. Even marrying another Finngall, knowing she could divorce him if necessary, would be a difficult undertaking. Most marriages were arranged, whether Christian or heathen. Love was not required nor expected. Mutual respect was the most that many couples could hope for. But Selia had loved Alrik, even at his worst. After being with someone she loved so completely, how could she now submit to a man she didn't care for? How could she allow him to touch her?

But keeping her boys safe—as well as this unexpected new life growing inside her—would have to take precedence over whatever reservations Selia had about remarrying. What if she didn't survive childbirth this time? What would happen to Geirr and Faolan then? Better for them to be the stepchildren of a good man than the orphans of a dead servant.

If Selia was able to find a man who treated her children well, that would have to be enough.

Their future security would be a fair trade for whatever she had to do to remain in a loveless marriage.

The weather cleared, with a fine wind. Selia's anxiety lessened as they neared Ireland. From overhearing the men talk, they would be in Dubhlinn very soon as long as the weather held out. Then on to find Dagrun in hopes the children could stay with her briefly while Selia and Ingrid looked for Ainnileas. As soon as Selia made a gown and had the slave collar removed, they could be on their way to Iceland.

Very soon she and the boys would be on another ship sailing away to start a new life in an untried new land. And if they could talk Ainnileas into taking them in Niall's ship, even better. They would be all together, safe, and maybe Selia wouldn't have to marry an Icelandic stranger after all.

Most of the men on the ship kept a wide berth from Ingrid after the incident with Brudd. Gunnar would speak to her, however, with a frequency that made Selia anxious. He was charming, and very handsome if one could overlook the mangled eye. Gunnar was married to Einarr's sister, but that meant nothing to most Finngalls. Einarr, and even young Leif, did not seem bothered by Gunnar's attentiveness to their lovely guest.

Ingrid was a strikingly beautiful woman. Her arrogance was inexplicably attractive to many Finngall men. Instead of being intimidated by Ingrid's confidence, Gunnar seemed to admire it. It was as though he saw her as a worthy challenge.

If Ingrid had any sense at all she would realize the danger of engaging in conversation with Gunnar. The man was charismatic, yes, and nearly as clever and perceptive as Ulfrik was, but Gunnar's calm demeanor veiled a viciousness of spirit Selia had never seen in any other man. And Ingrid knew this; she had heard the stories of

Gunnar One-Eye from Hrefna. She had seen firsthand how ruthless the man could be when he threw his sister's husband to his death and sailed away.

Why would she now talk with him and laugh with him? Was she interested in this pirate as more than just a way to pass the time as they sailed? Was Ingrid so fickle she had forgotten about her desire to find Ainnileas?

The ship clipped along at a good pace, bringing them closer to safety. The boys liked to stand by the rail and watch for schools of fish or the occasional whale. They had become bored and fidgety, tired of playing their game of rocks and sticks or watching the men play dice.

Whenever they reached land Selia would take the children with her to let them run as she collected firewood. Their eyes, especially Geirr's, were taking on a wild restlessness that begged for release. If only Selia had had the foresight to bring along the wooden sparring swords Alrik had made for them. At least then the boys would have an outlet on the ship for their abundance of energy.

Selia leaned over the rail to rinse out the slop bucket. She had so quickly grown accustomed to her role as thrall, it seemed second nature now. She had been the mistress of Alrik's farmstead, the wife of a great Hersir who owned dozens of slaves, and now she washed filth from a privy bucket. How quickly she had learned to take nothing as her due, for all could shift in an instant.

Selia heard Faolan's raised voice and turned sharply to look. What she saw made her blood run cold. Geirr was perched on his knees on the rail, gripping the sides as he leaned over to see whatever was in the water. Faolan held him by the hem of his tunic as he tried to pull him back down. No one else on the ship paid any attention to the boys. Selia dropped the bucket and sprinted toward them.

Geirr shifted impatiently, trying to persuade Faolan to let go. As Faolan pulled harder, Geirr moved to smack his brother's hand away. Just as Selia reached them, Geirr jerked too hard and lost his balance.

Selia watched in horror as her son fell from the rail and into the water. The splash cut short his surprised scream.

Without a second's hesitation, Selia clambered over the rail and jumped in after him. She sank for a moment but kicked her legs and was able to bob to the surface. She had never tried to swim but she had seen other people do it, and now thrashed her arms and legs in the direction of Geirr as though sheer force of will could make her a swimmer.

It could not. The cold, briny water hit her in the face and she convulsively swallowed. Then sank again, sputtering. Selia kicked in panicked frustration, desperate to save Geirr, to drag him back to the ship, but her arms and legs refused to move in the coordinated fashion necessary to keep her afloat. She swallowed more water and went under.

She was drowning. She was going to die. Her mind screamed in desperate prayer. *Please, let someone save Geirr . . .*

Suddenly, an arm snapped around her waist, pulling her to the surface. She coughed, twisting in a frantic search for Geirr, and sobbed with relief as she saw him being hoisted onto the ship by Gunnar's men.

Whoever had saved her now swam to the ship with her body in tow, and fumbled as he tried to heft her toward the hands waiting to pull her to safety. Selia was jerked up and over onto the warm, wooden planks of the deck, and she lay still, stunned to be alive.

She choked on her own breath, and rolled over onto her hands and knees to cough up a small puddle of water. She heard Geirr crying and tried to crawl toward him. Her body refused to cooperate, and Selia finally collapsed a few feet from him. She lay still again, just breathing.

A shadow fell over her and Selia opened her eyes. Einarr, dripping wet, stood above her. He had saved her life.

Selia met his eyes, then quickly looked away.

Chapter 22

Einarr said nothing. He walked away from Selia to join the crowd surrounding Geirr. Of course they had saved Geirr. His safe passage to Dubhlinn would guarantee them a fine reward. But why had Einarr saved Selia? Why would he risk his own life to save a thrall?

Ingrid clutched Geirr to her breast as she shouted at him. "What did you think you were doing?" she demanded. "You nearly died!"

"I'm sorry," Geirr moaned, twisting his head around toward Selia. He was talking to her, not to Ingrid.

Faolan knelt beside Selia, careful not to touch her. "Are you all right?" he asked. The word *Mamai* remained unspoken but was nevertheless more real than anything he had said on this journey.

Selia lowered her gaze and nodded at him. It was dangerous for Faolan to show too much concern for her. It would raise suspicion to worry about the welfare of a thrall after his brother had nearly drowned. Selia turned away from him, hoping he would understand.

"You can't swim, Hakon," Faolan continued with anger in his voice. "That was very foolish."

"On the contrary—that was very brave, young Fasti," a familiar voice assured. Gunnar stood over them. "Everyone should hope to have a thrall so loyal. I have half a mind to buy him from you and keep him on the ship."

Faolan rose and studied Gunnar. Selia watched him bite back the quick retort that surely leapt to mind, although his face grew flushed with emotion. "You will have to speak to my mother about that. Hakon has been with our family since before I was born. She is attached to him."

"As you and your brother both are," Gunnar said. "Although your sister doesn't seem to care as much."

"Edda is ill," Faolan replied.

"Yes, she is. Poor child. And your mother said the girl misses her father terribly. Was his death recent? What did he die of, exactly? I don't remember what Inga told me."

Faolan narrowed his eyes up at Gunnar. "He cut himself while hunting. The wound festered."

"Ah, yes. It's coming back to me now. That is what your mother said."

Selia rolled onto her side and began to cough. Anything to distract Gunnar from this conversation with Faolan. Her phony cough turned into a real spasm as she gasped for air.

"Inga," Gunnar called out. "Your thrall is ill. Should I carry him into the tent with your daughter?"

Ingrid scowled. "No," she replied. "Leave him there. He is a stupid boy."

Gunnar smiled down at Faolan. "So. It would seem your mother is not as attached to the boy as you thought. Maybe she will sell him to me after all."

One of Gunnar's men strode over and interrupted the conversation, thankfully. "Land, Hersir. Do we stop now or sail until nightfall?"

Gunnar considered this for a moment. "We shall stop now, I think. I would like some privacy to speak with Inga Elfradsdottir."

They pulled the longship into a leafy cove, and carried supplies onto the beach for the night. Although the air was still warm, Selia shivered as her wet, salty clothing dried against her skin. If only she could wrap herself in a blanket and rest for a bit.

As the shadows lengthened and the sun burnished everything it touched, Selia stopped to gaze at the beauty of her surroundings for a moment, breathing it in. The forest looked and smelled familiar, the trees and the earth calling to her of home.

She pushed aside her exhaustion. They were on land. But was it Ireland? Based on the conversations of the men, they should be near Ireland if not in it already. The question remained if they were on the mainland proper or one of the small outlying islands.

She must get to Ingrid somehow and ask her to find out. Because if they were indeed in Ireland, they must break with Gunnar and his men tonight and make the rest of the journey on foot.

From the way Einarr had scrutinized Selia, he might very well have guessed who she was. And Gunnar clearly suspected something was amiss. It had been a terrible mistake to come aboard his ship. It would be a miracle if they didn't all end up dead.

Selia broke the rules again and met Ingrid's gaze directly as she collected the satchel and the blanket they used as a tent. With her stare she willed Ingrid to understand she needed to meet with her privately. Ingrid brushed past her, knocking into her so hard Selia nearly fell.

"Come with me, children," Ingrid called. "We will find a stream to wash up. Bring the water flask, Hakon."

Gunnar overheard them and walked over. He met Ingrid's gaze and his voice was soft. "I would like to speak with you tonight, Inga."

Ingrid smiled at him. "Of course. Let me get the children washed and I'll be back directly."

Selia hefted the satchel over her shoulder and followed Ingrid and the children into the woods. They walked for a while, and Selia turned around a few times to be sure they weren't being followed. Finally convinced no one was watching, she grabbed Geirr by the arm and spun him around.

He met Selia's gaze, then she tugged him close in a fierce embrace. "I'm sorry, *Mamai*." Geirr's voice broke with emotion.

Faolan hung back for a moment, watching them, and Selia pulled him in as well. She held her children, feeling their heartbeats pounding in their young chests, and drew back to look at them again. With a start Selia realized Geirr had grown since she had hugged him last. He was nearly eye to eye with her now. She kissed them both, then turned to Ingrid.

"We need to change our plans, and quickly. Einarr may have discovered who I am. And Gunnar knows something as well. If we've reached Ireland, then we must leave tonight and walk the rest of the way to Dubhlinn. They won't follow us on foot."

Ingrid made a face at her. "I don't want to walk the rest of the way. It's too far for Eydis. Gunnar won't hurt us."

Selia gripped her arm. "Did you not see how he treated Brudd? A man wed to Gunnar's own sister? Of course he will hurt us!"

"Gunnar wants me for his mistress, Selia," Ingrid hissed. "He asked me last night. Gunnar said he would keep me in a fine house in Dubhlinn, and once his wife dies he will marry me. She is from a wealthy family so he is unwilling to divorce her."

Selia gaped, speechless. "What?" she finally sputtered. "Are you considering this?"

"Of course not." Ingrid waved a dismissive hand. "I came here to find Ainnileas. But does it hurt to let Gunnar think I'm considering it? It will keep us safe, after all."

"Have you gone mad? Gunnar Klaufason is a wicked pirate. Nothing good can come of this."

"I told him I was an honest woman and will be no man's mistress. Gunnar's wife is doing poorly. I told him when she dies he can ask my father for my hand."

"So you're encouraging his affections with a lie?"

"No. I'm buying us some time."

"And what does Gunnar want to talk to you about tonight, do you suppose? His plan to slit his wife's throat so he can have you honestly?"

"I have no idea what he wants to talk to me about. But I do know I'm tired of having to follow after you to fix your mistakes. If Einarr has guessed who you are, why do you think that is? How much attention did you draw to yourself by jumping into the water after Geirr? A thrall who clearly can't swim? How do you suggest I explain that?"

"Would you have me watch my son drown? You weren't even paying attention and you're supposed to be his mother!"

"You should have let one of the men go in after him. We wouldn't be faced with this dilemma right now if you had."

Faolan took Selia's hand. "Let's go now, Mother," he urged. "We don't have to go back. Let's leave and be done with these men."

Selia turned to him and caressed his small face. "We must wait until nightfall. As soon as they're asleep we will slip away. They won't realize we're gone until morning, and they won't want to waste time following us on foot. But we need to make sure we're in Ireland first, or we'll be stranded here."

Ingrid flung out both hands angrily. "Who said you were in charge, Selia? You're the one with the slave collar on."

Selia confronted her stepdaughter. "I don't care what you do, Ingrid. Stay with Gunnar One-Eye and keep his bed warm if you like. But my boys are leaving with me tonight. I'm not sure how you'll explain to Gunnar that two of your children disappeared with your thrall, but I'm sure you'll think of something."

Ingrid's nostrils flared. "I hate you, Selia Niallsdottir."

"And I you."

"I have no interest in Gunnar—I only want Ainnileas."

"Then find out if we're in Ireland. We'll leave tonight and you'll be with Ainnileas soon," Selia said through gritted teeth.

Ingrid snorted but kept her mouth shut. She pushed past Selia and turned back toward the camp, pulling Eydis by the hand behind her.

Chapter 23

Selia watched the flames smolder hot and red in the darkness. Most of the men were asleep, as were Ingrid and the children. The fire needed a bit more wood or it would go out soon. None of the men had made a move to stir the coals or add more wood in quite some time. Were they all finally asleep, then? Was it safe to wake Ingrid and the children to try to slip away?

Ingrid had confirmed from Gunnar that they were indeed in Ireland. The ship would reach Dubhlinn by tomorrow night if favorable winds prevailed. What to do? Should they take their chances and remain with Gunnar, knowing they would be safe in Dubhlinn soon? If Einarr had deduced who Selia was, he certainly was not acting upon it. Maybe his look of recognition had been her imagination playing tricks on her.

But even so, wasn't it safer to leave now and be free of these wicked men? Selia was torn. It was important to get to Ainnileas soon, and if they stayed with Gunnar they would be able to do so quickly. But extra time with Gunnar might be more trouble than it was worth. How far to walk, exactly? The distance would be hard on all of them, but especially on Eydis who had been ill for most of the journey. She was thin and pale and could barely be coaxed to eat. At least the child's seasickness would subside if they didn't get back on the ship.

Selia stared into the fire as her anxiety mounted. The night was so quiet she could hear her own heartbeat. Something felt wrong but she couldn't put her finger on the reason. There was a peculiar energy in the air, a thickness that shimmered just outside her line of vision. She pivoted sharply, catching sight of it for a moment, then she blinked and the apparition disappeared.

Selia shivered. It was only the smoke from the fire, nothing more. She jumped as she heard the rustling of something moving in the bushes, and a second later felt the rush of wings as though a bird flew past her face. The breeze carried the cloyingly sweet smell of rotten flesh, and Selia clapped a hand over her mouth to keep from crying out.

No. Not here. She had to get away from Gunnar and his men. They would kill her as a witch if they saw what was about to happen. Lurching to her feet she stumbled into the trees, forcing her body into an awkward run. It was so hard to move, so hard to make her legs work properly. The ground sucked at her feet to try to slow her down.

Her heart pounded in her chest and the drumbeat of her pulse moved higher, up to her head, the pain like a hammer as it thumped against her skull. The fluttering wings chased her and she fell as one hit her in the face. The birds circled her, cawing and pecking at her with their ugly, sharp beaks, and she swung her arms wildly at them as she stood up and ran again.

Her head hurt . . . it hurt so badly . . .

Where was her brother? She had to get away from the bad men, had to get away from the fire . . .

Selia blinked, long and slow, staring into nothingness. The quiet was absolute except for the soft sound of her own breath. She blinked again and the dark branches of the forest came into focus. Pulling the ragged edges of her mind together, stitch by stitch, as though she were mending a piece of torn clothing, she realized she'd suffered a spell. She had run into the woods to avoid Gunnar and his men seeing her.

But where was she? How was she going to find her way back again?

"That was the oddest thing I've ever seen," a voice rumbled behind her. "And I've seen some very odd things in my time."

Selia gasped and cowered against a tree. Who was there? What was she going to do now?

The man stepped closer. *Einarr Drengsson.* His eyes raked over her. "What exactly is wrong with you?" he asked. "Are you a witch?"

She almost answered him, then remembered she was supposed to be mute. Selia gestured toward the divot in her skull.

Einarr studied her. "You can stop pretending. I know you're not dumb. And I know you're not a thrall . . . *Selia.* Did you think I would forget you?"

With a shudder, she tried a change of tactics. "Please, Einarr," she whispered. "Don't tell Gunnar."

"Give me a reason why I should not tell my Hersir you have deceived him."

Selia blinked up at the man, her mind foggy after her spell. For the life of her she couldn't think of a reason. She felt her eyes well up with tears. "Because he'll kill us."

"Who is the woman, that Inga? Alrik Ragnarson's daughter, I would wager. Not his niece."

"I have silver, Einarr. I'll pay you."

Einarr continued on as if she hadn't spoken. "And that boy is yours, not Inga's. You can't swim but you jumped in after him anyway. Only a mother would have done such a thing. Is the other one yours as well? He has your coloring."

"They are still your cousins! They are your blood, Einarr. Your kin. Please don't give us away."

Einarr studied Selia for a moment. "What a shame you cut your hair. It was very beautiful." He took her chin and forced her to look up at him, and his lips curled in a predatory smile. "But your face is the same. There is nothing you can do to hide that face."

The look in Einarr's eyes made the shorn hairs stand up on Selia's neck. Something had changed drastically in his demeanor. She jerked back. "Don't."

He loomed closer. "Do you want to save your children?"

"I'll pay you! Don't do this—"

Einarr glanced over his shoulder. "Keep your voice down, little Selia. I want you all to myself tonight."

What could she do? If she ran, Einarr would return to camp and tell Gunnar who they really were. Gunnar would do something terrible to the boys. But Selia couldn't bring herself to simply allow Einarr his way with her.

She scrambled to her feet and gave him what she hoped was a fierce look. "Einarr Drengsson, I am married to your cousin. My children are your cousins. Your blood. You would not put them in danger. Stop this nonsense now. I will pay you very well when we reach Dubhlinn."

Einarr laughed and made a move to grab her. Selia darted to the side and he missed. "You would rape me, then?" Selia demanded. "You would dishonor yourself by forcing a freeborn woman?"

"It's not rape. It's striking a bargain."

"It is *rape*, Einarr. I am not willing. I will tell everyone you forced me. Stop this, now. Let me go and I will pay you well."

A darkness came over Einarr's features. "You're wearing a slave collar. How am I to know you're a freeborn woman?"

He reached for her again and this time Selia wasn't fast enough to get away. His strong fingers gripped her arm, digging in painfully.

"Let go!" Selia screamed.

Einarr spun her around and clapped a hand over her mouth, then picked her up and headed deeper into the forest. "Stop making so much noise," he hissed in her ear.

Selia struggled to break free. His hand was so large it covered both her mouth and her nose. She couldn't breathe. Panicking, she tried to turn her head for air, but Einarr held her still.

She was suffocating. Selia's desperate thrashing intensified as her vision began to dim. Einarr's grip on her face tightened and one of his fingers got close enough to her teeth. Selia bit down savagely and Einarr's warm blood filled her mouth.

Einarr shouted in rage and dropped her. She gulped a lungful of air, gasping, and didn't see Einarr's arm draw back until it was too late to duck. The impact of the blow knocked Selia off her feet and everything went black.

Selia came back to consciousness with Einarr's massive body on top of her. He was huge, nearly as big as Alrik, and his heavy chest pressed into her face as he lifted her tunic roughly.

She was lying on jagged, rocky ground and something dug painfully into her back. But Selia could focus on nothing except the throbbing in her cheek and eye, made worse by the pressure of Einarr's body against hers. The entire side of her face felt as if it were twice the normal size. She couldn't see out of her left eye and the pain was excruciating. She whimpered and squirmed underneath him in an attempt to twist her head away.

"Shut up," Einarr snapped. "Stupid bitch. I'll teach you to bite me. I'm going to pass you around to the men after I've had my fill of you. Then we'll see what Gunnar wants to do with your children."

Selia felt him fumbling to untie his breeches. Something knocked against her bare thigh, something cold and sharp. His dagger? She moved her fingers slowly, inching closer until she felt it. Yes, his dagger, dangling from his belt. Einarr had been so eager to force himself on her he had neglected to take it off. Thinking her too timid or too weak to fight back, the fool had left his weapon within her grasp.

She ripped the dagger from its sheath and drove it deep into Einarr's side, in the softness of his belly below his ribs, screaming in satisfaction as it sank up to the hilt. How dare he threaten her children?

Einarr made a noise of surprise and pain as he reared away from her and grappled for the dagger. Selia managed to get one foot up and she kicked toward his face as hard as she could, making contact with his throat.

He gurgled and collapsed on the ground.

Selia scrambled to her feet and ran, leaving Einarr to bleed out behind her.

Chapter 24

She ran blindly, holding up her arm to block the brush from hitting her wounded face. Every step felt like a hammer strike to her cheek. Selia had no memory of how she had gotten from Gunnar's camp to the spot in the forest where Einarr had found her. But Einarr had looked over his shoulder when she had shouted, so that must be the direction of the camp.

She wore only her tunic. Einarr had pulled off her shoes and breeches when she lay senseless, and Selia had been too panicked to look for them after she stabbed him with the dagger. She cursed herself for not at least finding her shoes. A cut on her foot would slow them down, and they couldn't afford that.

After a bit she heard the faint rumble of the sea, and turned toward the sound as she continued running. What if Einarr wasn't dead? What if he somehow managed to drag himself back to camp? She should have pulled the dagger out to bring on a quick death, as Gunnar had threatened with Brudd. She should have pulled it out and watched him die.

There was a faint red glow up ahead. Selia stilled and hid behind a tree. The camp. She peeked around the trunk, looking for any signs of movement from Gunnar's men, but there was nothing. Dawn hovered and everyone was still fast asleep, the fire little more than coals now.

Selia crept toward Ingrid and the children. They lay facing the fire, bundled in their cloaks. A man rolled over, snorting, and Selia froze. She stood quietly for several heartbeats and watched the man until she was sure he had gone back to sleep. She finally knelt beside Ingrid and put a hand on her shoulder.

Ingrid's eyes flew open and Selia covered her mouth before she could cry out. A shocked expression came over Ingrid's face as she realized it was her. Selia removed her hand.

"What happened to your face?" Ingrid whispered.

Selia ignored the question. "We have to leave. Now."

"Selia—"

"*Now*, Ingrid. Carry Eydis so she doesn't cry."

Selia woke the boys. They both gaped at the sight of her face but she held a finger to her lips to keep them quiet. She grabbed the satchel that held their meager belongings and pulled the boys into the forest, with Ingrid behind, carrying Eydis.

Geirr looked as though he were about to burst into tears. As soon as they were clear of the camp he took the satchel from Selia and slung it over his shoulder. "*Mamai*, your face!"

"It's nothing. I fell."

"How did you fall?" Faolan asked suspiciously.

"I had a spell. I ran into the woods so the men wouldn't see me. I fell."

"You've never fallen before."

Selia turned toward Faolan, biting her lip against the pain of the movement. "It was dark."

Ingrid piped up from behind them, huffing slightly as she carried a sleeping Eydis. "Why are we following the beach? We need to go inland or Gunnar will find us."

Selia was well aware of this. But somewhere, lying in the forest, was Einarr. Either dead or dying. They would have to follow the coastline far enough to get past where he'd fallen. Then they could turn inland. "We will. Soon."

"Why are you acting so strangely? And where are your shoes and breeches?"

"Ingrid! Just walk. Please."

They walked in silence for a time. Ingrid pouted but kept her mouth shut. Faolan was angry too; he knew Selia was hiding something. But Geirr walked beside her, quiet and protective, and after a while slipped his hand into hers. "Does it hurt?" he whispered.

"No."

Right before dawn they turned deeper into the forest. At a creek they stopped to fill their water flasks, and Selia took a moment to dump out the contents of the satchel. All of their food was gone. They had been eating the food Gunnar had brought aboard the ship as well as whatever fish or game the men were able to catch. They had a long walk ahead of them, perhaps a sennight or more, with no food.

Selia felt hot tears well up in her eyes and she blinked them away.

The excruciating pain in her face made it difficult to think clearly. She knelt beside the creek to splash cool water on her cheek, and nearly screamed with the agony of the movement. Selia took in a shaky breath and forced herself to assess the extent of the injury.

The focus of the pain was in her left cheekbone, and the flesh of her cheek and eye felt puffy and grotesque around it. Her eye had swollen shut almost immediately so it was impossible to tell if her eyesight had been damaged. Selia's careful fingers pressed the swelling on her cheek. Was that hardness in the middle of the puffy flesh her bone peeking through? Had her skin split from the impact of Einarr's hand?

"I'm hungry, Mother," Eydis said. Ingrid had been forced to wake her up and make her walk. She was a tiny girl but still, Ingrid couldn't carry her indefinitely.

Furiously, Ingrid confronted Selia. "So? What do you suggest we do now? We have no food and we don't know where we are. I should never have listened to you."

"I know where we are. Not far from Dubhlinn. The

forest is filled with blackberry bushes and the streams are heavy with fish. We will be fine."

Ingrid threw her hands up in disgust. "We would have been in Dubhlinn by tonight! Now we have to walk even longer, eating berries?"

Selia ignored her and turned to the children. "Look," she pointed, "I see a blackberry bush over there. Go and eat your fill, just watch out for the thorns."

The children did as instructed and Selia turned back to deal with her infuriating stepdaughter. She gritted her teeth as she spoke. "I had a spell, Ingrid. Einarr followed me and saw it happen. He realized who I was and said he was going to tell Gunnar. I stabbed him and left him in the woods. I don't know if he's dead."

Ingrid blinked at her for several long moments. "You stabbed Einarr? *You*?"

"Yes. Why is that so hard to believe?"

Ingrid snorted. "Because you're pathetic! You can't even pluck a chicken without crying about it. And now you're telling me you stabbed a man three times your size, and a warrior at that?"

Selia gestured wearily. "Believe what you will, Ingrid. But I'm telling the truth. That's the reason we couldn't stay with Gunnar. And why we had to follow the coastline, earlier, because Einarr is in the woods and I don't know if he's still alive."

Ingrid stopped laughing and her face turned serious as she studied Selia. For all her disagreeable personality, Ingrid was far from stupid. "He tried to force himself on you, didn't he? That's why you don't have all your clothes." Ingrid's hand went up toward Selia's cheek, making her flinch, then she dropped it back down at her side. "And he hit you."

Selia couldn't find it in herself to respond. She was so tired—so tired of all of it. Tired of running. Tired of pretending to be a thrall. Tired of putting up with Ingrid.

Would it have been worse to stay with Alrik in Norway? To have waited him out, knowing he would eventually be reasonable again? She had learned how to handle her husband—learned when she needed to back off and when it was safe to assert herself. She had done a good job of protecting the boys from his rages. Maybe she could have found a way to keep him from hurting Ainnileas.

Had she made a terrible decision to leave Alrik and come back to Ireland?

Selia closed her good eye and took a deep breath to center herself. Self-pity would get them nowhere. "No, Ingrid. That's not what happened. I went into the woods to relieve my bladder and I had a spell. I fell when I was running from Einarr. Nothing more than that."

They walked in silence for the most part. Ingrid, in a rare expression of kindness, ripped strips of fabric from the bottom of her shift so Selia could wrap them around her feet. The strips did nothing to stop the dampness from seeping in to her skin, but at least her feet were protected from the stones and sharp sticks of the forest floor.

In an effort to conceal their footsteps, they trod down the middle of the creek bed. Selia was relatively certain Gunnar's men wouldn't try to follow them on foot, but it couldn't hurt to be careful.

It was doubtful Gunnar would waste time looking for them in the forest. He knew they were headed to Dubhlinn, so he would most likely sail there and wait to obtain his revenge. It would be difficult to locate Ainnileas without Gunnar finding them first.

The next morning they had a bit of luck and came upon a road. It was not well-used, but easier to walk upon nevertheless. Selia sat to rest her weary feet for a moment as Ingrid and the children went to collect some berries. Geirr had speared a fish the night before with a stick he had sharpened. His catch had been woefully small, so Ingrid and Selia had let the children share it. Now, Selia was dizzy with hunger, and no amount of berries could take the edge from those pangs.

Just as when Faolan had been a babe in her belly, she could be ravenous one moment and violently ill the next. But Selia was unsure if all was well this time. There had been a few drops of blood down her leg since Einarr had attempted to force himself on her. Not enough blood to be her flow, but enough to make her wonder if the struggle had damaged the child in some way. Was she going to lose it?

And would that be so awful? The timing of this couldn't have been worse. It would be hard enough for Selia and the boys to start a new life without the complications of a suckling babe. Caring for her boys when they were babes had been a blur of exhaustion for Selia; midnight feedings, dirty nappies, and chasing them around to keep them from getting hurt. And that was with Hrefna and a farmstead of thralls to help. How could she possibly think she was capable of doing this alone?

Selia leapt to her feet as she heard the distinct squeak of wagon wheels headed in their direction. The canopy of trees blocked the view of the road, but there was definitely a wagon coming toward them. Selia sprinted across the road and pulled Ingrid and the children into the shelter of the forest. They sat motionless, waiting.

A few more squeaks and the wagon appeared. It was driven by an older man, small, thin and harmless-looking. His wagon was piled high with what appeared to be bolts of homespun wool fabric.

Selia did a rapid calculation of the amount of time it would take to weave so much cloth. There was more here than could reasonably be traded in a smaller market.

He must be headed to the market in Dubhlinn.

Making a quick decision, Selia emerged from the woods and darted in front of the oncoming wagon. The startled man pulled the horses to a stop.

"Boy!" the man called. "Mind the horses! I nearly ran you down." He paused, squinting his rheumy eyes at Selia. "Are you injured? What happened to your face?"

Selia nodded and kept her head down. She spoke in as deep a voice as she could muster. "I was traveling from Norway with my mistress and her children. The ship capsized and we washed ashore. Are we near Dubhlinn?"

"Not too far. I'm headed there myself."

Selia took a step closer. "My mistress will pay you well to hide us in your wagon and take us to Dubhlinn."

"Where is this mistress of yours?"

Selia motioned for Ingrid and the children, and they stepped forward. The man studied them with a frown. "Your mistress is a Finngall, I see. Why would you need me to hide you in the cart? What are you running from?"

Averting her gaze, Selia brought her hand up to touch her swollen cheek. Let him come to his own conclusions.

The man was silent for some time, as though deep in thought. "I don't like Finngalls, and I don't want any trouble. But you seem a good lad to have protected your mistress so. I will take you just outside the city and you can walk the rest of the way." He paused briefly. "You have silver, you say?"

They rode in the confines of the cart until well after nightfall. Ingrid and the children fell asleep, but Selia lay awake, listening to the rhythmic squeak of the wagon wheel.

Niall had owned a wagon very similar to this one. He would hitch it up and drive to Dubhlinn nearly every morning when he was home. Sometimes he would dock his ship at the smaller port at Baile Átha Cliath, and Selia and Ainnileas would return with him in the wagon to help him load his goods. They would all pile in together to go to church; Selia and Eithne in the back and Ainnileas up front with Niall.

There had been a slight irregularity in one of the wheels that caused the wagon to bump as the wheel went around. Selia had complained mightily about the bumpy wheel as a child. Now, the thought of those petty complaints made her cringe with remorse. Why hadn't she treated her father better when she'd had the chance? Why hadn't she spent more time with him when he was home, instead of bickering with Ainnileas?

The thought of Niall was like a knife in her heart. Her father was dead. Although back on Irish soil, Selia would never again feel Niall's familiar embrace. He had been dead for so long, but somehow being near to the place he had died made the grief fresh again. Tears welled in her eyes and she didn't bother brushing them away.

What she wouldn't give to be able to see her father one more time. To tell him she loved him.

To tell him she was sorry.

The wagon squeaked to a stop. "Lad," the man called over his shoulder, "this is as far as I will take you. Dubhlinn is just down this hill. Good luck to you and your mistress."

Selia waited with the children in the darkness. Ingrid had been gone for quite some time; Selia could see the first blush of dawn in the sky. What was taking her so long? How hard could it be to locate Dagrun's house? They had decided the safest thing was to find Dagrun and explain to her all that had happened. Hrefna had said Dagrun was a kind woman who would surely help them. She could hide them while they sent word to Ainnileas.

But Ingrid should have been back by now. Had Gunnar waited in ambush, knowing Ingrid would eventually show up at Dagrun's door? Or had Ingrid, in her foolishness, decided to look for Ainnileas herself? Ingrid was still as lovesick over him as ever. Time had not tempered the girl's rash nature.

There was a rustling in the brush up ahead. Selia leapt to her feet, her heart hammering in her chest. Only Ingrid would know where to find them. Unless it was an animal sniffing around? Selia put her arms out to keep the children behind her.

A man stepped into view and Selia screamed.

Alrik.

No. How had he found them? How could he possibly be here? Everything—all of it—had been for nothing. The boys leapt in front of her, brandishing their daggers. "Get away from her!" Faolan shouted.

"Selia," a voice called from the shadows.

Not Alrik's voice.

Ulfrik. And Ingrid was behind him.

A sob welled up from deep in Selia's belly and she took a step toward him, setting the boys aside. Another step and her knees gave out from under her. Ulfrik rushed forward and caught her just before she collapsed to the ground.

His arms went around her and Selia sank into his strong embrace. Ulfrik. He was here. After everything, he was here.

Selia held on to him, digging her fingers in as though Ulfrik was a rock on a stormy sea. She didn't know how it was possible, but he was here.

He pulled her in tighter, tucking her head under his chin protectively, cradling her like a child. His heartbeat was strong in her ear, safe and familiar. Selia's relief was so overwhelming, she could have melted into the forest floor.

Ulfrik.

"It's all right, Selia," he whispered. "Everything will be all right now."

Bonus: An Excerpt from Book Three of the *Sons of Odin Series: Oath Breaker,* Coming Soon from Soul Mate Publishing

Sometimes the right man has been there all along . . .

Selia has fled Norway and has divorced Alrik, her Viking husband, to protect her children from his berserker rages. His brother, Ulfrik, having loved Selia from afar, offers his protection. As Selia uncovers the man he is, love blossoms in her heart where there was only emptiness.

But will their newfound love survive when Alrik returns to claim what is his?

Chapter 1

Dubhlinn, Ireland
883 AD

Ulfrik rushed forward as Selia stumbled over the debris of the forest floor. He caught her before she fell, wrapping her in a tight embrace. She clung to him, digging her fingers in desperately as a drowning woman might, burying her face in his shoulder.

The ensuing fury that coursed through Ulfrik's body burned hot and quick, making it difficult to think clearly. Although Ingrid had prepared him for Selia's shocking appearance, the sight of her still seemed like a physical blow.

She let out a small, shuddering sigh, the sound of one exhausted who could finally rest, and Ulfrik felt the tension in her body ease as she curled in to him.

What had Alrik done to her?

The vibrant, spirited beauty of Ulfrik's memory had been roughly stripped away, replaced with the ghost of a woman who now trembled in his arms. His brother had broken her, crushed Selia like a fragile flower under his boot. He had reduced her to *this*.

Never in his life had he wanted to kill Alrik more than he did at this moment.

He tucked her in closer as though comforting a small child. Ulfrik would keep her in his arms for the rest of his life, if only she would allow it. "It's all right, Selia," he whispered. "Everything will be all right now."

"I can't believe you're here," she choked out. "I thought you were Alrik . . ."

"I know," he murmured. "I will never let him hurt you again. Any of you."

Ingrid had told him of the reasons for their flight from Norway. Alrik had snapped, nearly killing one of his own sons. It had been bound to happen eventually, and they were lucky no permanent damage had been done. Ulfrik knew only too well what his brother was capable of.

He gazed at the two boys who stood over them now, both appearing uncertain yet defensive. The handsome blond youth with Muirin's eyes he recognized immediately as Geirr. He'd been but a suckling child the last Ulfrik had seen him. The smaller boy must be the babe Selia had been carrying. Other than his coloring, he looked very much like Alrik, down to the hostile expression on his familiar features.

"Are you my father's brother?" the boy asked.

"I am."

"Then you are the reason for all of this."

"*Faolan*," Selia admonished weakly. "That is enough—"

Ulfrik shook his head. "It is all right." He rose and helped Selia to her feet. She seemed unsteady and he wanted to keep his hand on her, but the two boys stepped in protectively.

The golden rays of the rising sun dappled through the dark grove, catching Selia's face clearly for the first time. The smooth skin of her cheek was split, swollen and discolored. Ulfrik's breath stilled in his chest.

"Who hurt you?" he asked. He voice sounded calm to his own ears even as his insides shook with fury.

Selia dropped her gaze, bringing her hand up to her face as though ashamed. "No one hurt me. I fell."

He stared down at her for a moment. She was lying, that much was obvious. But why? The wound was too fresh to have been caused by Alrik. Who was Selia protecting?

Gunnar?

He knew Selia had bought passage out of Norway on Gunnar's ship. It was Ulfrik who had answered Elfrad Audunarson's door when Gunnar had come knocking, inquiring insistently about the mysterious woman Inga Elfradsdottir.

Had Gunnar been the one to hurt Selia? Cousin or not, a shallow grave would be the bastard's final resting place if Ulfrik learned his suspicions were true.

He motioned for the others to follow him, vowing to revisit this later when he could speak with Selia alone. "The sun is rising quickly. Come, this way."

Selia shivered in the dusty darkness under Ulfrik's cloak. She lay in the back of the cart with Ingrid and the children, covered with a heap of sweet-smelling straw. Eydis sneezed and Ingrid shushed her, just as the cart rolled to a stop.

"We're here," Ulfrik whispered. "But don't get out just yet. I want to make sure Gunnar's men aren't watching the house."

They waited for what seemed like an eternity for Ulfrik to return. Finally there was the sound of footsteps approaching, then Ulfrik's voice as he pushed aside the straw. "Hurry now, this way."

Morning had broken. Selia blinked into the harsh rays and got a brief glimpse of a large log dwelling, not long like Alrik's house in Norway but instead tall; two stories high. The house had narrow windows on the second story, shuttered over. Ulfrik urged them inside, then latched the massive carved door behind them.

Selia's eyes adjusted to the dim light as she stood in the main room of the house. A long plank table took up a good deal of the space, with two looms along the front wall. The side walls held sleeping benches. A welcoming fire burned at a large hearth in the back of the house, with twin doors on either side.

A stairway rose in the vaulted space to a loft above the middle of the main room, open to access the heat from the hearth below. A woman came down the steps, with three children behind her, two boys and a girl.

"Oh," the woman gasped, gazing at Selia with a sympathetic expression. She was tall and well formed, sharing her brothers' striking good looks. Her red-gold hair was plaited in a lovely design. Her eyes, however, looked very much like Hrefna's, and Selia's heart tightened in her chest at the thought of the woman she would never see again.

"Are you Dagrun?" Selia whispered.

"Yes."

"I'm sorry to come to you in such a manner. We didn't know what else to do."

Dagrun nodded. "I understand. Ingrid told us what my brother did. I will help you and your children any way I can."

Selia released a relieved breath. "Thank you."

The first obstacle was crossed; Dagrun would allow them to stay. The knot of anxiety in Selia's belly began to ease somewhat.

"Would you and the children like something to eat? Or would you prefer a bath first?"

The boys perked up immediately at the mention of food. Selia felt nearly faint with hunger, but a hot bath was the most wonderful suggestion she had heard in quite some time.

"I would like a bath, if it isn't too much trouble," she said quietly.

Dagrun smiled, revealing a missing front tooth. Alrik's sister was beautiful even with the imperfection, but Dagrun closed her mouth quickly and turned toward the back of the house where a few thralls stood in the shadows. "Draw a hot bath, and bring clean clothes for them all. And food, plenty of food."

The thralls scurried off, and Dagrun motioned for the three children behind her to step forward. The girl and one of the boys resembled her in coloring and build. The girl appeared to be about ten summers; the boy younger. The oldest boy had white-blond hair and a sharper bone structure, and seemed to be around twelve. "These are my children, Jora and Bjarni." She indicated the blond boy. "Valdrik Haraldson is my husband's nephew."

Selia flushed at the expression of shock she saw in the children's faces as they stared openly at the group of dirty strangers standing in their home. The girl, Jora, seemed scandalized at the sight of Selia's legs. She looked away briefly, then turned back to gape again.

Selia was acutely aware of the impropriety of her clothing. The thrall's tunic left her legs bare from the knee down. Somehow the disguise hadn't seemed nearly as awful until just now. She felt dirty, ugly, and exposed. Shifting uncomfortably, she pulled Ulfrik's cloak tight to cover her shame. Yet as soon as she walked, her legs would show again.

"These are my sons, Geirr and Faolan." Selia waved her hand to encompass the children. "Eydis is Ingrid's daughter."

Where *had* Ingrid gone? To the privy perhaps? Surely not to the bath. Yet the sooner Selia could bathe and change into appropriate clothing, the better. She had no desire to use Ingrid's tepid bathwater.

Dagrun studied the boys, her eyes resting on Geirr longer than on Faolan. Her gaze flickered toward Ulfrik for a moment where he stood behind Selia.

"Welcome to our home, children. Jora, show your cousins the house. Stay inside, and keep the shutters closed." Dagrun urged them along, and after a nod from Selia, Eydis and the boys followed the children.

Dagrun regarded Selia for a moment before she spoke. "I'm sorry my brother did this to you. I will help you as much as I am able to. My husband has no love for Alrik, and he will not be happy to hear such trouble has come to his home. He is away but will return soon, I think. Have you anywhere else to go, if . . .?" She trailed off.

If Elfrad Audunarson decided we can't stay.

Selia swallowed. "My brother, Ainnileas, lives in Baile Átha Cliath. I must warn him Alrik means him harm. Then, I plan to go to the Icelandic settlement. I have enough silver to start a new life there with the children." She felt her cheeks heat again at the mention of Ulfrik's silver.

Ulfrik spoke up from behind her. "Iceland? In the spring?"

"No." She turned to him. "Now—as soon as I know Ainnileas is safe."

Ulfrik and Dagrun exchanged a glance. Ulfrik seemed about to speak when one of the thralls entered the room and announced the bath was ready.

Dagrun nodded, then glanced at Selia, scrutinizing her injury. "Your eye looks very painful," she said. "I can stitch the wound for you after your bath. I'm not sure if it will heal cleanly, though. When did this happen?"

"I am not sure," Selia hedged.

Dagrun's expression relaxed. "So my brother did not do this?"

"No one did it. I fell." Selia stared at the floor as she lied.

"But Alrik put that collar on your neck?"

"Yes." The cumbersome metal slid on her neck as she nodded. "He thought to keep me from leaving him."

The shame of it all was just too much, to be standing here in front of Alrik's brother and sister, wearing a slave collar and dressed in rags, hair shorn to the scalp. Asking for help like a beggar. She wanted to sink into the floor.

Ulfrik leaned close to examine the collar, and Selia shrank from his touch. How must she appear to him? The woman he had expressed his undying love for was gone. In her place stood a dirty thrall, face disfigured, hair clipped to the scalp.

How disappointed he must be.

"I will send for a blacksmith to have this removed," Ulfrik assured, dropping his hand to his side. "Bathe now, and eat. Then we will speak further."

Selia stayed in the bath until the water grew cold. She soaped up three times, scrubbing the filth from her hair and skin. The soap stung the numerous scrapes and abrasions on her body from her struggle with Einarr and her flight through the forest afterwards.

There was a soft knock on the door, followed by a female voice. "Mistress, I have a clean gown for you. Would you like me to bring it in?"

Mistress. It had been quite some time since anyone had called her that.

"Yes, please," Selia answered. The thrall entered, placing a folded parcel of clothing on the bench next to the wooden tub. "Thank you." Selia spoke to the woman's downcast face.

The slave nodded and hurried out. Selia dried herself, hating the bristly feel of her hair as she toweled it. How long would it take to grow back? Or at least cover the awful dent in her skull?

The gown was a deep red shade, with a matching apron dress. It was a bit snug in the bust, but loose in the waist. A child's gown, cut for freedom of movement rather than alluring appearance. It must belong to Jora, Dagrun's daughter. The shoes, most likely Jora's as well, were too big, but Selia would have gratefully worn Ulfrik's enormous boots if it meant she didn't have to go barefoot any longer. Dagrun had also thoughtfully provided a wrap for her head, somehow understanding not only Selia's need to hide the shame of her shorn hair but to keep her exposed skin warm, too.

Clean and comfortable at last, Selia entered the main room where Dagrun and the children were seated at the long table. Platters of food lined the wooden planks; bread, cheeses, meat and sausages. Dagrun's children ate slowly, watching the strangers with fascination.

The boys and Eydis had shoveled food onto their platters and now ate like hungry animals, hunched over, stuffing their mouths as if afraid someone would come and snatch the repast away. Geirr paused for a moment to gulp from the cup of ale in front of him, spilling some down his shirt in his haste.

Selia was mortified. "I apologize for their lack of manners," she said to Ulfrik's sister. "It has been some time since they have had anything other than berries and fish."

Dagrun gave Selia a kind smile. "No need to apologize.

Sit, and eat your fill. I told the children to go ahead, but I wanted to wait for you."

Indeed, the woman's platter was untouched. Selia's cheeks heated once again. She shouldn't have stayed in the bath so long and made Dagrun wait.

She eyed the food, suddenly dizzy with hunger, and chose a hunk of succulent-looking sausage, dripping with fat and juices, as one of the thralls brought her a cup of ale.

Selia bit into the sausage and the familiar taste flooded her mouth. This had been her father's favorite meal; the very item Selia had bought in Dubhlinn when she first met Alrik. How appropriate that it would be her first meal back on Irish soil. She found herself blinking tears away as she chewed.

Dadai.

Dagrun was watching her. "You are very comely, Selia. As are your children. Your son Faolan favors you with his dark coloring. Geirr, though, looks like his father."

Selia swallowed her mouthful, pushing aside her sad memories to nod in agreement. "Like his father or his uncle. They look so similar."

Dagrun reddened and turned away, calling for the servant to bring more bread.

Selia reached for another chunk of sausage. Why did the woman seem so abruptly out of sorts? Had something upset her?

Perhaps, as she stated earlier, Dagrun worried about the reaction of her husband. Or perhaps Ingrid had told her aunt some lie about Selia. It certainly wouldn't be the first time her stepdaughter had disparaged her good name.

"Where is Ingrid? And Ulfrik?" Selia asked. Ulfrik had said earlier he would find a blacksmith to remove the slave collar. But it was unlike Ingrid to miss a meal. She had complained ceaselessly about the lack of proper food after they left Gunnar and his ship.

Before Dagrun could speak, little Eydis piped up from the other side of the table. "My mother went to find my father. My *real* father. His name is Ainnileas Niallsson."

Also by **Erin S. Riley** and **Soul Mate Publishing**

ODIN'S SHADOW:
BOOK ONE OF THE SONS OF ODIN SERIES

Obsession. Treachery. Revenge. Redemption. Certain themes resonate across the centuries.

In ninth-century Ireland, Selia is a girl on the verge of womanhood, frustrated by the confines of her gender and resentful of the freedom her brother boasts of. Intelligent and resourceful in a time when neither is valued in a female, she longs for an escape from her sheltered existence. Fascinated by the tales of Viking raids told by her maidservant, Selia's hunger for independence is fed through the stories of heathen ferocity she hears at the woman's knee.

A decision to sneak to the city's harbor to view the Viking longships leads to an encounter with Alrik Ragnarson, a charismatic Viking warlord whose outward beauty masks a dark and tortured mind. With the knowledge that her father is about to announce her betrothal to a man she doesn't love, Selia marries Alrik and within a day is on the longship bound for Norway and a new life.

While Selia's relationship with her new husband grows, her friendship with his brother Ulfrik grows as well. And as Alrik's character flaws come to light and tension mounts between the two brothers, Selia begins to have misgivings about her hasty marriage . . . especially when a secret from the past is revealed, one that threatens to destroy them all.

Available now on Amazon: <u>http://tinyurl.com/pubd6m6</u>

CPSIA information can be obtained
at www.ICGtesting.com
Printed in the USA
BVHW03s0201300418
514749BV00014B/84/P